The Hardy Boys

Read all the titles in the Hardy Boys Mystery series

Franklin W. Dixon

The Jungle Pyramid

The Firebird Rocket

·PARRAGON·

This edition published in 1996 for
Parragon Book Service Limited
Units 13–17 Avonbridge Industrial Estate
Atlantic Road
Avonmouth, Bristol BS11 9QD
by Diamond Books
77–85 Fulham Palace Road
Hammersmith, London W6 8JB

First edition published 1992 for Parragon
Book Service Limited

Printed and bound by Caledonian International
Book Manufacturing Ltd, Glasgow

The Jungle Pyramid

First published in a single volume in hardback in 1978 by
William Collins Sons & Co Ltd.
First published in paperback in 1989 in Armada

Copyright © Grosset & Dunlap Inc, 1978

The author asserts the moral right to be identified as
the author of the work

·1·
Gold Heist

FRANK Hardy turned the controls of a stereo radio. "I'll see if I can find some country music, Joe," he said to his brother. "Waiting for Dad to phone about a new mystery gives me the jitters."

"Same here," said Joe. "I wonder why he didn't tell us anything about the case he's on."

"It must be top secret."

The Hardy boys were sons of Fenton Hardy, a private detective who worked out of Bayport since retiring from the New York Police Department. Dark-haired Frank was eighteen. Joe was blond and a year younger. Their father had taught them most of what he knew about crime detection, and they sometimes helped him with his investigations but often took cases of their own.

A Kentucky hoedown came over the stereo, and a nasal voice sang the "Blue Grass Blues."

Joe was lying on the floor, his hands cupped behind his head. "It's just as well that Mother and Aunt Gertrude are out shopping." He chuckled. "This isn't their beat."

The country-western rhythm rose to a crescendo, then died away. Suddenly footsteps pounded on the front porch of the Hardy home. The door burst open and a plump, freckle-faced youth rushed into the room, clutching a rolled-up paper in one hand. He was Chet Morton, the Hardys' best friend.

"I got it!" he cried. "I got it!"

"Got what, Chet?" Joe demanded.

"My correspondence-course diploma!"

Joe turned off the stereo. "A real one? Well, congratulations."

"What's this diploma for?" Frank asked.

"Collecting more bottle tops than anyone else?" Joe needled their visitor, who always became involved with one hobby after another.

Chet looked pained. "That's kid's stuff. I thought you guys were detectives."

"Give us a clue," Joe suggested.

Chet did not reply. Instead he unrolled the paper and held it up for them to see. The words STATE COR-RESPONDENCE SCHOOL were blazoned across the top. The diploma certified that Chester Morton had passed an examination on the subject of gold artifacts, and it was signed by the president of the school.

Chet grinned. "That means I'm pretty good with the gold. Go ahead. Ask me questions. Want to know about Aztec masks or—"

The phone shrilled before he could finish his sentence. Frank seized the instrument and held it away from his ear so the other two could hear. Fenton Hardy was calling.

"Frank, Joe," he said hurriedly, "are you both there?"

"Yes, Dad," Frank answered. "Where are you?"

"I'm in Wakefield. That's a hundred miles from Bayport on the way to New York City. A consignment of gold has been stolen from the mint here. The case is too big for one detective, and I need your help. Come to the Archway Motel. Tell Mother and Aunt Gertrude where you'll be, but don't say there's any danger involved. Make it fast! Ah-ah-aaa—"

Mr Hardy groaned and ended his sentence in a gasp. Then the boys heard a scuffling noise.

"Dad!" Frank shouted frantically. "Dad, what's going on?"

Something hit the floor with a heavy thump, and there was a dragging sound. A door slammed in the background. Then silence. The three boys stared at one another in dismay.

"What—?" Chet began.

"Sh—sh!" Frank said and motioned to the phone.

Footsteps could be heard approaching. Someone breathing heavily picked up the receiver.

"Hello!" Frank said. "Hello?"

The phone clicked, and the line went dead.

"That wasn't Dad who hung up!" Frank exclaimed. "Something's wrong!"

"That's for sure," Joe said grimly.

"Try the motel desk," Chet suggested.

Frank dialled the Archway Motel and asked for Fenton Hardy's room. A moment later the clerk reported that there was no answer. Frank asked to speak to the manager. He introduced himself, then explained to the man that he had heard strange noises coming from his father's room.

"It sounded as if he were being attacked," Frank concluded.

"Attacked!" the manager exploded. "I'll check immediately and will call you back."

Frank hung up. "What do you make of it?" he asked his brother.

"Somebody must have sneaked up on Dad while he was talking on the phone," Joe said. "Someone he hadn't counted on."

"Probably more than one person," Chet added. "He could have taken care of himself otherwise."

"Not if he were hit by surprise," Joe argued.

The phone shrilled again. Frank picked it up.

"Mr Hardy's room is empty," the motel manager said. "I've also had him paged, but he doesn't answer."

"Anything wrong in the room?" Frank asked.

"No—except that the bedspread was half pulled off and some clothes were lying on the floor. When I see your father, I'll tell him you called. I'll also notify the police just in case your suspicions are correct." The manager hung up, and so did Frank.

"Dad must have been dragged from the room," the young detective theorized. "That could account for the bedspread. We'd better do something fast!"

"We'll have to go to Wakefield right away!" Joe said.

"How about my going along?" Chet put in. "I know all about gold. Maybe I can identify the loot." Then he added, "As long as it's not too dangerous to handle."

The Hardys were used to Chet's shying away from danger, but they knew they could rely on him when the sleuthing became rough. He had been helpful in many of their investigations.

"Okay, Chet," Joe said. "Call home and we'll be off."

"Leave your jalopy in our garage," Frank suggested. "Better get some clean clothes out of it."

Chet and the Hardys always carried extra clothes in

their cars in case of an emergency.

Frank quickly scribbled a note telling his mother and Aunt Gertrude that they were on the way to Wakefield to join Mr Hardy. He added that there was nothing to worry about. "Not much!" he thought to himself. "Just whether Dad's dead or alive!"

Joe backed the car out of the garage and soon the three boys were rolling down Main Street. Joe fretted at the wheel because traffic was heavy, but finally they got out of the city. He stepped up the pace and they roared towards Wakefield.

Mile after mile zipped away beneath their wheels. They passed farmhouses and pastures. At one spot chickens, out of their coops, fled squawking as the car rocketed by them.

Chet remarked, "If you should run over any of our feathered friends, stop so I can pick some up. Chicken soup is a great dish. I haven't had anything since breakfast but a couple of hamburgers and a bottle of lemonade."

Food always interested Chet, even in the middle of an investigation. The Hardys usually laughed at his remarks, but this time they said nothing.

"Okay," Chet said, "I get the message. I was just testing. Trying to cheer you up."

"I could use some cheering," Frank admitted. "Do you think Dad's been kidnapped, Joe?"

"I'm afraid so," his brother replied glumly. "Probably by the crooks who stole the gold."

"Don't jump to conclusions," Chet advised. "Anyway, your father has always managed to get out of tight spots because he's the smartest detective we know. Right?"

"Right," said Frank and Joe in unison.

"Let's talk about something else," Chet said.

"Like what?" Joe inquired.

"Like gold!" Chet answered. "Do you know the melting point of gold?"

Joe grinned. "Over a thousand degrees centigrade."

Chet looked crestfallen. "Oh, so you know that. Well, what can you dissolve gold with?"

"A mixture of hydrochloric and nitric acid."

"You Hardys know everything," Chet complained.

Frank decided to soothe their friend's feelings. "Not as much as you do, Chet. It's just that we ran some lab tests on gold for one of our clients."

The Hardys had a criminology laboratory over their garage, where they did scientific analyses for their clients. They matched fingerprints under the microscope and carried out chemical tests of poisons, explosives, and other materials from the scene of a crime.

While the boys were talking, they approached a hill with a stone wall on the right. Joe drove up as fast as he could within the speed limit. Suddenly a large station wagon hurtled over the crest of the hill. The driver, a burly man, was hunched over the wheel. He was on the wrong side of the road and racing directly at their car!

"Watch it, Joe!" Frank shouted.

Because of the wall, Joe could not move any farther to the right. With split-second timing, he swerved to the left. The station wagon swept past on the right. The Hardys' car skidded out of control for a moment, but Joe pulled it back into the correct lane and went on.

"Lucky you kept your cool," Frank complimented his brother. "There wasn't enough room for a penny between that station wagon and us."

"You can say that again," Chet remarked. "That knucklehead shouldn't be allowed to drive a kiddie car."

The three settled back for the rest of their trip to Wakefield, and Chet continued his lecture on gold. He described how prehistoric people used the yellow metal for jewellery, such as rings and bracelets, and later for money. He added that currently most of the gold was obtained from the deep mines in South Africa.

"The Russians," Chet revealed, "mine gold in Siberia and sell it on the international market. Headquarters for the gold exchange is Zurich, Switzerland."

"Perhaps the stolen Wakefield gold came originally from Siberia," Joe reasoned. "But who knows whether or not we'll ever see it."

"Talking about gold," Chet informed them, "there's an exhibition at the Early Art Museum in New York. Old Scythian artifacts. I hear it's fabulous."

"Sounds interesting," Joe said. "Maybe we can go there after we find Dad."

He turned left to get off the highway at the Wakefield exit, and ten minutes later drew into the Archway Motel parking lot. The boys went inside, where a teenage youth stood at the registration desk.

"Any message from Fenton Hardy?" Joe asked him.

"No. But I have one for Frank and Joe Hardy. Is that you?"

"Yes," Frank replied.

"Somebody called," the clerk stated. "Didn't give his name. Just said for Frank and Joe Hardy to come to the Stacy Hotel."

"How do we get there?" Frank asked.

"Go left to the end of the road, turn right, then right again at the second traffic light. It's a flea-bitten rat-trap in a rough neighbourhood. Watch your step."

"Will do," Frank said. "And thanks for the tip."

The drive to the Stacy took the boys into an area of run-down houses and dismal streets. Local toughs sauntered by, glowering at them.

"I hope we don't run into street gangs," Chet remarked. "A guy could be mugged in this end of town without half trying."

Joe parked in front of the Stacy. The boys climbed out and stood on the pavement, gazing up at the grimy exterior of the hotel. A bewhiskered tramp strolled up the street towards them. He was dressed in old clothes, battered shoes, and a slouch hat. They stepped aside to let him pass.

Abreast of them the tramp suddenly turned and deliberately bumped into Joe. "Follow me," he snarled, "if you know what's good for you!"

·2·

The Subterranean Vault

REACTING instinctively, Frank and Joe grabbed the tramp's arms to keep him from pulling a knife or a gun. Chet waved a fist under the man's nose.

"Fellows, hold it!" said a familiar voice. "I'll go quietly."

The tramp was Fenton Hardy! As the boys showed their surprise, he whispered, "Don't give me away. Play my game."

"Okay," Frank replied. "But we're glad to see you." Aloud he said, "All right, Harry, we'll buy your dinner."

He led the way into the hotel, where they sat down at a table in a secluded corner of the dining room. The other customers looked seedy, and the waitress chewed gum loudly as she took their order. When the food arrived, Chet seized his knife and fork and began to eat with gusto.

"I was in my room," Mr Hardy said in a low tone, "when a couple of men came in—"

He broke off as he noticed that the waitress was still standing near their table, flipping through her order pad. Then he said loudly, "A couple of men came in and asked me if I wanted to buy an encyclopedia."

The waitress went to another table to present the bill. Mr Hardy resumed his story. "They jumped me while I was talking to you on the phone, and slipped a cloth saturated with chloroform over my face."

Frank nodded. "We heard a thud and figured somebody was dragging you out of the room."

"Right. When I came to, I was in an old abandoned garage. I—" Mr Hardy suddenly changed the subject and talked about finding a job at the Wakefield timber company, since the waitress again stood within earshot. After she had left, he continued, "That girl seems rather nosey. Well, anyway, I picked the lock, got out, went to my car, and put on this disguise. Then I called the Archway Motel from a pay phone and left the message about meeting me at the Stacy."

"What's it all about?" Frank asked.

"The Wakefield Mint has been robbed of a big consignment of gold bars. The haul is worth over a million dollars!"

Joe whistled. "That's a big deal!"

Mr Hardy agreed. "I've been hired by John Armstrong, the administrative assistant to the director of the mint. He asked me to keep this secret. That's why I couldn't tell you what the investigation was about. Then I received a threatening phone call warning me to get off the case. At that point, I decided I'd better send you an SOS."

"Good thing you did," Frank said.

Mr Hardy went on, "Incidentally, Chet, I'm glad you came along. That fist you waved under my nose seems like a lethal weapon."

Chet tried to grin, but was not very successful since his mouth was full of baked potato.

"Got any leads, Dad?" Joe asked.

Fenton Hardy shook his head. "Not really. I assume the pair who chloroformed me belong to the gang that stole the gold. Beyond that, nothing."

Frank and Joe ruminated over their father's experience as they finished the meal. Chet downed his last mouthful of apple pie. As the waitress was adding up the bill, Frank handed his father a ten dollar bill.

"There, Harry, that should help you out for a while," he said.

"Thanks, my boy," Mr Hardy replied, speaking in the whine of a tramp down on his luck.

Leaving the hotel, he whispered to Frank, "Stay at the Shadyside Motel down the street tonight. Meet me at my car at nine in the morning. It's parked in a private garage at 10, Pine Street. The people who own it are away, so I'm using it as my dressing room. I can change my disguises there without being seen."

The elder Hardy slouched away into the darkness, and the boys drove to the Shadyside Motel, where they spent the night. In the morning they met Mr Hardy as arranged. The detective no longer looked like a tramp. He had stashed the old clothes and the fake whiskers in the trunk of his car and resumed his usual appearance.

"Mr Hardy, you sure fooled me last night," Chet said.

"That was the idea," the sleuth told him. "If my disguises didn't fool everybody, I'd be in big trouble. Boys, suppose we take your car."

Frank got behind the wheel. "Where to?"

"The Wakefield Mint."

The mint was a square two-storey building. Faced with white stone, it had rows of narrow windows along the first storey. The ground floor was sheathed in stone and steel.

The foyer inside contained a collection of coins and medals produced by the mint. A crowd milled around the main exhibit, a medal representing Captain John Smith at Jamestown.

Fenton Hardy showed his pass to a guard, who escorted him and the boys down a corridor, through a door lined with steel bars, to the office of the administrative assistant.

John Armstrong was a friendly-looking man who wore horn-rimmed glasses. He got up from the swivel chair behind his big desk and shook hands with Mr Hardy, then with each boy, as he was introduced.

"They've helped me on previous cases," the investigator explained, "and I'll need them to assist me on this one." He described the kidnap attempt.

Armstrong expressed concern, then said he had no objections to the boys participating. "Perhaps, then, you can solve our problem quicker," he remarked. "I want this case cracked before Director Wadsworth gets back from his vacation. I'm responsible for the mint while he's away, you know."

"Mr Armstrong, suppose you clue us in," Frank suggested.

Armstrong looked grave. "First, let me remind you that there must be no leaks about the theft. We don't want any publicity in the news media."

"Mum's the word," Chet vowed.

Joe inquired about security precautions.

"The best," Armstrong stated. "See this panel on my desk? It monitors the entire mint. We have hidden television cameras watching every square inch of the building. Our security equipment includes trip wires, photoelectric plates, and laser beams. If anybody gets in their way, sirens go off and warning lights flash on the panel."

"It sounds as if you're better protected than Fort Knox," Joe said. "How come the gold was stolen?" '

"That's just it," Armstrong said, looking bewildered. "The equipment must have been turned off. It was back on the next morning, however."

"What about the guards?" Frank asked.

"That's stranger yet," Armstrong went on. "One was posted at the outer door, one at the inner steel door, and one here in my office, monitoring the mint through the TV cameras. They were supposed to alert the rest of the night shift if anything happened, but they didn't."

"In other words, they went off with the thieves," Chet said.

"No. They're here!"

"You mean they helped the thieves get in, then let them escape with the loot, and stayed behind?" Joe was incredulous.

"Yes. That's what's so strange," Armstrong replied. "They claim nothing unusual happened at any time that night. The police questioned them after they were arrested but they're sticking to their story."

Frank shook his head. "It doesn't make sense. Where was the gold taken from?"

"The subterranean vault," Armstrong said. "Come on. I'll take you down there."

He ushered the group to his private elevator and pushed the button. The elevator descended three floors. The doors opened and Armstrong led the way to a steel door, where a guard was on duty. He spun the dial until the combination clicked-and pushed the door inwards.

The boys gaped. Gold bars about a foot long were stacked in rows on racks that stretched across most of the room. A yellow gleam shimmered under fluorescent lighting. A couple of men in shirtsleeves were counting the bars and entering figures in a ledger.

Chet's eyes bulged. "There's got to be a million dollars in here," he practically shouted.

"More than that, young man," Armstrong said. "We're missing twenty-five bars. Each weighs over twenty-seven pounds, and with gold selling on the international market at a very high rate presently, that consignment comes to more than a million."

He gestured towards an empty rack near the door. "That's where the stolen bars were when we closed the vault for the night. The thieves must have carted the gold out of here and round to the outer door at the rear of the building. That's where they made their getaway."

Frank was peering at the nearest row of gold bars. "Why, they're stamped with the hammer and sickle," he noted.

"Same as the missing gold," Armstrong replied. "The Russians traded it through middlemen in Zurich, who sold it to us."

He conducted them out of the gold room and through the subterranean vault to a freight elevator. They emerged at the rear door of the mint . A guard let them through into a receiving area, where some armoured cars were parked.

"I'm late for a meeting," Armstrong said and excused himself. "Please look around all you want and we'll talk later." He went back to his office.

Frank quickly surveyed the lot. "Nothing to stop the crooks once they got the gold this far," he concluded.

"Right," Joe agreed. "But how did they get this far? We'll have to talk to the guards."

"You go ahead," Mr Hardy said. "I'll carry on my investigation here at the mint and talk to the employees."

"And I'm going to have breakfast," Chet stated.

Frank chuckled. "Your second breakfast, Chet."

"Got to keep my strength up if I'm going to solve this case," the stout boy replied airily.

Frank and Joe dropped Chet at a snack-bar and drove to police headquarters. They identified themselves to the sergeant at the desk.

"You're Fenton Hardy's sons?" the officer asked. "That's good enough for me. Around here, we admire your father's work. Come on! I'll let you speak to the prisoners from the mint. Funny thing about them."

"Funny?" Joe prodded.

"They've got to be guilty," the sergeant said, "but they've taken a polygraph, or lie-detector, test. It says they're telling the truth!"

The three men looked sullen. They were Herb Ponty, Fred Walters, and Mike Nicholson. Ponty did most of the talking.

He admitted they had been on duty the night the gold had vanished. He himself had been stationed in Armstrong's office at the monitor. "Walters was posted at the outer door to the receiving area. Nicholson guarded the steel door to the gold room."

The Hardys cross-examined the men. Had they left their posts during the night? Had they gone to sleep?

"No, not us," Ponty replied defensively. "It's our job to stay awake. Anyway, it wouldn't have made any difference. A thief trying to get in would have kicked off the alarm system."

"You could have turned off the alarm," Joe asserted.

"If I had," Ponty argued belligerently, "would I have hung around to be arrested? I'd have left with the thieves."

"Yes," Frank said, "but the gold is gone. Have you three any idea how the crooks pulled off the heist?"

"No, we don't remember seeing anything unusual all night," Ponty declared. "When Mr Armstrong opened the vault the next morning, the gold wasn't there and we were arrested."

Frank and Joe realized they could not get any more information from the prisoners and headed back to the Wakefield Mint.

The boys picked up Chet at the snack-bar as he was drinking his third milkshake. Then they rode back to the mint, where they told Fenton Hardy and John Armstrong about their talk with the accused men.

"How many people know the combination of the vault door?" Frank asked Armstrong.

"As I told your father, only Director Wadsworth and I. You see—"

A screaming siren cut him off. Red and blue lights flashed on the monitor panel. A moving blur appeared on one TV screen.

Armstrong gasped. "There's a thief in the vault!" he cried.

·3·

"Deep Six F.H."

JOHN Armstrong rushed into his private elevator. Fenton Hardy and the boys crowded in on his heels. The elevator descended three floors and then the doors opened.

The noise of the siren was nearly deafening in the subterranean vault. A guard stood at the door of the gold room, which was wide open. He turned towards Armstrong.

"Unauthorized person inside, sir," he announced. "The door was open and he got in."

"I left it open, Porter," Armstrong confessed. "I thought Millard and Lajinski had nearly finished counting the gold and would close it when they came out. My mistake."

"They hadn't finished when the siren went off," Porter replied.

He led the way inside. The two men in shirtsleeves were still there, talking to a third, who looked embarrassed.

"I didn't know a laser beam crossed the gold room," he protested. "I got in the way by accident when I came in to see why the door was open."

Frank stared at him. "If you're an employee of the

mint, why don't you know about the alarm system in the vault?"

"I'm new here," the man replied sulkily.

Porter nodded. "That's true. We took him on three days ago. He hasn't had time to learn the ropes, but he'll catch on."

Armstrong ordered that the siren be turned off and sent the man to his post; then he escorted his visitors to his office. He sat down in his swivel chair and mopped his brow with a large handkerchief from his breast pocket. Mr Hardy took a stuffed leather easy chair. The boys occupied a couch.

"Mr Armstrong," Frank began the conversation, "you were saying that only you and Mr Wadsworth, the director, know the combination to the steel door of the gold room. Do you think somebody else could have learned it?"

"I suppose someone could in spite of all our precautions," Armstrong admitted. He added, "The gold was shipped from the Swiss Gold Syndicate in Zurich. The bars might be smuggled back there for resale by a shady international financier. I'd better send an agent to Zurich to investigate."

Fenton Hardy smiled. "Two agents," he suggested. "I dare say Frank and Joe will volunteer. They're on their spring vacation."

"Will you, boys?" Armstrong asked eagerly.

The Hardys quickly agreed. Chet looked crestfallen, but said nothing. Armstrong turned to him. "You're included if you want to be."

"Oh, great!" Chet said, and smiled again.

"The place to begin is the Swiss Gold Syndicate," Armstrong pointed out. "They handle transactions on the world-wide gold market, and know about this theft. I'm sure they'll be glad to co-operate. I'll set up an interview for you."

He made a long-distance call to Zurich. While he spoke, the expression on his face changed from a frown to utter surprise. When he hung up, he said, "I think we have our first clue!"

"What happened?" Fenton Hardy asked.

"I didn't speak to Johann Jung, the director of the syndicate. He's in South Africa, inspecting gold mines, and won't be back till next Monday. But his assistant just told me that he received a phone call from a man who said that he should watch out for the Wakefield gold. It is expected to be sold in Zurich illegally in about two weeks."

"Wow!" Frank said. "Who was the caller?"

"He didn't identify himself. But I hope you can find out. You're supposed to be in Jung's office on Monday at two in the afternoon."

Fenton Hardy arose. "That gives us some time for sleuthing here before you leave," he said. "I have a notion the crooks have already flown the gold out of the Wakefield area or are about to. Transporting it by truck on the highway would be too risky. I'll alert the airlines. You boys check the charter carriers. Also scout around and see if you can find a private airstrip where a plane could take off with a cargo of gold bullion. I'll meet you at the garage later."

The three boys went out and got into the Hardys' car. Frank turned on the ignition and headed towards the centre of town. Suddenly he circled around the block and stopped at a phone on the corner.

"Frank, what's up?" Chet asked.

"I think we should check out Mr Armstrong's story."

Chet's eyes widened in astonishment. "*He* isn't a suspect!"

Joe spoke up. "Frank's right, Chet. Everybody's a suspect in this case."

Frank found Armstrong's address in the phone book and the address of Wakefield's only charter airline. They drove first to the man's house. A motherly woman answered the door.

"Mr Armstrong is not at home," she told them. "I'm Mrs Wright, his housekeeper. Mr Armstrong is a bachelor."

Frank mentioned the night of the gold theft. "Was Mr Armstrong at home that night?"

"Oh yes. He returned from the mint in time for dinner, as usual. And he didn't leave the house till the following morning."

Frank thanked the housekeeper and the boys resumed their drive to the centre of Wakefield.

"That clears Mr Armstrong," Frank commented. "He was in bed when the gold vanished from the mint." In a few minutes Frank parked in front of the Carrier Consolidated office on Main Street. The boys went inside. They looked around in surprise. The office was a dusty cubby-hole. A pile of canvas bags lay in one corner, and a half-filled coke bottle stood on the counter. An old plaque on the wall proclaimed that Carrier Consolidated would ferry any cargo anywhere.

"This place could use a clean-up," Frank muttered. "If only Aunt Gertrude were here! She'd give the guy in charge a piece of her mind."

"I'll see if he's in the back room," Joe said. He went

around behind the counter. Suddenly a hand pointed a round metal barrel at him through the doorway!

"Watch out!" Chet whispered hoarsely. "He's got a gun."

Before Joe could move, a heavy-set individual came through the doorway. "Look here," he said. "This is our newest fire extinguisher. Point it like a pistol, pull the trigger, and presto! It shoots foam all over the blaze. Neat idea, eh?"

"Neat is right," Joe answered. "I thought it was a real pistol."

The man put the fire extinguisher on the shelf behind him. "Carrier Consolidated, at your service," he said.

"Any flights to Zurich, Switzerland?" Frank asked.

"Sure. What's on your mind?"

"We're working on a deal involving a shipment," Frank said.

The man reached for a ledger. "We have two flights to Zurich this month: a cargo of tin and a shipment of timber. The next flight will be in approximately a week. What's the weight going to be?"

"Uh—about two hundred pounds."

"No problem."

"Okay. We'll let you know when the deal goes through," Frank said, and thanked the man for the information.

As the boys were leaving the office, they almost ran into a woman who came through the door and walked up to the counter. She was the waitress from the Stacy Hotel!

Frank nudged Joe as he started to close the door behind him. "What do you know about that?" he whispered.

"Let's see if we can hear any of their conversation," Joe replied and left the door open a crack.

The three friends stood still and pressed their ears against the door, but there was only the sound of muffled voices.

"What now?" Chet asked. "This is strange."

"Let's go to the Stacy and check up on the waitress," Frank suggested. "Maybe she had a reason for being nosey last night."

They went to the hotel and spoke to the manager. "We'd like to talk to your pretty, red-haired waitress," Frank began. "Is she in?"

"No, it's her day off," the man replied with a grin. "But there's no use in trying to date her."

"Oh?" said Frank.

"Sure. Her husband runs the Carrier Consolidated Office. He'd give you a hard time."

The boys wanted to roar with laughter, but instead pretended to be embarrassed and left quickly.

"What do you know!" Frank said when the boys were back in the car.

"That you're some smoothy," Chet needled him.

Joe was serious. "Maybe both the husband and the wife are involved in our case."

"What do we do now?" Chet asked.

Frank started the engine. "Let's see if we can find a private airstrip."

The highway curved round Wakefield to the north, east, and south. An undeveloped area lay to the west. They decided to scout in that direction. Frank parked at a dead end, and the boys crossed a field on foot. Then they plunged into the woods.

For two hours they tramped between groves of trees

and thick bushes. They stumbled over stones and fallen tree trunks. Brambles tore at their clothing and scratched their hands. Doggedly they puffed up hills and down into ravines.

Finally Chet halted and sat down on a boulder, perspiration streaming down his face. His breath came in great gasps. He held up a hand and let it fall limply into his lap. "Fellows, I've had it!" he announced.

Joe grinned. "Don't give up now, Chet! You're getting rid of that spare tyre round your middle. Besides, you've got to walk back out of the woods!"

Chet groaned. "Don't remind me."

Frank was surveying the ground beyond the boulder. Suddenly he called to the others. Joe raced over. Chet followed slowly.

"What's up?" Joe asked eagerly.

"Tyre marks on the ground!" Frank exclaimed. "A car went right through the woods!"

"It probably came from the dirt road we crossed a couple of miles back," Joe theorized. "Where did it go?"

"Let's find out," Frank urged.

Trained woodsmen, the boys followed the tyre marks. They noted how the dried-out, brown grass was flattened, and how the vehicle had run over bushes and around trees. Silently the three sleuths pursued the trail through a thicket to where the woods ended. All the trees and shrubs had recently been cleared away in the shape of an oblong.

"It's an airstrip," Frank said in a low voice. "Do either of you see a plane?"

"No," Chet answered, and Joe shook his head.

They scouted around the airstrip in Indian file, with

Frank in the lead. They had nearly returned to their starting point when Joe noticed sunlight gleaming on metal in a grove of trees.

"I'll investigate," he offered. Dropping to the ground, he crawled to a large bush, peered through the bare branches, and saw a car parked in the grove. Nobody was in sight, so he waved to his companions to follow him.

The car was old and battered. Scratches on the bumpers showed it had been driven a long distance through the woods. It had no licence plates.

Finding the doors unlocked, Joe opened the glove compartment and took out a sheet of paper lying inside. Frank and Chet peered over his shoulder as he read a short typewritten message.

DEEP SIX F.H.

·4·

Stop Thief!

THE boys were shocked. Frank felt cold chills run up and down his spine.

"I'll bet F.H. stands for Fenton Hardy!" he exclaimed.

"And deep six means get rid of him," Joe added grimly.

"No wonder your dad said it was a dangerous case," Chet put in. "We'd better let him know the gang's after him."

They marched back to the dirt road and on to their car. Joe drove to the garage, where Mr Hardy was already waiting. Frank quickly explained to him about the airstrip near the Wakefield Mint and the car hidden in the clump of trees.

"Here's what I found in the glove compartment," Joe said, handing him the message.

Mr Hardy read it thoughtfully. "This ties in with that phone call I received," he said. "Whoever stole the gold wants me off the case. When he realized that his warning had no effect, he and his pals decided to use other measures."

"What now, Mr Hardy?" Chet asked.

"Leave the car where it is. Don't let on to anyone that

31

you've seen it. I'll keep the area under surveillance and see who comes back to the spot. That might break the case wide open. I only hope," he added wryly, "that the person who is to receive this message has not seen it yet!"

Frank looked doubtful. "I think Joe and I shouldn't go to Zurich, Dad. It's too dangerous for you to be here without us."

Joe supported his brother. "We'll stay in Wakefield and help you out in case of trouble."

Fenton Hardy shook his head. "I realize the danger," he confessed. "But I'll watch my step, and take my assistant, Sam Radley, off his case to give me a hand if necessary. We must look into the Zurich angle, and my sons are naturals for the assignment. Chet, if your folks consent to your going, too, I'm sure Frank and Joe will be glad to have you along. Go home to Bayport and arrange for your flight."

Reluctantly the boys drove away early the next morning. On the way Chet begged to stop in New York to see the gold exhibition at the Early Art Museum before returning to Bayport.

The Hardys consented and they went on to New York City. Joe spotted a parking lot only a few blocks from the museum. They left the car and walked to the building. A large sign over the entrance read: SCYTHIAN GOLD. The words below stated that the art objects had been sent to the United States by the Soviet Union under a cultural-exchange programme.

Chet assumed a learned expression. "The Scythians lived in an area that now belongs to Russia," he intoned. "That's why they have the Scythian gold. They dug up a lot of it in places where those guys camped."

Frank smiled. "Very interesting, Chet. We'll hear the rest of your lecture later, Professor Morton."

The boys were the first viewers to arrive at the museum. The man in charge of the exhibition was a Russian with jet-black hair and a black spade-shaped beard. He wore black clothes and a ring with a large black stone, which gleamed as he gestured.

"I am Ivan Orlov," he introduced himself. "Perhaps you would care to have me describe our Scythian gold."

Chet waved a hand. "That won't be necessary," he declared. "I'm a pro when it comes to gold."

Frank nudged Joe. He concealed his mouth with his hand and whispered, "Chet's up to his old tricks, telling the experts he knows more about their subject than they do."

Joe grinned. "Let's see if he gets away with it."

Orlov gave Chet a dubious look. "I do not doubt you, my friend," the Russian said, "but surely—"

"I'm a correspondence-course graduate in golden artifacts," Chet told him. "And I've got a diploma to prove it."

"I have never heard of such a title," Orlov said coolly. "But please go inside." His black ring reflected rays of light as he gestured towards the first room of the exhibition.

The boys entered, noticing a sign with the words ANIMAL CHAMBER. Large locked cases held gleaming gold figures of horses, dogs, bulls, deer, mountain goats, tigers, and many other species.

"Those Scythians were big on animals," Chet observed. "They made gold representations of everything that moved."

The Bayporters walked through the display, marvelling at the high quality of the Scythian art. They stopped before a huge vase ornamented in gold with the figure of a tiger leaping towards the horns of a defiant bull.

"Siberian tiger," Chet identified the big cat.

The next case contained nothing but replicas of horses, large and small, reclining and standing, jumping and galloping.

"Don't tell me, Chet," Joe said. "Let me guess. The Scythians rode a lot."

"Right. They were terrific riders."

A small figurine in the lower left-hand corner caught their interest. It was a golden horse, rearing on its hind legs. The animal was perfectly modelled with uplifted head and tossing mane.

"I'd like to own that one," Joe remarked. "I'll bet Mother would put it on the mantel in our living room."

Frank grinned. "Aunt Gertrude would surely keep it polished," he added.

While they sauntered around the Animal Chamber another visitor came in and looked at the display with intense interest. He was a middle-aged man with grey hair, dressed in a pin-striped suit. Under his right arm he clutched a leather briefcase, his hand tightly grasping the handle as if he were afraid somebody might snatch it from him.

As the stranger stepped back to get a better view of the figurine of the rearing horse, he bumped into Joe. The briefcase fell to the floor. The man instantly reached down and picked it up.

"Excuse me," he apologized in a high-pitched voice tinged with a slight Spanish accent. "I did not see you."

"No harm done," Joe said cheerfully.

The boys went into the next room, the Ornament Chamber. Every case gleamed with rows of Scythian rings, necklaces, bracelets, pins, brooches, earrings, buckles, and other items of personal adornment.

In an authoritative voice Chet told his friends about the dress of the ancient tribe. "The Scythian girls went in for gold in a big way," he said, "and the men, too. Everybody wore—"

He was interrupted by a frenzied shout from the Animal Chamber. "Stop, thief!"

Alarmed, the boys hurried out into the hallway. At the far end they saw the stranger with the briefcase and the Spanish accent push through the revolving door. A guard dashed from the Animal Chamber and ran after him. The three Bayporters joined the chase.

When they reached the street, however, the fugitive had already hailed a taxi and was speeding away in the traffic.

"What luck!" Frank fumed. "And there isn't another cab in sight."

"Mr Orlov will be furious," the guard said, his voice trembling with fear. "But I noticed it too late—"

"Exactly what happened?" Frank asked.

"That man ran out of the Animal Chamber. I became suspicious and checked. I found that the glass in one of the display cases had been cut open. A figurine was missing. I alerted Orlov and took off after the thief."

"Was anyone else in the room at the time?" Frank queried.

"No. Mr Orlov had gone to his office. Oh, just before the robbery a tall blond man came out of the room and buried his cigarette butt in the bucket of sand in the hallway. I appreciated that because we don't want a fire in the museum. The man went upstairs. In a moment the thief appeared. Obviously he waited until he was alone in the room, then stole the figurine."

The boys found Orlov in the Animal Chamber in front of a display case. A piece of glass had been cut out neatly, and the figurine of the rearing horse that Frank had admired was missing.

The Russian was extremely agitated. He demanded to know what had become of the thief.

"He got away, Mr Orlov," the guard replied. "Jumped into a taxi."

Orlov began wringing his hands. "Americans! You cannot trust them. I never should have brought the gold here. Our government will be very angry!"

"Maybe we can help you recover the piece," Frank offered. "We have been doing some detective work. Unfortunately, the thief seems to have left no clue."

"I don't know about that," Chet spoke up. "While you were staring after that taxi, I picked this up from the pavement. Maybe the guy dropped it!"

He held up a telegram. The others crowded around and read the message.

PEDRO ZEMOG. TAKE CONSIGNMENT TO ZURICH. A.P.

·5·

The Bulging Briefcase

CHET grinned with a self-satisfied expression as the others read the telegram. "The Hardys aren't the only detectives around here." He chortled.

Joe scratched his head. "But what does the message mean?"

"Search me," Chet replied.

Frank turned to the Russian curator. "Mr Orlov, does the name Pedro Zemog suggest anything to you?"

"Nothing!" Orlov answered. "Nothing!"

"What about A.P.?"

"Nothing."

The Hardys wondered about the briefcase Zemog had been carrying. Had he opened it in the museum and slipped the figurine inside?

"I saw nothing!" Orlov said.

The guard added, "The thief did not open his briefcase when I saw him. As a matter of fact, he acted as if it were made of solid gold, and he held it very tightly."

"Your police had better do something about getting my ancient horse back!" Orlov exclaimed impatiently. "This theft could be a serious matter between our two countries."

"Yes," Frank agreed. "You'll have to report it right

away. But perhaps we can help you. Mr Zemog is headed for Zurich according to this telegram. We're planning to go there ourselves. Mr Orlov, would you like us to try to find the thief?"

Orlov stared at him. "You—but who *are* you?"

Frank introduced himself, Joe, and Chet and told Orlov about his father's work.

The Russian became interested. "You are going to Zurich? Good. I will let you pursue the case in Switzerland."

Joe had a sudden thought. "What about the tall blond man? If he's still upstairs, he might be able to tell us something about the thief."

Orlov gave the boys permission to search the building. They rushed upstairs, but could not find anyone who fitted the blond man's description. They returned and reported their failure.

"He must have left by this time," Orlov said. "Too bad we did not think of looking for him sooner."

"Maybe the guy didn't know anything was wrong and simply strolled out after he looked at the exhibition," the guard added.

Frank and Joe promised Orlov they would stay on the case. Then they went with Chet to the parking lot.

"Let's stop at police headquarters," Frank suggested. "We may be able to explain the loss of the gold horse better than Mr Orlov."

He took the wheel and a few minutes later they were talking to the lieutenant on duty. He agreed to cooperate. Hearing their names, he asked if Frank and Joe were the sons of Fenton Hardy. When he learned that they were, he said, "Fenton is a great detective. I'm glad to hear you're following in his footsteps."

After the lieutenant heard the description of the suspect, he shrugged his shoulders. "Middle-aged man with grey hair, pin-striped suit, carrying a briefcase. Hundreds of men in New York match that description. But I'll put out a bulletin on him and alert the airlines. Who knows? We might be lucky."

The boys thanked the lieutenant and drove to Bayport. After dropping Chet at his house, the Hardys hurried home.

They found their mother in the living room, reading a magazine. She was a pleasant woman who worried about the cases her husband and her sons handled. But she had confidence in them and knew that they had squeezed out of tight situations many times.

"Frank, Joe," she greeted them. The boys hugged her. "I'm relieved to see you. What have you been doing?"

"Pretending we're gold bugs," Joe said with a chuckle.

Another voice interrupted. "Bugs? We don't want any bugs in this house! What are you boys up to now?"

The speaker was their Aunt Gertrude, Fenton Hardy's sister, who lived with the family. She was often stern with her nephews, but they knew she was very fond of them. Miss Hardy admired their skill in solving mysteries, although she tried not to show it.

Joe laughed. "Aunt Gertrude, these aren't the kinds of bugs you sweep out the back door with your broom."

"We're not talking about entomology, the science of bugs," Frank added with a grin.

"Goldology would be more like it," Joe quipped.

Gertrude Hardy sniffed. "You boys can keep your ologies and your bugs," she stated firmly. 'Now, if you please, explain your explanation.''

"Dad's trying to recover a shipment of gold that was stolen from the Wakefield Mint,'' Frank told her, "and we're helping him. As a matter of fact, we'll be going to Zurich, Switzerland, as soon as we can get a flight.''

"Isn't that a risky adventure?'' his mother asked.

Frank reassured her. "We'll interview the director of the Swiss Gold Syndicate and ask if the gold has been routed through there.''

"You might get buried by an avalanche,'' Aunt Gertrude remarked. "What will you do then?''

"We'll wait for a Saint Bernard dog to find us,'' Joe needled his aunt. "Seriously, though, we'll be all right.''

"We don't want to stay away too long,'' Frank said. "Not when we have your delicious pies to come back to.''

Gertrude Hardy smiled and smoothed back her hair. She could never resist a compliment about her cooking, and promptly invited her nephews into the kitchen for cherry pie and homemade whipped cream.

The next morning Chet phoned. He was glum. "Dad says I have to stay home and help on the farm,'' he reported. "Have fun, fellows, and round up the gold heisters.''

Frank and Joe flew out of Kennedy Airport the following evening. They would have liked to stay in the city longer to see if they could trace Pedro Zemog, but could not book a later flight that would get them to Zurich in time for their appointment with Johann Jung.

Their jet zoomed up from the runway, climbed into the sky, and circled over New York's skyscrapers. Frank and Joe settled near the rear and got a good view of the Empire State Building, the towers of the trade centre, and the tip of lower Manhattan. Soon the plane gained altitude and all they could see below them were puffy white clouds.

"I wonder if there's a connection between the Wakefield gold and the Scythian treasure," Frank said thoughtfully.

"Could be," Joe replied. "Both came from the Soviet Union."

"And it's our job to find both," Frank reminded his brother. "The consignment mentioned in the telegram Zemog dropped—could it be gold bars that vanished from Wakefield?"

"Good question," Joe replied. "Maybe we'll find the answer in Zurich."

He slipped out of his seat into the aisle and went for a drink of water near the centre of the plane. Then he strolled up front and finally started back. He noticed a man with grey hair, dressed in a dark brown suit. Though he was asleep, he guarded a briefcase under one arm.

Joe paused a moment. "That guy resembles the thief from the museum, Pedro Zemog," he thought. "Too bad he's asleep. I wish I could find out if he speaks with a Spanish accent."

Joe went to ask a stewardess. She replied that the man had not spoken so she did not know.

Joe returned to his seat and informed Frank of his suspicion. Frank immediately made a trip to the front of the plane. On his way back he glanced at the man, who was still sleeping.

When Frank returned, Joe asked, "What do you think?"

"Hard to tell. We're looking for a guy with a Spanish accent. Let's wait till he wakes up. If this passenger is not Zemog, we could get into real big trouble by accusing him of being a thief."

"But didn't you see the bulge in his briefcase?" Joe asked. "It could be the gold horse."

"Joe, the man had to go through the detection centre at the airport. A gold object would have been spotted and he would have been arrested."

"That's right," Joe had to admit.

"We'd better sit tight until we get to Zurich," Frank urged, "unless we hear him talk in the plane."

The stewardess arrived with a late dinner, which the boys lost no time in eating. After that, they checked on the suspect again. He had obviously not eaten and was still sleeping.

The boys returned to their places, pushed the reclining seat as far back as they could, and slept as the jet thundered towards Europe. When the Hardys awoke, they saw a magnificent view through the window. Snow-covered mountains spread far and wide beneath their plane. Tall peaks towered towards the sky. Villages nestled in the valleys.

"We're over the Alps!" Joe exclaimed.

Frank glanced at his watch. "By my reckoning, we're over Switzerland already."

Over the loudspeaker a stewardess advised passengers to fasten their seat belts. The jet hissed over Lake Zurich, which extended from the city to the high mountains. The pilot kept on course and came down for a perfect landing at the airport. He taxied to the terminal, braked to a stop, and shut off the engines.

Frank and Joe stood up and tried to reach the suspect, but passengers blocked the aisle. The man in the brown suit waited at the head of the line to disembark. Within minutes, he was off the plane.

Watching him through the window, the Hardys saw him hasten to the terminal and into the building. Finally Frank and Joe arrived too. By the time they passed through customs, their quarry was headed towards the exit with long, swift strides. Lugging their suitcases, the Hardys pursued him as fast as they could. They caught up with him at the taxi rank.

He whirled and glared at them when Frank spoke to him. "We're interested in what happened in New York," the boy said.

An expression of fear came over the man's face. Suddenly he hurled himself at Joe, bowling him over backwards. Joe collided violently with Frank. The impact caused both the Hardys to lose their footing. They fell to the pavement in a heap.

A taxi bore down on them at full speed!

·6·

Over the Cliff!

INSTINCTIVELY resorting to judo, Joe rolled to the right of the speeding taxi. Frank did a somersault to the left.

The vehicle careered between them and jolted to a halt. *"Was ist los?"* the driver shouted at them. *"Was machen Sie denn da?"*

The Hardys scrambled to their feet. Frank tried to apologize in his high school German: *"Entschuldigen Sie bitte."*

The driver responded with a tirade in German before going on to pick up a fare.

Frank straightened his jacket. "Joe, I think he was telling us off for scaring him. What happened to Zemog?"

"He's gone!" Joe said glumly, looking at the passengers lining up for taxis. "He must have disappeared while we were nearly getting run over by that cab."

They walked to the end of the line and finally got an empty taxi. Frank told the driver to take them to the William Tell Hotel. At the desk, they signed identification cards and received a room key. They set their luggage inside and tidied up their appearance, then went to the Zurich police headquarters.

Frank explained to an English-speaking captain,

44

named Hartl, that Pedro Zemog, a suspected thief, was somewhere in the city. Joe inquired whether the Swiss authorities had any information about the man.

The officer checked through the files and made a phone call. Then he turned back to the Hardys.

"Pedro Zemog has no criminal record in our country," he informed them. "But we will watch for him. Tell me where you are staying, and we will call you if we learn anything."

"Thank you," Frank said. "We're at the William Tell for the next few days."

The boys returned to their room and unpacked, then contacted the Swiss Gold Syndicate.

Mr Jung's assistant told them there had been no more anonymous phone calls. "I asked a lot of people around town," he said, "but found out nothing. I doubt anything will transpire over the weekend. Since Mr Jung is coming back Monday, perhaps the caller will try to get in touch with him personally."

Frank thanked the assistant and hung up. "What do we do now?"

Joe shrugged. "Let's see the town."

Taking the elevator to the lobby, they found people at the registration desk or following porters who carried their luggage. Others inspected items in the souvenir shop and relaxed in comfortable chairs. The Hardys paused to look at postcards on a revolving stand. Joe twirled it.

"Hey," said a young American, "you just took the card I wanted." A youth about Frank's age peered at them from behind the revolving stand.

"Sorry about that," Joe apologized. "I didn't know you were on the other side."

The two boys started a conversation and Frank joined them. The youth said his name was Rory Harper. He was in Switzerland to see the country and do some skiing.

"Listen," Rory said, "I'm here with three girls, my sister Alice, my girl friend Jane Owens, and their friend Karen Temple. They're standing over there by the window. Want to join us for a coke?"

Frank and Joe peered in the direction of the window and broke out in grins after glimpsing three very attractive teenage girls.

"Sure, we'll be glad to," Frank said.

After introductions, the Americans sat down at a low table in the lobby and ordered drinks. Rory's group talked about home and their vacation in Switzerland.

Karen set her glass down on the table. "Joe," she said, "do you ski?"

"A little," Joe answered. "So does Frank."

"That's great!" Alice exclaimed, "We're leaving today. Want to join us for the weekend?"

Frank and Joe looked at each other. "We don't have to be back till Monday morning, Joe," Frank said.

"And there's nothing we can do here in the meantime," Joe added.

"Good. Then it's all settled," Rory said. "We can rent our gear at the lodge. Let's go!"

The young people went to their rooms and quickly packed warm clothing in an overnight bag, then met in front of the hotel. They hailed a large taxi and the driver let them off at the railway station.

On the way to the nearest ski resort, they watched the beautiful landscape as the train snaked up the mountains. They exchanged cheerful banter.

"I hope you guys are pros," Rory said. "You'll have to move fast to keep up with me."

"That's right," his sister added. "Rory is fast—on his rear end!"

"Aw, Alice, don't say that!"

Jane giggled. "We should modify that statement. Sometimes he's fast on his stomach, too! I'll never forget that time in Vermont when he slid down head first."

"Oh, that was a bad spill I took," Rory admitted. "My hat went one way, my goggles another, the poles almost hit another skier, and if the safety straps hadn't held the skis, they would have arrived at the lodge without me."

"What were you trying to do, wind up in the hospital?" Joe kidded.

"No," Karen said. "He was just trying to imitate Herman the German, who did a somersault over a three-foot mogul."

"He's one of our instructors up there," Jane explained. "Only Rory can't ski nearly as well as he can."

When they arrived at their destination, they hitched a ride to the lodge with a friendly farmer, who chugged along the road in a small truck. As soon as they got there, they rented skis, boots, and poles.

Rory and the three girls had brought ski clothes. The Hardy boys each bought a tracksuit to wear.

Sunlight glistened on the packed snow of the slopes, and skiers looked like coloured dots on a white sheet.

After the Americans had bought their lift tickets, they lined up for one of the chairs. Joe paired off with Karen, Frank with Alice, and Rory got on the lift with Jane.

"Wait for us when you get up there!" Rory yelled to the first pair.

"Will do," Joe called back as he watched a girl in a red suit expertly parallel down the slope.

When they arrived at the top, they surveyed the mountain. Alpine peaks formed the skyline around them. The snow-clad terrain dropped away at their feet into a steep run. A colourful white sign with an arrow read: AUTOBAHN-EXPERT ONLY.

Frank held up a hand. The rest gathered around him in a circle.

"Have any of you skied this slope before?" he asked. He received only negative answers.

"Then we'd better take the Mouse Run over there first. That's intermediate," he advised.

Joe and the girls agreed, but Rory shook his head vehemently. "No, that's too easy for me," he said. "I'm going to take the Autobahn and beat you all to the bottom. See you later!"

He gave a strong push with his poles and began to parallel over the lightly-packed, powdered snow.

"We'd better not let him go alone," Frank called out. "If you girls think you're up to it, let's follow him."

"We'll make it," Jane said.

Frank led the way to the starting point and pushed off with his poles. Joe and the girls followed. The slope took them in a long semi-circle and once narrowed to a steep trail, where they had to go in single file. When it widened again, Frank swiftly decreased the gap between himself and Rory and caught up with him about three hundred feet from the bottom.

"Hey, slow coach!" he yelled as he overtook the other boy.

Rory tried to catch Frank, but hit a slippery spot and fell.

This gave Joe and the girls enough time to pass him, and they waited at the bottom with Frank.

"Did you say you were a pro?" Karen joshed him.

"I hit an icy spot," Rory said lamely. "My luck!"

"No excuses," Jane said and laughed. "Just do better next time."

Rory looked at the Hardys. "You guys ski well," he admitted.

"We go to Vermont quite a bit," Frank said.

They spent an hour or so skiing the Autobahn and surrounding slopes, then they rode up a different lift, which took them to a trail called St Gotthart's Pass. A barricade blocked the way and a sign read: DANGEROUS SNOW CONDITIONS. TRAIL CLOSED.

"We don't want to ski down there," Frank observed. "Let's go to the right and get another run."

"Aw, that sign doesn't mean a thing," Rory said flatly. "I'm not afraid to ski down there. According to the map, this connects with a slope called Rim Run, which sounds interesting. Let's go anyway!"

He quickly slipped around the barricade and was halfway through the first turn before Frank could convince him not to go.

"Girls," Frank said, "take another run. We'll meet you at the bottom."

"Okay," Jane said. "But be careful."

Joe followed his brother, who was having trouble on the slippery surface. "Rory is crazy!" he fumed. "He's going to kill himself and us along with him by going down this death trap!"

Uneven and rocky under the snow, the trail was

narrow, the ridges precipitous, and the gorges deep.

"This is like Russian roulette," Frank muttered to himself. "Guess wrong, and it's your last chance. It's over the edge, and somebody else picks up the pieces at the foot of the cliff!"

He was relieved when he saw he was catching up with Rory. "I'll head him off," Frank thought.

But Rory seemed determined not to be passed. He skied at top speed along ridges and past gorges. Reaching a steep decline flanked by an icy cliff, he looked back over his shoulder to see how close Frank was.

The gesture caused him to lose his balance. He slipped head over heels on the ice and lay still!

Wondering how badly his friend was hurt, Frank drove himself forward with his ski poles, his eyes on the crumpled form in front of him. His left ski hit a boulder hidden in the snow. His feet shot out from under him and he landed on his back. The momentum carried him into a long slide on the ice. Frantically he tried to stop himself, but it was no use.

Frank Hardy slid over the cliff!

·7·

The Confrontation

Joe skidded to a stop near the top of the cliff, where he had seen Frank vanish.

Rory rose and shook his head woozily. "What happened?"

Joe did not explain. "Go get the ski patrol, pronto!" he yelled.

Rory realized the seriousness of the situation instantly and quickly fixed his skis. Then he schussed down the treacherous trail as fast as he could.

Joe, meanwhile, had taken off his skis and edged himself over the cliff. Frank was clinging by his fingers to a stone ledge about two feet from the top. Beneath him there was a ragged drop.

"Hold on, Frank!" Joe shouted. He climbed on to the ledge. Planting his feet as firmly as he could, he gripped his brother by the arms and struggled to pull him up.

Frank tried to anchor his feet against the cliff, but it was of no use. His skis, dangling on his ankles by the safety straps, clattered on the rock.

"Just hold still," Joe advised. "I sent Rory to get help."

A few minutes later two men from the ski patrol arrived. A rope was dropped over the edge of the cliff, and Joe reached out to catch it. He tied it around Frank, who was drawn to safety by the men above.

"Thanks," Frank said gratefully. "Thanks a lot."

"You should have more sense than to ski down here," one of the men chided. "Don't you realize we close these trails for a good reason?"

"It wasn't Frank's idea." Joe came to his brother's defence. "Rory wanted to get the connection to Rim Run—"

"You can get it another way," the man said curtly. "Now follow us down and don't try it again!"

The boys put their skis back on and made it safely to the intersection of Rim Run. From there it was not far to the bottom, where they met Rory and the girls in the lodge. He was drinking a mug of hot chocolate and was glumly stroking the pigeon's egg on his forehead.

"Boy, do I have a few choice words for you!" Frank said, anger welling up in him again.

"Oh, please don't!" Rory said, rolling his eyes and pointing to his head. "I've ruined my beauty externally and it doesn't feel so hot internally either!"

The Hardys laughed. "Serves you right, my friend," Joe said. "And I think now we'd better stop!"

The skiers returned their equipment and found an inexpensive guesthouse in which to spend the night. The following day the Hardys skied till early afternoon, then said goodbye to their new friends, who planned to stay for a few more days. Frank and Joe took the train back to Zurich.

At the William Tell Hotel, Frank phoned police headquarters and spoke to Captain Hartl.

"We're still looking for Zemog," he informed the boy.

"Any clues?"

"Negative."

After lunch the following day the boys walked to the Swiss Gold Syndicate. It was nearby in a grey limestone building.

"Looks like a fort," Joe commented.

"Sure does," Frank agreed. "It's made of stone and filled with gold."

The brothers identified themselves to one of the guards, who escorted them to the office of the director. It was a large room with a high ceiling, thick rugs on the floor, and small stone-framed windows.

Johann Jung, a tall, dark-haired man, greeted them in perfect English. "I'm glad you're here," he said. "We've had another call this morning."

"Anonymous again?" Joe asked.

"Yes. It seems that a small-time crook has got wind of the fact that the Wakefield gold is to be traded on the black market and wants to capitalize on his information."

"What did he say?" Frank asked eagerly.

"He told us to deposit five hundred Swiss *marks* in a small pedestrian tunnel in the old section of town. When he finds the money, he'll leave the information he has."

"Could be a big hoax," Frank said. "He might take the money and run."

Jung nodded. "That's possible," he said. "On the other hand, the Wakefield gold robbery is not known to anyone here except myself and the staff. How did he find out about it?"

"Shall we take a chance and pay him, then?" Joe asked.

"I have already," Jung said. "He wanted the money at two o'clock. I sent someone to deposit it."

"Can your man stake out the place and see who our anonymous friend is?" Frank asked.

"I doubt it. The fellow picked an excellent spot for this type of thing. The tunnel is short, narrow, and dark, and many people use it. Anyone waiting inside or on either end would be obvious."

It was not long before there was a knock on the door. A young man entered and handed Jung an envelope. "I deposited the money, sir. This is what I got in return."

Jung took the envelope. "Thank you, Hans. Did you see the man?"

Hans shook his head. "I waited about ten minutes after I left the money before going into the tunnel again. In the meantime, too many people walked through it. I have no idea who took the five hundred *marks* and left this envelope."

"Okay. Thank you."

Hans left and Jung opened the message. It read: "If you want to find out about the Wakefield gold, go to Auerbach's."

"What does that mean?" Frank asked, puzzled.

"Auerbach's is a restaurant in Niederdorf," Jung said. "Maybe you'd better check it out. I'll give you directions."

Half an hour later Frank and Joe walked into Auerbach's. A few people sat at scrubbed wooden tables. The boys approached the elderly man in an apron, who waited on them, and started a conversation in their high school German.

The wrinkle-faced Swiss grinned. "You Americans?" he asked.

Frank nodded. "I'm glad you speak English."

"I lived in Chicago for ten years," the man said.

They found out he was Xaver Auerbach, the owner. After some general comments on Zurich and their travels, Frank said, "We hear people around here trade in gold."

The man looked at him suspiciously. "I don't know what you're talking about."

Joe pulled out a ten dollar bill. "A friend told us to come here if we wanted to buy gold."

Slowly Auerbach took the money. "The only person I hear talking about gold around here is Karl Pfeiffer, and it seems to me he's more talk than action. He usually drops in at five for something to eat."

"Thanks," Frank said. "We'll see him then."

But at five Karl Pfeiffer did not appear. At six there was still no sign of him. Frank slipped Auerbach another bill. "Maybe we could talk to Pfeiffer at his house," he said. "We really can't wait around here any longer."

"He lives at nine Annastrasse, three blocks from here to your right. The basement apartment."

"Thanks."

The boys found the address and knocked on the door. A sloppy-looking man in his thirties answered.

"Karl Pfeiffer?" Frank asked.

"*Ja*."

"You speak English?"

"*Ja*. A little."

"What do you know about the Wakefield gold?"

"Nothing."

"That's not what you've been saying at Auerbach's," Joe put in.

Pfeiffer looked scared. "I don't know what you're talking about. I—"

He looked up as a police car halted in front of the building. Then he whirled around and hurried into his apartment as two officers approached.

"Hey, Pfeiffer, wait!" Frank called out. He ran after the man, who had opened a window on the other side of his living room and was about to climb out.

"Hold it!" Frank said and pulled him back just as the policemen entered the apartment.

"Vielen Dank fuer die Hilfe," one of the officers said, thanking Frank for his help. Obviously they had come to arrest Pfeiffer!

Frank tried to explain why the Hardys wanted to talk to the man, but the policemen spoke little English and the boys' German was not fluent.

"Let's go with them to headquarters," Frank suggested, "and talk to Captain Hartl."

"Right," Joe said. "It'll be interesting to find out why they nailed Pfeiffer."

The officers did not object to the boys accompanying them to headquarters. When the group arrived, one of them showed Frank and Joe into Captain Hartl's office. They explained what had happened, and the captain looked puzzled.

"Pfeiffer was seen at the scene of a burglary this morning," he said. "That's why we brought him in. He's a petty thief, but is not known to be a smuggler. Why don't you wait here and I'll talk to him."

The captain was gone for about fifteen minutes. When he returned, he held two envelopes in his hand. "This is a rather amazing turn of events," he said. "Look what we found on Pfeiffer!"

One envelope contained five hundred Swiss *marks,* the other a few gold coins. In the upper left-hand corner of the second envelope were printed the words *Wakefield Mint*.

"Wow!" Frank exclaimed. "What a clue! Pfeiffer is involved in the gold heist!"

"I don't think so," Hartl said. "He told me the whole story. Pfeiffer was approached by a man last week and paid to spread the rumour about the Wakefield gold. The stranger also gave him the envelope with the coins for future use. Then he told him to call the Swiss Gold Syndicate and arrange for them to pay him five hundred *marks* in exchange for the information about Auerbach's."

"Who hired Pfeiffer?" Frank asked.

"He doesn't know. But I know Pfeiffer. He's been in and out of our jail several times. I think he's telling the truth. He was set up by someone who wanted to mislead you!"

"What did the stranger look like?" Joe asked. "Maybe it was Zemog."

"I asked Pfeiffer that," Captain Hartl replied. "The fellow was tall, thin, and in his early thirties. He spoke German without a trace of an accent and Pfeiffer thinks he's either German or Swiss. That doesn't sound like Zemog."

"It doesn't," Frank had to admit.

"If I find out anything else about this case and Zemog, I'll contact Mr Jung," Captain Hartl promised.

"Thank you very much for your help," Frank said and the boys left.

"Let's go back to the hotel and call Jung," Frank

said. "I'm sure he'll be glad to hear the police recovered his five hundred *marks.*"

A short while later Frank and Joe took the elevator to the fifth floor of the William Tell Hotel. The door clanged open and they stepped into the corridor. At the same time, a man was about to enter the next elevator, which was going down. The boys looked straight at him. He stared in return.

"Pedro Zemog!" Frank exclaimed. Zemog still clutched his briefcase, shielding it with his arm. Then the elevator door closed.

"He's headed for the lobby!" Joe cried.

They reached the lobby and looked around. There was no sign of Zemog.

The desk clerk could not tell them anything about Pedro Zemog, but he did say a man named Jones, who matched their description of Zemog, had been in room 506 and had just checked out of the hotel.

Back on the fifth floor, the Hardys noticed that the door of 506 was open. They went in. The bed was mussed, the drawers half-open, the closet door ajar. A quick tour of the room revealed nothing.

"Zemog didn't leave a single clue," Frank said in disappointment.

"Maybe he did," Joe answered, as he reached into the wastebasket beside a table. He drew out some shredded yellow paper. Carefully he fitted the torn pieces together.

"It's a telegram!" Frank said, looking over his brother's shoulder, as Joe put the last piece in place. The boys were puzzled as they read the message:

PEDRO ZEMOG. TAKE CONSIGNMENT TO MEXICO CITY. A.P.

·8·

A Warning

FRANK and Joe stared at each other, wondering again if the telegram referred to the gold stolen from the Wakefield Mint.

Finally Frank shook his head. "It can't be. I think the telegram indicates that the consignment referred to has been in Switzerland and is now to be shipped to Mexico. But the crooks wouldn't be so foolish as to bring the gold to Zurich secretly and then spread a rumour that it would be sold here!"

"I see what you're getting at," Joe agreed. "The rumour was created to keep us far from the place where the Wakefield gold has been, or will be, taken. So Zemog's instructions don't refer to it."

"Right. But let's phone Captain Hartl about the telegram, anyway. We still want to find Zemog for the museum."

Police Captain Hartl promised to alert the airlines about the fugitive's planned trip to Mexico, but said, "Since Zemog called himself Jones at the hotel, he's obviously travelling under an assumed name. That creates a problem. What are your plans?"

"I think we'll go back to Wakefield," Frank said.

"Good idea. If we find Zemog, we will get in touch

with the Early Art Museum in New York."

"Thank you very much," Frank said and hung up.

The boys packed and flew home the next morning. When they arrived, their mother greeted them with hugs. "I'm so glad you're back," she said. "I hope you weren't in any danger."

"Well, Frank did a cliff-hanger," Joe said, laughing. He described the skiing party and his brother's accident.

"Why, Frank, you could have been hurt!" Mrs Hardy exclaimed.

"Mother," Frank assured her, "I knew what I was doing. And anyway, Joe was watching and came to the rescue."

"I wish the two of you wouldn't take such chances." Mrs Hardy sighed.

"Chances? What chances?" said Aunt Gertrude at the doorway. "Have you boys been up to some of your hare-brained stunts again?"

After hearing the story, she shook her head. "You must have nine lives, like they say cats do."

Frank thought, "I used one up on that cliff."

"By the way," Mrs Hardy put in, "a man named Ivan Orlov phoned and asked for you. I told him you'd be back today. He refused to say what he wanted."

A short while later, the phone rang. Joe answered. The caller was Orlov. "So you are back from Zurich," he said. "Have you brought the Scythian figurine with you?"

Joe confessed that he and Frank had failed to retrieve the golden horse. He described how the boys had spotted Zemog at the Zurich airport and at the William Tell Hotel, and said that the police were looking for him.

"Why did you not have him arrested? Why did you not take the figurine from him?" Orlov demanded.

"We lost him both times."

"Lost him!" Orlov stormed. "You mean you and your brother permitted him to escape?"

"That's about the size of it," Joe said.

"Size? What does that mean—size?"

"It means you're correct, Mr Orlov."

"You have brought back no clue from Zurich?"

"Yes, as a matter of fact we have," Joe stated. He told the curator about the shredded telegram in Zemog's abandoned hotel room and the message referring to Mexico City.

"You must follow him!" the Russian declared, excited. "You must go to Mexico City at once and find the gold horse! I will pay your expenses!"

Joe informed Orlov that they could not do this until they heard from their father. "He and my brother and I are involved in another case," he explained.

Orlov became angrier. "Another case? What case could be more important than mine? Are you leaving me—how do you say it—in the lurch?"

"Mr Orlov, if our father can spare us, we'll be glad to pursue your case. But we'll have to check with him first."

"This is too confusing," Orlov complained. "All I can say is that if the gold horse is not restored to me, it will be . . . most unfortunate for your country!"

The Russian hung up so vehemently that Joe felt a painful buzz in his ear.

"Wow! Next time he calls, Frank, you talk to Comrade Orlov!" he said, holding his ear.

"What's up?"

"He's mad at us because we didn't bring his gold horse back from Switzerland. Now he wants us to leave at once and chase Zemog around Mexico City."

The phone rang again. Frank answered it.

"If it's Orlov," Joe muttered, "say I'm off on a moon flight."

This time Fenton Hardy was calling. "I'm in John Armstrong's office and we have you on conference call so we both can hear your report on Zurich," the detective said.

"It was not a success," Frank said and told about their visit to the Swiss Gold Syndicate, the false lead, and the arrest of Pfeiffer.

Mr Hardy and John Armstrong agreed that the rumour was undoubtedly a diversionary tactic which the thieves had cunningly used to mislead the Hardys.

Frank told his father about Zemog and the stolen figurine from the Early Art Museum in New York. "Orlov wants us to go to Mexico City," he said. "But we told him that we could only work for him if you don't need us any more."

"Well, I'm up against a stone wall right now," Mr Hardy said. "Let me talk to John."

The two men conferred for a few minutes, then Mr Hardy came back on the line. "When you mentioned Mexico City, John remembered something he had been told just the day before the burglary," the detective said. "It had slipped his mind, but now it seems as if it might be a clue!"

"What is it?" Frank asked eagerly.

"One of the guards mentioned that he saw a private plane flying rather low over the mint with the words 'Mexico City' on the fuselage. John paid little attention to it at the time, but now we're beginning to think that perhaps the plane landed on the hidden airstrip here in Wakefield and waited for the gold to be flown out."

"Oh, Dad, that's a great theory!" Frank said, excited.

"The only thing is," Joe put in, "how do you know Mexico City was the plane's destination?"'

"You don't," Mr Hardy said thoughtfully. Again he conferred with Armstrong for a few minutes, then he said, "John thinks that even if the plane didn't fly to Mexico City, it might have been based there. Since there's nothing for you to do here at this point, he wants you to fly to Mexico and see if you can track down the plane while you're looking for Zemog."

"We'll be glad to check out the Mexican angle," Frank said. "And Orlov will be pleased, too. We'll leave as soon as we can. What's new in Wakefield?"

"No clues," Mr Hardy replied. "I scouted around the airstrip in the guise of a camper and kept the abandoned car under surveillance for three days. No one went near it."

"Was the car stolen?" Frank asked.

"Yes. The owner has it now. By the way, John said if you need any help in Mexico he'll be glad to pay the expenses. He wants that plane tracked down as fast as possible."

"We'll ask Chet, Biff, and Tony to go along," Frank suggested. "This way we can split up and divide the legwork."

"Excellent idea. And good luck!"

Biff Hooper and Tony Prito were two more of the Hardys' close friends. Biff was a husky six-footer who knew how to use his fists. Olive-skinned Tony was a

carefree youth who was always ready for an adventure.
Like Chet, the two boys had helped Frank and Joe solve
some of their mysteries in the past. Frank phoned them
at once. "Big doings!" he said. "Make tracks over here
in a hurry or get left out!"

Twenty minutes later a series of loud, gunlike reports
sounded in the street. Chet's battered jalopy rattled up
to the Hardy home, backfiring all the way. Chet was at
the wheel, with Biff and Tony beside him. He brought
the vehicle to a jolting stop at the kerb and turned off
the ignition. The jalopy stopped its bucking and sub-
sided.

Tony jumped out and stretched. "Oh, my aching
back!" He groaned.

Biff extricated his long legs from under the dashboard. "When you ride with Chet, you hurt all over."

Chet grinned. "How come you guys let me give you a
lift if my jalopy scrambles your anatomy?"

"We never learn," Biff said.

The three hurried up the front steps. Frank and Joe
were eating large pieces of cherry pie on the porch. "Go
right through," Joe told their friends. "Aunt Gertrude
is ready for you."

Chet, Biff, and Tony went to the kitchen and reappeared with slices of pie. Tony sat down in a rocking
chair, Biff perched on the porch railing, and Chet
reclined in a hammock, balancing the loaded plate on
his belt buckle.

"Okay," Tony said, "let's have it."

"It had better be good," Biff warned.

"The cherry pie suits me," Chet countered. "But I
know what the Hardys are up to."

"What?" Biff demanded.

"Gold!"

"Chet's right," Frank revealed. He briefly told them the story of the Wakefield and Scythian gold. "We are working on both cases," he concluded.

"Next stop—Mexico City," Joe added. "How about you guys joining the expedition, all expenses paid?"

"Wow!" Chet exclaimed, and the other two were equally enthusiastic.

"It might be dangerous," Frank warned.

"We'll outsmart our enemies," Tony vowed.

Chet levered the last piece of pie from his plate into his mouth. He chewed and swallowed with a blissful expression. Then he put out a hand and pushed on the railing, causing the hammock to sway back and forth.

"You fellows can have the crooks," he declared. "I'll stick to archaeology. The Aztecs lived in Mexico City, and had tons of gold. I'd love to see their ancient masks."

Frank shook his head. "You may not have a chance, Chet. Our assignments are the Wakefield gold and the horse figurine Orlov wants back."

Chet gave in. "Well, as long as I get to see somebody's gold. Aztec or Russian, it's the same difference."

The others laughed. They were used to their stout friend making jokes when danger lay ahead.

The five spent the rest of the evening planning their expedition. The next morning they drove to the airport and caught a flight to Mexico City. Upon landing, Frank proposed that the group split up and see if they could find the plane from Wakefield.

Chet was to check with the tower, Biff and Tony were to talk to the pilots, and the Hardys would question the mechanics.

Chet went to the tower and discussed the mystery plane with the dispatcher.

"Mexican airlines have many craft marked 'Mexico City'," the man pointed out.

"This is a private plane," Chet replied. "It flew down from the U.S.A. about a week ago."

The dispatcher checked. "I have no record of the one you describe," he said.

Meanwhile, Biff and Tony had been circulating through the offices of the airlines, questioning pilots. None could tell them anything about an aircraft marked "Mexico City".

Frank and Joe had better luck. The fifth mechanic they interviewed had serviced a private plane with that marking. Its pilot was a young man.

"I heard him mention Palango," the mechanic said.

"Palango?" Joe asked. "What does that mean?"

"I think it's an archaeological term. Better ask Professor Carlos Alvarez at the university. He can tell you all about archaeological digs around here."

"Thanks for the information," Frank said.

He and Joe held a conference near one of the runways. Planes took off and landed, taxiing up to the terminal. Crews removed baggage as lines of passengers alighted.

"It's sure noisy here," Joe said.

They walked to a hangar servicing private planes. A small aircraft stood near them on the runway, ready for takeoff. They could see the pilot checking his instruments.

While they were talking, Chet joined them. Biff and Tony came up at the same time.

"No luck," Chet reported.

"We drew a blank, too," Biff said.

Frank told them not to worry. "We got a clue from one of the mechanics."

"The plane was here, and the pilot mentioned the word Palango," Joe added. "Professor Alvarez at the university might be able to tell us what that means."

"You see?" Chet said triumphantly to Biff and Tony. "The Hardys always get their man. They'll find the gold!"

His words were overheard by the pilot of the small plane near them. He had just climbed out of the cockpit and proved to be a hulking figure in overalls. He carried a long wrench in his right hand.

The man stared at the boys, his brows furrowed. Then he sidled up to them. "What are you guys doing here?" he scowled. "And who are you?"

"Who are *you?*" Biff retorted boldly.

"My name's Murphy, and they don't call me Rumble for nothing. Understand?"

"Understand," Chet said hastily. He was not about to tangle with a man carrying a wrench.

"What are you after?" the pilot demanded.

"Gold," Chet said.

"It has to do with Palango," Joe put in.

Rumble Murphy stepped towards them. Glowering, he slapped the wrench menacingly against the palm of his left hand. "You'd better go home right now if you want to stay healthy!"

·9·

Chet's Mistake

RUMBLE Murphy brandished his wrench. Chet stepped back for fear of being hit, but Tony stood still, his hands on his hips. Biff assumed a karate stance.

"That sounds like a threat!" Frank said.

"It *is* a threat!" Murphy snapped.

"What do you mean?" Joe asked.

"You'll find out soon enough if you butt in where you're not wanted."

Joe stepped foward and looked the pilot straight in the eye. "Come on, Murphy!" he demanded. "Why are you threatening us?"

The man's answer was a punch that struck Joe on the jaw. Joe staggered backwards and toppled over. Biff and Tony caught him as he fell.

Murphy ran to his plane and jumped in. The boys raced after him. Suddenly Frank shouted, "Hit the ground!"

They all plunged face down on the runway. A landing plane sped towards them. They felt a gust of air as one wing passed over them with inches to spare! Shakily, the boys got to their feet.

"Lucky you shouted, Frank," Biff said, "or we would have been mowed down."

68

They watched helplessly as Rumble Murphy took off. He became airborne and vanished into the clouds scudding across the sky.

"Murphy's a real pro when it comes to flying," Frank observed.

Joe rubbed his jaw. "My guess is he's a boxer," he said. "That guy hit me really hard with that haymaker."

The boys walked to the airport terminal.

"We must find out about Palango," Tony remarked.

"Let's set up an appointment with Professor Alvarez," Frank suggested.

Biff clapped Chet on the shoulder. "You're the expert on archaeology, Chet. We elect you to contact the professor."

Chet grinned. "I'll be glad to. Just lead me to the phone."

He made the call to the university. Alvarez said he would welcome the visitors next morning.

The boys claimed their baggage and took a taxi to the hotel at which they had chosen to stay. After freshening up, they decided to use their free time sightseeing.

In the lobby, Frank inquired at the desk about a guide, and soon a wiry Mexican with wavy, black hair appeared.

"You want to see Me-hee-co?" he asked the travellers with a friendly grin. "My name is Juan and my car is outside. It will cost you only a few pesos."

They made a deal with the guide, who led them to an old car with crumpled bumpers and a crack in the windshield.

"This must be fifty years old," Joe presumed. His companions were thinking the same thing. Feeling somewhat dubious about its reliability, they climbed in.

Juan started the engine, which wheezed and then made a put-putting sound that seemed about to choke off at any moment. He released the brake and chugged away from the hotel, dispensing tourist information as they rattled along.

First he took them through Mexico City's main square. "The *Zocalo*", he informed his passengers. "Our great plaza."

The area was dominated by the cathedral. They saw the national palace, the library, the School of Fine Arts, and other public buildings in and around the plaza.

Traffic whizzed every which way. Their guide stepped on the accelerator and headed into it. His passengers braced themselves as he raced ahead of one car and braked sharply to avoid another.

"Chet, this is worse than your jalopy!" Biff muttered out of the corner of his mouth.

They reached a beautiful broad boulevard. The car bumped along past trees, office buildings, crowds of pedestrians, and benches where tourists and citizens relaxed. Next came the markets of Mexico City, colourful areas with shops and outdoor stalls. Most of the vendors were selling fruits and vegetables.

In the Merced Market, Chet tapped the driver on the shoulder and told him to stop. Juan pulled into a side street.

"What's up, Chet?" Frank asked.

"Come on. I'll show you."

They got out and followed him and he walked to a stall with succulent Mexican dishes. The aroma of tacos, tortillas, enchiladas, and chilli filled their nostrils.

Chet closed his eyes and inhaled rapturously.

"We might have known," Joe said with a chuckle. "Chet never passes up any chow."

"I'm with him this time," Frank said.

The rest echoed the sentiment. They ordered a tortilla for each, including the driver, then strolled around the market, examining stall after stall. Juan talked to them animatedly, and occasionally conversed with the merchants in Spanish.

Chet, Biff, and Tony paused to look at some prints of Mexico City. Frank and Joe wandered down a side street into a dingy alley.

"*Señores*, permit me to tell your fortune!" The speaker was an old woman with piercing black eyes and a black lace veil over her hair. Her shop had an astrological chart of the heavens on the open door. *Señores*, only a few pesos!" she urged them.

They went in and found her shelves covered with curios—herbs to be distilled for poisons, signs of the zodiac, and dolls with pins stuck in them.

The woman grabbed Joe's hand and began to read his palm. "You have had a recent misfortune," she said.

Joe rubbed his jaw, which was still sore from Rumble Murphy's punch. "Right," he replied.

Frank extended his hand. "How about reading my future?" he suggested.

The woman surveyed his palm. Her eyes narrowed. "What do I see here?"

"That's what I want to know," Frank said.

"Much gold!"

The Hardys were startled. They tried to query the woman. Finding she would say no more, they paid her and left the shop.

"Could she know about the gold we're after?" Joe wondered.

"Anything's possible," was Frank's opinion.

The Mexican guide continued the sightseeing tour by driving to Chapultepec Park, a broad green area of woods and a lagoon, where entire families were enjoying the outdoors. Children played amid multi-coloured shrubs, bushes, and flowers. Fountains spouted water.

"Chapultepec," the guide said. "That word means 'grasshopper' in the Aztec language."

His battered car huffed and puffed as he pointed it up the hill. At the top he parked in the grounds of Chapultepec Castle, a white stone building with rounded arches and a tall oblong tower. A piece of sculpture on the terrace represented a huge grasshopper.

Inside, the visitors were streaming through the various halls. The boys from Bayport joined them. They saw costumes worn in Mexico City since Aztec times and the apartment once occupied by Emperor Maximilian, who ruled Mexico during the American Civil War.

"What happened to Emperor Max?" Joe asked.

"We shot him," Juan said laconically.

They climbed up to the roof garden for a view of Chapultepec Park. Frank turned his head. A man with grey hair, wearing a dark suit, was on the other side of the garden. He held a briefcase! Frank tapped Joe on the shoulder and pointed.

"Zemog!" Joe gasped.

The brothers pushed through the crowd, turning and twisting in the press of bodies. At one point they were stopped by a solid wall of visitors and had to detour around them. Struggling and panting, they inched foward. At last they got to the other side.

The suspect was gone!

Frank and Joe hurried through the rest of the castle, only to draw a blank in every hall. They ran out to the terrace. Zemog was not there either.

"This is getting ridiculous," Joe fumed. "Zemog pops up in the craziest places, and when we follow him, he dissolves into thin air!"

"We let him escape again, as Orlov would put it," Frank agreed. "Which isn't saying much for us!"

"I'm beginning to think it's Zemog's ghost who's giving us this problem." Joe chuckled.

The boys strolled around the terrace until they found Juan and their friends.

"What happened?" Biff asked. "You took off so fast we didn't even have a chance to offer our help!"

"We think we saw Zemog again," Frank explained. "And as usual, he escaped."

"What do we do now?" Chet asked.

"I think we should finish our sightseeing tour at police headquarters," Joe suggested.

Everyone agreed, and Juan took them to their destination. The boys thanked him for the tour, paid him, and went inside.

The sergeant at the desk spoke English well and listened to their problem with interest. He checked his records for Zemog, but found nothing.

"Zemog is not a Mexican name," the sergeant said. "Unless he uses an alias, we should be able to track him down without too much difficulty. I will check all the hotels and see what I can learn."

The boys returned to their hotel for the night. After breakfast the next morning, they taxied to the university to meet Carlos Alvarez. The professor's office was lined with rows of books on archaeology.

He identified Palango at once. "It is an archaelogical site not far from the great ruins of Chichén Itzá on the peninsula of Yucatán. Palango was recently discovered and digging has just begun. It lies in the same area as a lost pyramid of the Mayas. Fifty years ago a hunter reported seeing the pyramid. But since then, every attempt to find it has failed. What is your interest in Palango?"

Frank said that somebody might have flown gold from Mexico City to Palango.

Alvarez was puzzled. "I don't know why anyone would do that. Usually it is the other way around."

He gave them a little lecture on gold, noting that the Aztecs moulded it into fine art pieces. "Their artifacts are so good many people cannot tell the difference between Aztec and Scythian."

Chet puffed out his chest. "Oh, I can always tell Aztec stuff!" he boasted.

Alvarez smiled. He took a small piece of gold representing the head of a child from his drawer. "What do you make of that, my friend?"

Chet held the gold in his hand. "That's Aztec, all right."

"No, it comes from the Inca civilization down in Peru," Alvarez corrected him.

Chet turned red in the face. His companions snickered, but Alvarez was indulgent. "An easy mistake to make." He soothed Chet's feelings.

That ended the session with the professor. The boys, deciding to run down the Palango angle at once, went to the airport and chartered a plane to Yucatán.

Three hours later they were on their way. The pilot flew across central Mexico, took the long leg of the journey across the Gulf, and zoomed past the shoreline over the jungle, thick with trees and tropical vegetation.

Suddenly the engine began to sputter. The boys looked at one another in alarm.

"What's happening?" Frank asked tensely.

"I don't know," the pilot replied. "I had everything checked out before we left. But this is definitely trouble."

He worked the controls frantically. But it was of no use. The engine cut out and the plane nose-dived towards the jungle!

·10·

The Boa Constrictor

DOWN, down they plunged! The jungle seemed to be rushing up to meet them and presently they could see the upper branches of the trees!

The pilot fought desperately to bring his plane out of its nose-dive. At the last moment, the engine came to life, and he regained control. They swooped down, then climbed just above the trees. Now he was able to zoom back to a safe altitude.

The pilot mopped his brow. "I don't understand what happened. I double-checked everything before we left Mexico City."

"Could be somebody doesn't want us to get to Palango," Frank observed in a shaky voice.

The plane flew across Yucatán and came down for a landing at Mérida, the main city in the northern Mayan region. The boys climbed out. All were shaken by the near crash.

"*T-t-terra firma* for me," Chet stuttered.

"For me, too," Biff added.

"The Mayas had the right idea," Tony said. "They never fooled around with planes."

The Hardys tried to cheer their pals. "We got here, didn't we?" Joe pointed out.

"Better than hacking our way through the jungle," Frank declared.

The pilot inspected his plane. "Somebody tampered with the engine," he said grimly. "I'll have to repair it."

His passengers checked with airport officials to see if anybody had seen a private plane marked "Mexico City". Nobody had, so the boys decided to go right on to Palango. Frank rented a jeep and drove to Chichén Itzá. All of them marvelled at the ruins of temples and pyramids that once were the centre of the Mayan culture of northern Yucatán. They asked a policeman about Palango.

"Take the dirt road north-east," the man replied, "and then follow the jungle trail. The Palango dig is at the end of it."

The boys set out, with Biff at the wheel of the jeep. The dirt road ended and the jungle trail began. It was so rough and bumpy through the dense tropical vegetation that they felt sore and bruised. Even the well-padded Chet complained. "I'm not made to be a rubber ball," he said.

Biff shifted into low gear. "We should have rented a Sherman tank," he grumbled.

Joe laughed. "How about a swamp buggy?"

The jeep bounced over a large bush. An enormous hole loomed directly ahead! Biff stepped on the brake and the jeep halted at the edge of the hole with a jerk that nearly sent Chet flying over the windshield.

Frank pointed to a pile of fresh earth beside the trail. "Somebody dug that hole recently. I wonder—"

A splintering sound interrupted him. A giant tree beside the trail began to sway. It toppled towards the jeep!

Biff reacted instantly. He put his foot down, wrenched the wheel to the left, and scooted into the jungle undergrowth flanking the trail just before the tree fell with a crash. The boys ducked as the branches lashed over the jeep. Then Biff cut back out on to the trail beyond the hole and stopped.

He sighed with relief. "Anyone hurt?" he asked.

The others said no, then Frank proposed that they look around before going on.

The boys walked to the fallen tree. As Chet inspected the tangle of heavy branches, he remarked, "It's lucky we got out from under."

"The tree would have smashed us," Tony agreed.

"Look at the trunk!" Joe declared.

It had been chopped nearly all the way through!

"Someone was setting a trap for us!" Tony exclaimed.

Frank nodded. "He dug the hole to make us stop, cut the tree with an axe till it was barely standing, and then pushed it over to make it topple on us."

Biff clenched his fists. "That means he must still be around here somewhere. I'll take him apart if I lay my hands on him!"

He ran back up the trail. Frank and Joe took the underbrush on one side, Chet and Tony the other. The boys scouted through the area but found nothing except scuffed footprints near the base of the fallen tree.

"He got away!" Biff lamented.

"We may as well call off our search," Joe said. "It would be like looking for a needle in a haystack, only this haystack is the Yucatán jungle."

An hour later the group bounced into Palango. A Mayan temple had been partially reclaimed, and nearby a deep excavation revealed further work in progress. Several tents had been set up in a cleared area. Four Americans were there along with a dozen Mexicans, descendants of the Mayas, who had been recruited to help with the dig.

The leader of the archaeological expedition came forward to meet them. He was tall and handsome with black wavy hair. "I'm Steve Weiss," he introduced himself. "It's a surprise to see you. Usually visitors don't get this far in the jungle."

Frank explained that he and his companions were trying to find gold.

"We have already found quite a bit!" said a voice behind them.

The boys turned to see a man wearing white shorts and a pith helmet. He had a superior smile on his face, as if to say that he was doing the visitors a favour by speaking to them. He carried a swagger stick, which he slapped against his leather boot.

"I'm Melville Courtney, assistant archaeologist on the dig," he announced. "I'm also a Hawkins man."

"He means Hawkins College," Joe thought.

"We have already found gold, son," Courtney repeated, "and are scarcely in need of your assistance on that score. The Mayas buried the gold. We retrieved it after much exertion and loss of perspiration.

"I'm sure you realize," Courtney continued, "that your help would be superfluous."

"A job is not what we have in mind," Frank told him.

"Do you have armadillos in mind?" asked a woman who had just walked up. She had golden hair and a heart-shaped face. She wore a denim shirt and slacks.

"Rose Renda, our biologist," Steve Weiss introduced her. "She just joined us a few days ago."

Chet scratched his head and gave her a blank look. "Armadillo freak?"

"As you no doubt know," Rose explained, "an armadillo is an armoured animal native to these parts. It's about five feet long from snout to tail in the biggest species. The armour on its back is approximately three feet long. The problem I'm researching is this: how is the armadillo related to the glyptodon?"

Now Tony looked blank. "What's a glyptodon?"

Rose smiled. "You mean, what was a glyptodon? It lived millions of years before the armadillo, was about nine feet long, and had five feet of armour. The armour was completely smooth, and had a number of hinges that permitted it to turn more easily."

"And you want to find out how the glyptodon evolved into the armadillo?" Tony asked.

"Yes," Rose replied.

A man carrying a rifle joined the party. He was over six feet tall, slim, and quiet.

"This is Frank Pendleton," Rose said, "our jungle guide. He knows everything about this area."

"I should after twenty years," Pendleton said, smiling.

"I take it you hunt, too?" Tony said with a glance at the man's rifle.

"No. The gun is strictly for self-defence against the dangerous animals of Yucatán and the jungles south of Brazil. I've seen them all."

"You mean jaguars?" Biff asked.

"That, and big snakes—boa constrictors, for instance."

Chet grimaced. "I hope I don't meet one."

"You never can tell what you may meet in the jungle," the guide responded. "I—"

"Time for chow," Weiss interrupted.

Melville Courtney slapped his swagger stick against his boot again. "Dinner is indeed served, such as it is," he said in his high-pitched voice. "Beans and coffee. Really!"

"However you say it," Weiss laughed, "we're all ready to eat." He invited the Bayporters to share their fare, and they sat in a circle on the ground.

After a while Frank asked, "Has anybody here seen a private plane marked 'Mexico City'? We're trying to find it."

No one had.

Joe put the next question to the group. "Have you ever met a man named Pedro Zemog?"

Again, everyone said no.

"Rumble Murphy?"

As the men shook their heads, Rose said, "Why are you looking for these people?"

"Because we're trying to solve the mystery of a gold theft," Joe replied. He told the group about the Wakefield heist and the theft of the ancient horse from the Scythian collection.

Courtney coughed. "Mr Zemog and Mr Murphy are obviously not gentlemen," he stated. "I would not care to associate with them."

"But they're part of our mystery," Joe pointed out.

"I don't think you'll solve your mystery here," Weiss said. "There's no reason for these gold thieves to bring their loot down here. They'd stick to Mexico City."

Rose lowered her coffee cup. "It looks as if you boys

have come a long way for nothing."

Chet grinned. "Not me. I want to look at the Mayan gold you found, because I have a graduate's diploma in gold artifacts."

"What in the world is that?" Rose asked.

Chet explained about his correspondence-course.

Courtney gave him a supercilious look. "That is not like a degree from Hawkins," he stated.

Chet looked hurt.

"Well, it's an interesting title," Steve Weiss interjected to make Chet feel better. "Sure, you can see our gold. The Mayas buried it to keep the Spaniards from getting it. Palango was once a thriving Mayan city. It was subordinate to Chichén Itzá, which you passed through to get here. You must have seen the temple-pyramid there."

"Yes, we did," Frank said.

"Well," the archaeologist continued, "Chichén Itzá also had its Temple of the Warriors, its Court of the Thousand Columns, and its Observatory."

"Observatory?" Tony asked. "Did those people study astronomy?"

"Oh, sure, and in a big way. They kept records of the stars and planets so they could be sure their Mayan calendar was accurate. They needed to know which days of the year to hold their religious festivals and other ceremonies."

"Palango was minor compared to Chichén Itzá," Pendleton put in. "But it did have a pyramid—the lost pyramid."

"Boy, how can you lose a pyramid?" Biff quipped. "Kind of careless."

Rose laughed. "The fact is that jungle growth covers

everything in a very short time indeed."

Weiss nodded. "And the jungle's had almost five hundred years to cover the pyramid. When the trees, moss, vines and creepers have done their work, you can walk close to a Mayan building and never spot it."

Pendleton continued. "We know the lost pyramid is about twenty miles from here because a hunter spotted it fifty years ago. But he didn't give the location. Even if we knew that, it would be very hard to hack our way through the jungle. There's vegetation, the heat, and the insects. As things are, every attempt to find the pyramid has failed because it's like looking for a minnow in the Gulf of Mexico."

"We may never discover it," Rose added, "but we expect to run into a lot of armadillos. The jungle here must be loaded with them."

"It is," Pendleton assured her. "We'll go out after armadillo tomorrow. Like to go along with us, fellows? You can help capture one."

Biff spoke for them all. "That would be great!"

Weiss dug into the camp stores for more tents. Frank and Joe pitched the one they would share on the edge of the clearing near the Mayan temple. Branches of large trees, which surrounded the ancient building, were festooned with moss, giving the scene an eerie look.

The Hardys said good night to their friends and were sound asleep when they were awakened by a terrified shout from Biff's tent. It woke up others in the camp and brought footsteps pounding in his direction.

Joe snapped on his pocket torch and opened the flap of his friend's shelter.

"On the ground!" Biff cried.

"It's a boa constrictor!" Chet bellowed.

·11·

A Mysterious Shot

BIFF crouched at the rear of his tent and eyed the big snake apprehensively. His friends formed a semi-circle at the open flap of the canvas, not daring to get too close. The boa constrictor flicked its tongue menacingly.

"What'll we do?" Chet wailed.

"Step aside!" a woman ordered. Rose Renda walked into the tent. She was carrying a large canvas bag, the mouth of which she opened by releasing a draw-string. Just then three Mexican workmen, alerted by Pendleton because of their experience in handling snakes, joined the group.

The jungle guide teased the boa constrictor with a stick until it struck ferociously. As its head hit the ground, Pendleton's hand flashed out and closed on the neck just behind the head.

Two of the other men grabbed the reptile round the body, while the third seized the lashing tail. The four lifted the boa off the ground and dropped it, tail first, into the open canvas bag that Rose was holding. Then they crammed in the sinuous body, and finally Pendleton shoved the head, instantly pulling his hand away. Rose drew the mouth of the bag taut.

"This will make a fine addition to the Mexico City Zoo," she commented.

"The zoo can have it," Biff muttered.

Pendleton told everybody to go back to sleep and stop worrying. "It's almost unheard of for a snake of this size to invade an archaeological dig," he told them.

"This one," said Frank, "must have lost its way."

"Poor, crazy mixed-up snake," Joe said with a grin.

That broke up the tension and all the boys went back to their tents. In the morning, they joined Rose, Pendleton, and Courtney on a trek into the jungle in search of an armadillo. Pendleton wore the rough clothes and floppy hat of an experienced jungle guide. Courtney appeared in spotless white ducks, wearing his pith helmet and carrying his swagger stick.

"Melville, you'd better leave your helmet behind," Pendleton urged.

"It's part of one's dress in hot climates," was the reply. "I wish to dress correctly."

"That's when you're out in the sun. We'll be under the trees and you'll need air. You'll be too hot with a helmet on."

Courtney insisted on wearing his helmet, however, so the guide shrugged and dropped the subject.

The party started their trek into the steaming jungle. Frank and Joe decided to say nothing but to keep their eyes open for a plane flying overhead. They might spot the one they suspected!

Insects stung them and sweat poured down their faces. As Pendleton had predicted, Courtney felt the heat worst of all because of his helmet.

"Ditch it!" the guide advised.

"A Hawkins man never gives up," Courtney replied.

"Have it your way, but we have quite a distance to go before we reach armadillo country."

They slogged forward, taking regular breaks since it was so difficult to advance. Late in the afternoon, the guide suggested, "Let's call it a day." The others willingly agreed. They opened crackers and tinned meat, and ate dinner.

Then Rose gave a talk on armadillos. "They're rarely found together," she stated. "When we spot an armadillo, we'll run him to earth. He'll try to reach the security of his burrow before you get there. If you head him off, he'll roll up into a ball and stay put."

"Why does he do that?" Tony queried.

Rose smiled. "He hopes whoever's bothering him will get tired of waiting for him to uncurl and go away."

"What are the chances of finding one tomorrow?" Chet asked.

"Pretty good. Yucatán has been the home of the armadillo for thousands of years. According to a Mayan myth vultures turn into armadillos when they grow old. There are plenty left here."

In the morning, the march resumed. Insects swarmed around the hunters and Frank swatted a mosquito. "They're as big as robins," he complained.

"Big as crows," Joe corrected him, knocking one off his cheek.

After hours of pushing through the jungle undergrowth, Rose noticed an anthill that had been broken open. "An armadillo did that," she said, excited. "Ants are number one on his menu."

Pendleton told the group to split up. "Look under bushes and in burrows. If you flush an armadillo, sing out. The rest of us will come on the run."

Courtney slapped his swagger stick against a tree. "I will direct the capture," he offered.

"I'll bet he will," Frank whispered to Joe. "He's not about to touch an armadillo."

They separated to look for their quarry. Rose tried to pick up a trail at the ravaged anthill. Pendleton continued straight ahead in the direction they had been taking. Courtney stabbed into the bushes with his swagger stick, looking as if he hoped never to see an armadillo in his life.

Chet, Biff, and Tony moved beyond Courtney into the jungle. Frank and Joe went to the left. "There's one thing we won't find in here," Frank remarked.

"What's that?"

"The Mexico City plane. You couldn't fit even a helicopter into this jungle with a shoehorn."

"That's right. Well, let's concentrate on the armadillo."

They split up. Frank vanished among some moss-laden trees. Joe took a route over a carpet of jungle vegetation. The undergrowth slowed him considerably. Vines caught at his clothing, and creepers tripped him. A green parrot fluttered down on to a bush and squawked at him angrily, but he laughed as a hare stood upright on its hind legs, twitching its nose as he passed.

Presently Joe found an armadillo burrow, which he probed with a branch. It was empty. He went on, but after a while his legs were tired. He paused beside a tree in an open space of the jungle to rest. *Wham!* A rock slammed into the tree, inches from his head! It bounced off and flew into a thicket.

Joe hit the ground in a headlong dive. He crawled

over a tangle of creepers and pulled himself into a crouching position behind another tree. Gingerly he peered around the trunk. No one was in sight.

A sharp report cut through the stillness of the jungle. A shot! It had come from behind him! Joe dodged into the underbrush and stealthily moved in an arc towards the spot where the shot had been fired. He saw no one.

His companions had heard the shot, and ran up to see what had happened.

"Somebody used me for a clay pigeon," Joe told them. "He fired right at me!"

Frank turned to Pendleton. "You're the only one carrying a weapon. Did you fire at Joe?"

"Of course not." The jungle guide strenuously denied the charge. He opened the breech of his rifle. "Look for yourself. It hasn't been fired."

"Who could it be, then?" Biff wondered.

Tony sighed. "We're obviously not the only ones here in the wilderness."

"Maybe it was a Mayan hunter after armadillo," Pendleton suggested. "Mayas love armadillo steaks."

"Or the guy who dug the hole and tried to conk us with a tree," Frank said to Joe in a low voice. "Matter of fact, that's more likely."

"That would mean we're being watched constant-ly," Joe said in alarm.

Frank nodded. "It is a possibility."

The searchers began beating the undergrowth. An armadillo, evidently startled, bolted from behind a rock. It was about three feet long, with a pointed snout, long ears, and a long tail. The armour fitted over its back like a half-shell.

The animal hit Biff a hard blow on the ankles, knocking him off his feet, then raced past. Everybody chased the armadillo, crashing and stumbling through the jungle undergrowth.

The creature veered into Chet's path. As he lunged for it, his foot caught in a creeper, and he fell with a crash. The Hardys, too close behind him to stop, piled on top of the stout boy in a tangle of arms and legs. Frantically they scrambled to their feet and resumed the chase.

The armadillo did an about-face and raced between them. It ploughed into Courtney, bowling the Hawkins man over. His pith helmet rolled into the underbrush. He got to his feet slowly, retrieved the helmet, brushed it with his sleeve, and placed it on his head, looking embarrassed.

"I won't associate with any armadillo," he declared, seating himself on a stump and rapping it with his swagger stick. "I will wait here."

The animal reached its burrow, but Pendleton, too quick for it, seized the armadillo and pulled it out, kicking and squealing. The creature resisted briefly before quieting down in the guide's arms.

The other searchers arrived. The boys stroked the armour, which was composed of hide with a series of plates around the body, giving it flexibility.

"So that's an armadillo!" Tony marvelled.

"Yes, indeed," Rose answered. She scratched its ears with her fingertips.

"Isn't that dangerous?" Chet asked apprehensively. "You might lose a finger."

Rose shook her head. "Armadillos have few or no front teeth, so they can't bite." She held the animal while Pendleton took a collapsible wire cage from his pack. They eased their captive into it and the jungle guide pulled the straps over his shoulders. The cage rode easily on his back.

"Mission accomplished," Pendleton said.

"Right-o!" Courtney exclaimed. "We may now leave this jungle, of which I have had quite enough."

Frank spoke. "I'd like to scout around here a bit longer."

Joe and his friends agreed enthusiastically, but Pendleton objected. "We'll have to get back to the dig. Do you want to stay here alone?"

"Is there any reason why we shouldn't?"

"Not really. We're on an elevation where the mosquitoes aren't bad. I don't think you'll see any dangerous animals, either. Can you find your way back?"

"Sure," Frank said. "We'll go by the compass. Since we came from a north-easterly direction, we'll return that way."

"Good enough," Pendleton replied. "You stay then, and we'll be on our way."

Courtney doffed his pith helmet. *"Adios,"* he said solemnly, and Rose waved goodbye.

As the three explorers disappeared into the jungle, their footsteps died away in the distance.

The boys walked in the opposite direction, noting the jungle flowers and animals as they went.

"There are a million monkeys here," Biff judged.

"And a billion parrots," Tony added.

"What do we do if we meet any Mayas?" Joe asked.

"Talk Mayan to them," Frank quipped.

By nightfall the boys were extremely tired. Making a hasty meal of their rations, they set up camp beneath towering trees.

Frank could not sleep. He kept thinking about the strange events that had taken Joe and him to Switzerland, then to the jungles of Yucatán. It appeared that they were finally on to a clue—the plane marked "Mexico City". But where was it?

He sat up and turned his head. Everything was pitch black. Suddenly through the darkness he saw a light. It moved in a circle and went out. Frank rubbed his eyes.

The light flashed once more, swaying back and forth for a few minutes, then went out again. In a moment the signal was repeated a third time.

Now fully awake, Frank reached over and shook his brother.

Joe yawned. "What is it, Frank?"

"A light out there! Look!"

The beam remained stationary for a few seconds. Then it started moving once more, vanished, and reappeared a moment later.

Frank jumped up. "Hurry, Joe, we'll have to find out what this means!" He grabbed his compass and the two slipped through the jungle, guiding themselves by the mysterious light. After about half a mile, they reached a clearing.

The full moon revealed a weird sight. A stone building covered with jungle vegetation towered towards the sky. The vines and creepers spreading up the uncanny edifice from base to summit seemed like writhing serpents and disguised the building completely. The mysterious beam came from the summit.

"That's a torch!" Joe said in a low voice. "Somebody's up there. What's he doing, Frank?"

"Joe, I believe he's signalling a pal. But why?"

·12·

The Jungle Pyramid

THE Hardys entered the clearing and cautiously approached the eerie edifice. It was more than a hundred feet high, tapered towards the summit, with indented rows of stone steps rising from the bottom to the top. The base was formed of massive stone blocks. On the summit stood a temple.

"I'll bet it's the lost pyramid!" Frank gaped.

"No wonder it got lost," Joe whispered. "Rose was right. The jungle covers everything!"

Close up, they could see where winds had blown earth over the stone blocks. The seeds of plants, vines, creepers, shrubs, and flowers had imbedded themselves in the earth and sprouted in profusion.

Joe looked up towards the light on the summit. "Let's find out what's going on," he whispered.

"Easy does it," Frank counselled. "We don't want to scare the person off. First we'll explore the ground round the pyramid. Whoever is up there might be signalling an accomplice down here."

Stealthily the two boys slunk past the staircase in the centre of the façade, noting that it lead up to the temple entrance. As they turned the corner, Joe bumped into an upright slab of stone covered with raised squares and bearing strange symbols.

"Glyphs," he thought.

They went on with their search. At the back of the pyramid, they saw the carved figure of a monstrous snake undulating down over the stone blocks. Eyes of obsidian glinted at them in the semi-darkness. The open mouth revealed oversized fangs. Plumes bedecked the head and neck.

"The Feathered Serpent of the Mayas!" Frank said.

He and Joe had seen statues of this mythical creature many times since their arrival in Mexico. They knew it was the principal god of the Indians who had lived in Mexico before Columbus came to America.

Circling the pyramid, the boys returned to their starting point. "Nobody down here but us," Joe said in a low voice.

The light was still showing on the summit. Suddenly, at the door of the temple, it went out.

"The man's gone inside," Frank observed. "This is our chance."

Slipping and sliding, the Hardys silently climbed the steps to the top of the pyramid. Frank edged his way into the entrance of the temple. They did not see the light, and he whispered, "Maybe there are inner stairs to the top."

"Then we can take him by surprise," Joe said. He stepped forward, feeling his way along the wall. The boys did not want to use their pencil torches because they might alert the person inside to the fact that they were stalking him.

Suddenly Joe plummeted out of sight!

"Joe!" Frank whispered hoarsely. "Joe! Where are you, Joe!"

Receiving no answer, Frank fished out his light and

played the beam across the interior. At his feet the edge of a long stone incline dropped into utter darkness. Frank was horrified. Had Joe plunged down into a Mayan dungeon? If so, he might be hurt! He might be unconscious! He might even be—! "Joe!" he called. "Are you all right?"

Then he heard Joe's voice behind him. "I'm okay, Frank. I just took a ride on a Mayan roller coaster!"

Frank breathed easier.

"It's leading outside to the steps in the back," Joe continued. "I landed next to the Feathered Serpent. He didn't blink an eye."

Frank kept the beam of his torch shining over the end of the inclined plane. The boys decided it must have been used to lever heavy objects up to the higher levels of the pyramid.

"No freight elevators for the Mayas," Joe joked, "They did everything with muscle."

"Not so loud!" Frank warned. He played his beam round the lower chamber of the temple. It flashed over a pile of clay pots and stone figures in a corner.

"Where are we?" Joe asked.

"It looks like a storeroom, Joe. They kept supplies here until they were needed upstairs." The light from Frank's torch crossed a tall stone column in the opposite corner. Frank brought it back into focus. The column was a rectangular stone block standing on end, about as tall as the boys. The same face was repeated four times from top to bottom, the visage of a large cat, its fangs bared in a savage snarl. "The jaguar god," Frank whispered.

"As Chet would say, I hope I never meet up with him," Joe said.

Frank now pointed his torch towards the ceiling. It showed row after row of petroglyphs, which they could not read.

"I understand," Frank said, "that Mayan script has not been completely deciphered yet."

The Hardys circled the chamber. The only opening was a low doorway. Frank ducked under it, followed by Joe, into a small, empty room. A quick search showed it had no other outlet.

A rustle at the doorway made Frank snap off his torch. The boys whirled in the defensive stance of karate experts. The sound came directly towards them in the darkness!

The Hardys had a strategy for such confrontations. They counted silently to three, then Frank snapped on his light. At the same time, Joe leaped on the intruder. He received a whiplash across the face, and went down in a tangle of branches!

Frank chuckled in spite of the danger. "A bush! The wind blew it in here!"

Ruefully Joe extricated himself and got to his feet. "Next time, I'll look before I leap!" he said.

The Hardys went back through the first chamber. "We'll have to use the outer stairs to get to the top of the temple," Frank declared. "I hope the guy inside won't see or hear us."

He pocketed his torch; then the boys went outside and manoeuvred over to the staircase. The steps seemed to rise endlessly above them, steep and narrow. The footing was difficult, and clouds gathering across the face of the moon created a dark, murky atmosphere.

"Don't fall!" Frank muttered. "It's a bumpy road to the ground."

They got about a third of the way up, gripping vines to steady themselves and making sure of a foothold on every step, before they were interrupted. Something moved among the vines near Frank's right hand. Pulling his fingers away, he got out his light and shone the beam on the fluttering leaves. A menacing snake raised its head, stared at him for a few seconds, then slithered on to the bough of a small tree. It vanished among the creepers.

Frank felt his heart pounding. He had almost placed his hand on a fer-de-lance, one of the most poisonous snakes of the Yucatán jungle!

"You're no snake charmer," Joe whispered. "Don't fool around with our lethal companions."

They resumed their climb. A black object hurtled through the air at them. Joe ducked in time to avoid getting hit on the head, but lost his footing and toppled off the step! Frank grabbed his brother in mid-air and held him until he could regain his foothold.

The trajectile veered to one side and landed on a bush. A harsh croak jarred their ears.

"A raven!" Frank whispered. "He almost got us!" As they continued their climb close to the summit, Frank paused and looked up. The smoother stone of the temple gleamed through tangled tropical growth that sprouted on its roof and spilled down the sides, waving wildly in a rising wind. The entrance was a dark oblong in the front wall. Total silence reigned over the jungle pyramid.

Frank gestured to Joe not to make a sound. They moved slowly and carefully up the rest of the steps. The final one brought them to the sacrificial chamber. On it stood a platform with four feet on each side. The walls of the temple behind it were made of pink-red stone rising some twenty feet into the air. A doorway led into the interior, and blank walls extended on each side of the doorway. The roof was flat.

Frank and Joe stole to one side of the entrance and peered in cautiously. A shaft of moonlight gleamed through an opening in the opposite wall. There was no sign or sound of life in the temple.

"Do you think the guy heard us and ran?" Joe asked in a whisper.

"If he did, let's see what he was up to," Frank said.

As the boys entered, Frank fumbled for his torch. Just then something rustled in a dark corner, and the next instant a man jumped out at them! He flattened Joe with a wild swing, then grappled with Frank!

The pair staggered back and forth in a furious test of strength until the assailant gave ground. Frank pressed him back. They swayed through the doorway and over to the staircase.

Joe recovered slowly from the blow. He felt woozy, but got to his feet. Then he realized he was alone in the temple. His brother and their attacker were gone!

"Frank!" he shouted. "Frank!"

The name echoed out over the jungle, but Frank did not answer. Frantically Joe rushed through the nearest doorway, which was the rear exit, and circled around the temple to the front.

There he could see Frank and the stranger still locked in combat! Joe rushed to help his brother, but before he could reach the spot, Frank and his attacker had lost their footing!

With a scream, they pitched down the main staircase and fell towards the bottom of the jungle pyramid!

·13·

A Strange Figure

JOE leaped forward and clutched wildly at Frank, but his fingers missed by inches!

Three new shapes were suddenly visible on the steps in the moonlight. Three pairs of arms caught Frank and his antagonist in mid-air. With great relief, Joe recognized Chet, Biff, and Tony!

The boys pulled Frank free. He stood to one side, panting from his struggle, while Biff gripped his adversary in a bear hug. The two wrestled fiercely on the temple staircase.

The man tripped Biff, who tumbled into a tangle of creepers. The assailant leaped up the steps, but Tony brought him down with a tackle around the ankles. Chet sat on him and grinned.

"Had enough?" Chet inquired.

"Chet's a bit overweight," Tony pointed out.

"I—can—tell—that!" the man gasped. "Okay. I give up!"

The boys pushed their captive up to the summit and backed him against the temple wall in the darkness.

"You guys came just in time," Frank said to his friends. "How did you get here?"

Biff said he had awakened to discover that Frank and

Joe were gone. "I noticed a light and figured you must have seen it, too. So I woke Chet and Tony and we decided to back you up in case you were in trouble. We found what we think is the lost pyramid, and we saw a fight on the top."

·"We came up the Mayan escalator," Tony quipped. "Stone blocks and leg power."

Biff looked at their captive. "Say, who is this guy?"

Joe took out his pencil torch, snapped it on, and shone it in the man's face.

Rumble Murphy!

"What are you doing here?" Frank asked the pilot.

"None of your business!" Murphy grunted.

"Let's tie him up," Frank suggested. "One of us can watch him, while the rest are searching the place. There should be some clue as to what our friend was doing in the pyramid."

The boys bound Murphy's hands with Joe's belt, and tied his ankles with Tony's. Biff volunteered to guard the pilot, while the others went over the temple and pyramid with a fine-toothed comb.

First they entered the section of the temple where they had been before. It had a high ceiling. A raised altar stood at one end and a row of stone idols at the other. Here the priests of the Mayan religion apparently had presided over ceremonies to the gods.

"Wow!" Tony said as he played his light over the altar. "This is where the Indians prayed to the jaguar god and the feathered serpent."

Frank nodded. "Right now I'm not interested in the feathered serpent, but in some clues as to why Murphy was here."

The boys looked in every nook and cranny, and were

about to give up when Joe called out, "Hey, fellows! Come over here!"

The others ran up to him. Joe pointed to a bulky sack concealed behind a statue of the jaguar god. Together, the boys dragged it into the centre of the room.

"It's heavy as lead!" Tony exclaimed.

Excited, they opened it.

"Gold!" Chet cried in awe as they pulled out one object after another. First came a disc representing the sun. Small figurines followed. Finally there were dozens of ornaments—headdresses, bracelets, and rings.

"I don't believe it!" Frank said. "This stuff is price-less!"

"All Mayan," Chet added. "It takes an expert in golden artifacts to know that."

Joe upended the sack and shook out the contents. "The Scythian horse isn't here," he said, a note of disappointment in his voice.

But Chet was ecstatic. "Who cares! You were look-ing for one little figurine, and see what you've found instead!"

"Not the Wakefield gold, either," Frank said.

"Let's take one thing at a time," Tony suggested, "and confront Rumble Murphy with the evidence. Maybe he'll enlighten us as to the origin of this treasure."

"Good idea," Frank said, and the boys began put-ting the glittering objects back into the sack.

"Remember the fortune-teller in Mexico City?" Joe asked his brother. "She said there was much gold in your future. Maybe she meant this."

Frank laughed. "Who knows?"

The boys carried the sack outside and showed it to Biff. Murphy mumbled under his breath.

"Okay, Murphy," Frank said. "You may as well tell us what this is all about."

Murphy glared as his captors surrounded him menacingly.

"Come on, talk!" Biff hissed and moved his bulky figure closer to the pilot.

"All right, all right," Murphy grumbled. "I handle Mayan artifacts. Take them by jeep to Chichén Itzá, then fly them out of Mexico for international buyers."

"Did you ever see a figurine of a rearing horse?" Tony inquired. "A Scythian piece."

Murphy shook his head. "I told you I handle only stuff that's found right here in Mexico—Aztec, Mayan, Olmec—no Scythian gold."

"How did you find the pyramid?" Frank queried.

"I spotted it one day when I was flying low over the jungle. Later I discovered a way in by jeep from Chichén Itzá. And I saw it was the perfect hideout because nobody else knew where it was, so I stored my loot here."

Frank changed the line of questioning. "Why did you threaten us at the airport in Mexico City?"

"Because your fat friend said you were after my gold!"

"*Your* gold?" Frank was puzzled.

"He said you always find your man, and you'd find the gold. I don't know anyone else smuggling gold around here, so I figured you were after me! Who do you work for, anyway?"

Frank grinned. "The Wakefield Mint."

"What!"

"Never mind. But we had nothing to do with you. If you hadn't signalled tonight, we would never have suspected you."

Murphy mumbled again, but said nothing aloud.

Biff said, "You were the one who dug the hole in the trail from Chichén Itzá and then caused the tree to tumble on us! You almost killed us!"

"I did no such thing," Murphy grumbled, but the boys knew he was lying.

"And you tampered with the engine of our chartered plane," Joe accused. "After you dug the hole you flew back to Mexico City and waited for us!"

"And you took a pot shot at Joe today," Frank added.

Murphy did not reply.

"Why were you signalling with the torch tonight?" Frank asked.

"What signal?" Murphy asked defiantly.

"Don't play dumb," Frank said. "If we hadn't seen your light, we never would have found you or the pyramid."

"A buddy of mine flies over here at night at a certain time to let me know if we found a buyer. I don't know which night he's coming, so I signal, then he drops the instructions. He didn't show up tonight."

"Why did you take a chance with us so close by?" Tony asked.

"I didn't know you were still here," Murphy said glumly. "I thought you had left with the others."

By now the sun had begun to rise and a soft mist hung over the jungle.

"What'll we do with him?" Chet asked.

"Murphy must have a jeep around," Frank replied.

"We'll have to deliver him to the nearest police station in Chichén Itzá."

Rumble Murphy looked at them with squinting eyes. "Do you have to be that drastic? Look, I could cut you in on the loot. This stuff is worth a bundle of money. If you don't want to handle it yourselves, I'll pay you in cash. Fifty-fifty. What do you say?"

"No," Frank said laconically.

"All right. I'll give you seventy-five percent. That's robbing me, but what can I do?"

"Forget it, Murphy," Joe said. "We're not thieves."

"You're crazy! Do you realize what you're turning down? Listen, I'll give you everything, but don't take me to the cops!"

Frank ignored the plea. "Where's your jeep?"

Murphy realized that he had lost and started to scream at the top of his lungs. Suddenly he fell silent and would not utter another word.

"I'll go find the jeep," Frank offered. "It has to be around here somewhere. Hey, look!"

He pointed to a stranger entering the trampled area around the pyramid. He was a man dressed in the white suit worn by modern Mayas, with a wide-brimmed straw hat on his head. He edged around the pyramid in a suspicious manner.

"So, there's your accomplice, Murphy!" Joe exclaimed. "Let's meet him, gang. Biff, want to guard our friend again?"

"Sure thing," Biff replied as Frank, Joe, and Chet took the steps down as fast as they could, followed by Tony. They circled the pyramid, taking the direction opposite from that used by the man in the white suit.

They met him at the corner. He had the light-copper

colouring of an Indian. Lank black hair extended down to his shoulders. His cheeks were round and a scar ran across the right side of his face. He looked startled when he saw them.

"Are you looking for Rumble Murphy?" Joe asked.

The man responded in a rapid flow of Spanish. Though the boys had studied the language in high school, they could not follow him because he spoke so fast and with a strange inflection. Joe asked him to repeat slowly what he had just said, but the man stared at him blankly.

Chet had an idea. "Let's try sign language," he suggested. "I'll take it from here."

He touched the man on the shoulder, turned, and pointed into the jungle. He made a long sweep with one arm towards the pyramid.

"What does that mean?" Joe wondered.

"I'm asking him where he comes from, and how he got here," Chet explained.

"Well, you could have fooled me," Joe said.

The man smiled, shrugged, and spoke again.

"We're getting nowhere fast," Frank protested.

The boys decided to bring the man face to face with Murphy. One of them might give something away. They were discussing the best way to arrange the confrontation when the man suddenly spoke English.

"Bayport seems to be on the ball!"

·14·

The Aztec War God

THE boys gasped. The voice was unmistakably that of their father!

"Dad!" Frank cried out. "I don't believe it!" He scrutinized the coppery face closely. Then he grinned. "I should have known. The colour of your eyes doesn't fit your make-up!"

Mr Hardy chuckled. "A bit of make-up and cheek pads can do a lot to change one's appearance. And I can always squint when necessary."

"But, Dad, we thought you were investigating the case in Wakefield," Joe said. "What's up?"

"It's a long story," Mr Hardy said. "And it was John Armstrong's idea."

"You mean he doesn't trust us?" Frank asked.

"Well, he thought you could use some reinforcement. Actually, he decided all of a sudden that I was wasting my time in Wakefield. Since he had some business in Mexico City, he asked me to come along. We left the day after you did. When we arrived, John took care of his appointment in the city, while I asked questions around the airport about the mysterious plane."

"Same as we did," Joe said. "And that's how you found out about Palango?"

105

"Palango? What's that?"

"An archaeological dig near here," Frank said. "That's where we ended up."

Mr Hardy shook his head. "No one mentioned Palango to me. But I was tipped off that Rumble Murphy was smuggling gold, so I hid in his plane all the way to Mérida."

"Wow!" Chet looked at the detective in admiration. "Neat sleuthing!"

"Well, I almost lost him when we arrived," Mr Hardy continued. "I had to rent a jeep while his was already waiting. But I caught up with him and followed him here."

"Did he stop on the way?" Frank asked.

"Yes, in the jungle, for about an hour. He got out of his jeep and disappeared into the woods. Then another car came along the trail, nearly ran into a hole, and barely escaped a falling tree. I saw it from a distance."

"That car was ours!" Frank cried out.

Mr Hardy stared at the boys. "You'd better tell me all that's happened to you," he said gravely.

The boys described their adventures for their father, then Joe asked, "Dad, what did you do when you saw the pyramid?"

"There wasn't much I could do," Mr Hardy said. "I pitched a tent nearby and kept observing Murphy so I could be sure he didn't have a gang of people working here with him. Yesterday he left the place and I followed him into the jungle. There were people close by and he shot at something, maybe to scare them off."

"He shot at me!" Joe declared. "But he didn't scare us away!"

Mr Hardy nodded. "I was hoping he'd leave for a

while so I could search the pyramid, but he went right back."

"Did you see the lights last night?" Frank asked.

"No. I must have dozed off. This morning I decided I'd better do something. So I disguised myself and was on the way to confront Murphy when I met you."

"We've taken care of Murphy already, Mr Hardy," Chet announced and they reported their adventure of the previous night.

"Murphy admits he's a smuggler," Biff said. "We found his loot. Great stuff—gold by the sackful!"

"Unfortunately it wasn't the Wakefield gold, or the Scythian figurine, either," Frank said.

Mr Hardy tried to cheer his son. "Even if Murphy and Palango were false leads, you discovered an illegal smuggling operation. The Mexican government will be very grateful to you, and Murphy deserves to be put out of business."

Frank nodded. "You're right. We were just about to take him to Chichén Itzá and hand him over to the police. If necessary, we'll take him to Mérida."

"Good thinking. We can use his jeep and mine. Let's go get him," Mr Hardy said.

The group walked up the steps of the pyramid to where Biff was guarding Murphy. Biff marvelled at Mr Hardy's disguise, and the thief glowered at them. "I want to see a lawyer," he snarled.

"You'll see one in town, Murphy," Mr Hardy said. "First we'll take you and your loot out of here."

The boys untied Murphy's ankles and led him to their father's jeep. He was put in the front seat, while Tony and Biff rode in the back to make sure the smuggler would not try to escape.

The others had soon located Murphy's vehicle and Frank climbed behind the wheel with Joe and Chet as passengers. The jeeps took a long detour that Murphy had discovered was the easiest route through the jungle. Arriving in Chichén Itzá, they turned the man and his gold over to the authorities.

The police deputy was gratified. "We knew a smuggler was operating in this area, but we never could catch him. You have done us a great favour!"

After Murphy was led away, Frank said, "I don't see any reason to go back to Palango. What do you think, Dad?"

"I agree. Let's drive to Mérida and get a flight from there to Mexico City. Then we can see what Armstrong has in mind."

In Mérida, Mr Hardy called John Armstrong at his hotel to tell him when they would arrive. He picked them up at the airport. Looking harried, he mopped his brow with his handkerchief.

"What's new, Fenton?" he asked.

"No news of the mint thief, John. We didn't find the stolen gold in the jungle," Mr Hardy replied, "but the boys nabbed a smuggler." He told Armstrong about their adventure.

Armstrong sighed. "While you were away, I checked with the police on Zemog. Nothing positive there either. But I'm sure the answer—"

"Look!" Joe interrupted and pointed to a small plane with the words "Mexico City" on the fuselage. It was just taking off on the runway.

Joe memorized the craft's number, and the excited boys went to check with the control tower. They found out that the plane belonged to Carlos Calderón.

According to the pilot's flight plan, he was bound for Mérida.

"I think he's going to Palango," the official in the tower told them.

"Results at last!" Joe said jubilantly as they went back to tell their father and Armstrong what they had just heard.

Armstrong was enthusiastic. "You see? We'll have to go there right away!"

They took a flight the following morning. Mr Hardy would stay in Mexico City to testify against Murphy, who was being transferred for his hearing the next day. Armstrong and the boys flew to Mérida, where they rented two jeeps and once more drove to the dig. When they arrived, their archaeological friends greeted them with loud shouts.

"Thank goodness you're all right!" Rose cried out. "We thought you were lost in the jungle! Frank Pendleton went out looking for you but had no luck!"

"We ran into an unexpected adventure," Frank said. After introducing John Armstrong, he told about Rumble Murphy and the pyramid.

Steve Weiss was incredulous. "This is absolutely fantastic!" he said.

"Well, we didn't find what we were after," Frank said. "But the plane we were looking for has supposedly flown to Mérida and its owner, Carlos Calderón, was planning to come here."

"Carlos!" Steve exclaimed. "He's a good friend of ours, an archaeology student who visits once in a while. He does graduate work at the University of Mexico. Right now he's out in the jungle with a couple of our men. Should be back any minute, however."

"Why didn't you tell us his plane has 'Mexico City' on it?" Joe asked.

"I didn't know. He told us he had bought a small plane recently, but I never saw it."

Just then three men appeared at the excavation site. Two were Mexican workmen, the third a handsome young fellow with wavy black hair and a bright smile.

"Hey, Carlos!" Steve called out. "These people want to meet you."

He introduced everyone, then Frank asked Carlos if he had ever been in Wakefield, U.S.A.

The young man was surprised. "No, I have never been out of Mexico. Why do you ask?"

"We're trailing a private plane marked 'Mexico City' that took off from an airstrip near Wakefield."

"When was that?" Carlos asked.

Frank gave him the date.

"Wait a minute," Weiss intervened. "At that time Carlos was here at the Palango dig with us."

Melville Courtney had been listening. Now he slapped his swagger stick against his boot and addressed the boys. "My dear chaps, you will have to look elsewhere for your culprit. My goodness, how suspicious you are!"

"I realize you have a case to solve," Steve Weiss said. "But I hope you'll stay and lead us to the lost pyramid. We'll go out tomorrow and do a preliminary survey. After that we'll take a work gang and begin clearing away the vegetation."

Frank and Joe looked at Armstrong, who nodded vigorously. "Of course we'll stay. We'll be glad to guide you to the place." To Frank he said in a low tone, "I don't believe Calderón is as harmless as he seems.

Maybe someone else flew his plane. We'll stay here and keep him under surveillance."

Steve Weiss and his group were excited about the lost pyramid, and they could hardly wait to explore it. "We're glad you caught that smuggler," Steve told the boys. "We just dug up a lot of artifacts, and he might have stolen them. Look here." He showed them small statues, images of the Mayan gods, an assortment of weapons and knives, and some tablets bearing petroglyphic inscriptions.

"This is our masterpiece," he declared, holding one up for all to see. "It's an image of the Aztec war god. The Aztecs traded with the Mayas of Yucatán."

The image was a shining gold mask. The features were contorted into a ferocious scowl, and the jade eyes reflected the sunlight in shimmering blue-green.

Weiss handed the mask to Frank, who examined it and passed the piece round the circle. Everybody was thrilled by the Aztec war god. Chet and Carlos were fascinated.

Armstrong handled the mask. "Feels like solid gold," he announced. "I'd say it's as valuable as one of our larger bars in the mint."

He began to speak with Chet, Carlos, and Pendleton about the quality of gold. Later that evening, the four sat up after the others had gone to bed. Just before he fell asleep, Joe heard Chet retire to his tent.

A rattling noise woke Joe up hours later. It came from the tent where the artifacts were kept. Joe crept towards the tent, straining his eyes to see in the darkness. A figure stole out and walked towards the jungle.

"Whoever he is," Joe thought, "he's stealing the valuable gold mask!"

· 15 ·

Lethal Reptiles

FOR a moment Joe stared at the thief, who was slowly strolling along in the darkness. Then the young detective crept back to his tent and wakened Frank.

"Someone's taking off with the golden mask!" he whispered into his brother's ear. "We'd better stop him!"

Frank bolted out of his sleeping bag. "Go after him," he said. "I'll wake the others and we'll be right there."

Joe ran from the camp as quietly as he could in order not to alert the thief. The man might run into the jungle and disappear into the night! He saw the thief, still walking slowly in the moonlight, and caught up to him. "Stop!" Joe commanded. "Don't go any farther!"

He expected the thief to whirl round and attack him, and was ready to fight. Instead, the man turned slowly, holding the mask over his face, and said nothing!

By now Frank and the others ran up. "Joe, did you get him?" Frank called out.

"Right here," Joe replied.

"Who is he?" Steve Weiss demanded.

Joe stared at the thief, who stood motionless, his face hidden behind the ancient image. "Come on," Joe said, "take that thing away and stop playing games!"

The man did not move. Joe grabbed the mask and pulled it from the thief's face.

Carlos Calderón!

"Carlos, what are you doing with that mask?" Steve Weiss asked, incredulous. "You're not trying to steal it, are you?"

"Of course he is," Armstrong declared. "He took it and then tried to make a getaway. I suspected him all along!"

Weiss took the mask from Joe. "I don't know the explanation," he said, "but Carlos is not a thief. I'm sure of that."

"Weiss, you're out of your mind," Armstrong exploded. "We've caught him red-handed!"

Carlos stood perfectly still, saying nothing. He looked at the rest with a fixed stare.

"He's sleepwalking!" Tony exclaimed.

"No, that's not it," Frank said. "A sleepwalker would have awakened after all this commotion."

Rose walked up to Carlos. She peered deep into his eyes. Made passes with her hand in front of his face, and spoke to him. He did not react.

"He's in a trance," the biologist said. "I think Carlos has been hypnotized. I've studied the subject and I know all the signs. A hypnotized person looks just the way Carlos does."

Frank became excited. "Somebody hypnotized Carlos and made him take the gold mask!"

Chet scratched his head. "But who?"

"Nobody in this camp," Weiss said. "None of us is a hypnotist."

"Could it be somebody hiding in the jungle?" Tony suggested. "The guy met Carlos, hypnotized him, and told him to get the mask. A confederate of Rumble Murphy's, perhaps."

"You may be right," Joe said. "It's one more mystery for us to solve."

Weiss tapped a finger against his chin. "I've just thought of something. Aztec masks of the gods were supposed to have a hypnotic effect on worshippers in the temples. I wonder if the mask could have hypnotized Carlos."

"Nonsense!" Armstrong objected. "He wasn't in a trance when I left him last night. He stole the mask deliberately!"

"Why not ask him?" Biff suggested. He shook the student. "Carlos! Wake up!" he commanded. "Wake up!"

Carlos did not respond.

"It's no use," Rose said. "He can't hear you. Besides, it's dangerous to wake up a hypnotized person suddenly. It could affect his mind and impair his memory. Let him sleep it off."

"Just like that?" Pendleton queried.

"Right. Most hypnotized people pass into ordinary sleep and wake up normally. In extreme cases, a doctor is needed. All we can do is see how Carlos comes out of this."

Weiss led the way back to camp. Rose guided Carlos by the elbow. She deposited him in his tent while Steve replaced the gold mask with the rest of the artifacts from the dig.

"I'll stand guard outside Calderón's tent," John Armstrong offered, "and make sure he doesn't escape."

The others went back to sleep. In the morning, Carlos came out of his tent to join the group for breakfast.

Armstrong, who was still on guard, grabbed him.

"Hey, let go of me!" the student objected. "What's the idea? I can walk on my own."

"We saw that last night," Armstrong replied sarcastically.

"What are you talking about?"

"About the way you tried to walk off with the gold mask!"

"John, you don't make any sense at all," Carlos said, looking puzzled. "*You* took the mask back to the tent before we went to bed, not I!"

"Come on, the others will tell you," Armstrong said, dragging the student to the breakfast area.

Everyone seemed to stare at him in a strange way. Carlos began to feel uncomfortable. "Is anything wrong?" he asked. "John said something about my walking off with the mask. What is this?"

"Carlos, what is the last thing you remember last night?" Frank Hardy asked.

"Well, Chet, John, Pendleton, and I talked about the mask and admired the beautiful craftsmanship. Then John took it back to the artifacts tent and we all went to bed."

"And then?"

"Then? Nothing. I went to sleep! What in the world are you getting at?"

"You walked off into the jungle with the mask in the middle of the night," Armstrong said. "Don't deny it because we all saw you!"

Carlos stared at the man in utter astonishment, then turned to Steve Weiss. "Steve," he said, and his voice was shaking with fear and bewilderment, "what is this man trying to do to me? You know I'm not a thief. I didn't touch that mask after I went to my tent. You people all know me. Please, won't anyone stick up for me?"

Rose walked over to the student and put her arm round his shoulders. "Calm down, Carlos. Something happened last night, and we have a pretty good idea what. You were hypnotized and started to walk away from the camp with the mask. Moreover you didn't react to anything we said to you."

"Hypnotized! But—but I don't remember anything of the sort."

"You wouldn't, so don't worry about it."

Carlos sat down and put his head into his hands. "I can't believe it. I just can't believe it."

Armstrong did not speak out loud, but said to Frank in a low voice, "I don't either. I think he's putting on an excellent show. Let's ask the authorities to investigate his story."

Frank was inclined to believe Carlos, but since he worked for Armstrong, he did not contradict him. "Sure, Mr Armstrong, we'll check him out as soon as we get back to Mexico City."

Carlos stood up again and looked at everyone at the table. "Who hypnotized me?"

"We don't know," Steve said. "Must have been an outsider who stole in here."

"I haven't talked to any outsiders since I arrived!" Carlos argued.

"Who knows?" Pendleton put in. "Someone could have come into your tent last night and commanded you under hypnosis not to remember ever meeting him."

"But why would anyone want to do that?"

"Possibly so that you would take the mask and deposit it somewhere in the jungle."

"What—what if it happens again?"

"It won't. We'll keep an eye on you. Relax," Steve told him. "And now let's get to work. We're going to find the pyramid today. Remember?"

He organized a party, including Pendleton, the Hardys, and himself. Armstrong decided to watch Carlos; and Biff, Tony, and Chet would help Courtney to list artifacts from the dig.

"We don't have to hike as we did last time," Frank said. "I have a pretty good idea of how to find Murphy's trail from here. Let's take the jeep."

Frank found the way without difficulty, and even though it was a roundabout route from Palango, the searchers reached the pyramid within a few hours.

The archaeologist and the guide were ecstatic. "This is absolutely phenomenal!" Steve Weiss exclaimed. "We've finally found the lost pyramid! Frank, Joe, you can't imagine how grateful we are to you!"

The Hardys grinned. "Don't forget, we discovered it by accident!"

While Steve and Pendleton entered the structure, Frank and Joe reconnoitred the jungle round it and plunged into the underbrush.

"I believe Carlos was hypnotized," Frank said. "What do you think, Joe?"

"I'm with you. I hope whoever did it won't come back and put all of us in a trance!" He took out his machete and began to hack through the jungle growth. Frank did the same. The keen blades of the long knives easily sliced through the vegetation, lopping off vines, creepers, and tree branches.

The boys reached a clearing, where they paused for a conference on what to do next. "If we go any farther," Frank said, "we might lose our way. The undergrowth is dense around here. How about going back?"

Joe nodded. "Look! There's a path. Want to try it?"

"Sure. Why not?"

The new route took them downhill into a swampy region of the jungle. They found a sluggish creek and tramped along its banks until it widened into a fast-moving stream.

A steamy haze rose from the ground. Black mud clung to their shoes. Grassy hillocks were slick with wet grass, and tree boles slanted crazily from the bank out over the water. Moss hung from the branches like long, heavy ropes.

"Let's pretend we're monkeys," Joe proposed. "We'll swing from one tree to another on the moss and avoid getting our feet wet."

Frank chuckled. "Okay, Tarzan, you lead the way. I'll follow when I see how you make out."

Frank tripped over a root, and fell headlong into the ooze, breaking his fall with his hands. He pushed himself up into a squatting position and washed himself in the stream before proceeding.

The boys hiked along the stream, which flowed roughly in the direction of the pyramid. Massive tree roots compelled them to make a detour inland. They came to a rocky ledge, where ferns covered the mouth of a small cave.

Joe poked a branch into the darkness of the cave. *Whoosh!* A black snarling form flashed out at him! He ducked by reflex action. The creature just missed his head and zoomed up on to a branch overhead. Savage eyes glared down at him. Sharp fangs snapped.

"It's a bat!" Frank exclaimed.

Joe shuddered. "A vampire bat. Let's get out of here before his buddies in the cave come out!"

They hurried round to the bank and continued tramping downstream. The river gradually broadened until it extended a hundred yards across. The Hardys stopped to survey it.

A snout broke the surface and rose into the air, revealing a long head with tiny reptilian eyes. The body floated like a log. A pair of jaws opened, revealing a row of wicked fangs. A heavy tail whiplashed the water. A similar reptile rose beside it. Then another, and another.

"Alligators!" Joe exclaimed.

"There must be a school of them!" Frank cried. "Come on, let's get out of here!"

He turned and climbed up the embankment. Joe started to follow him, but slipped in the mud. Wildly he flung his arms out in a desperate effort to maintain his balance. A hillock broke loose under his foot.

With a scream, Joe toppled into the river and was swept by the current towards the lethal reptiles!

·16·

Unexpected Revelation

ONE alligator spotted Joe in the water and eagerly moved towards him. Three others followed with open jaws!

Frantically Joe swam against the current. He was a strong athlete, but the swift-moving waves carried him downstream away from the bank. The alligators gained on him, slithering through the water like torpedoes!

Frank ran to a bend in the stream. He tore a long creeper from a tree and tossed one end far out into the water in his brother's path. Joe grabbed the creeper as he went past.

"Help—me!" he yelled.

Frank braced himself on the bank and tugged on the creeper. As he drew it in, Joe kicked his feet and began to move faster through the waves. But the alligators were still gaining on him!

As Joe reached the shallow water, Frank dropped the creeper, held on to the tree branch with one hand, and extended the other out over the stream. Joe grabbed it and Frank pulled his brother up the bank.

A rasping crunch sounded just behind Joe. One of the alligators hurled itself out of the water in an effort to close its jaws on its prey. Missing by a hair's breadth, the giant reptile splashed back into the waves.

Joe lay high on the bank, gasping for breath. "Frank," he panted, "you were better than the U.S. Cavalry galloping to the rescue!"

"Well," Frank replied, "I figured that if you insisted on playing tag with a bunch of alligators, you might need help in a hurry."

When Joe recovered, the Hardys found that the bend in the stream carried it away from their starting point. Frank got a fix with his compass on a direct march through the jungle, and half an hour later the boys arrived at the pyramid.

Steve Weiss and Frank Pendleton had made sketches and layouts and were about ready to leave. "What happened to you?" Steve asked Joe, who was still wet from his swim.

"I was in a racing meet with some alligators," Joe said and told them about his adventure.

Steve shook his head. "Please don't pull any more stunts like that! We haven't had any casualties so far, and we'd like to keep our record clean."

When the group reached Palango, the Hardys showered and changed their clothes, then washed those they had worn and hung them up to dry in the late afternoon sun. Then they recounted their adventures to Chet, Biff, Tony, and Armstrong.

"Any news on this end?" Frank asked.

"Nothing," Biff said. "Tony and I inspected the surroundings now and then, but spotted no one at all."

Armstrong frowned. "I'm not surprised to hear that. I still think Calderón's guilty."

"What do you suggest we do?" Frank asked.

"Let's go back to Mexico City and check with the authorities."

Next morning the group thanked the people at the dig for their hospitality, then rode back in the jeep to Mérida and took a plane to Mexico City. They found Mr Hardy at the Montezuma Hotel, which he and John Armstrong had made their headquarters while staying in Mexico.

"Rumble Murphy has been indicted," he reported, "and the police have arrested his Mexico City contact, a man by the name of Hank Corda. But there's no evidence that they were involved with the Wakefield heist. What did you find out in Palango?"

Frank described the incident with Carlos Calderón and the gold mask. He mentioned the suspicion that the young man had been hypnotized.

"That's possible," Fenton Hardy mused. "Hypnosis has been used before in crimes."

Armstrong stirred in his chair. "Calderón is our prime suspect! I want a thorough investigation of him. Take all the time you need. You've got to solve the Wakefield theft!"

The boys promised to get to work right away. First they went to the university and checked on Carlos. The administration confirmed that he was an archaeology student, top man in his class, and was doing work financed by the government. Carlos enjoyed the highest reputation in academic circles.

At police headquarters Frank and Joe were told that Carlos Calderón had no criminal record. The officer in charge made a call to the Department of Aviation to confirm that Calderón held a pilot's licence.

"The story Carlos told us checks out," Frank advised

his buddies as they walked towards a shop to have soft drinks.

"Does anybody think Carlos was working with Rumble Murphy?" Joe asked. "Frank and I doubt it."

Their friends agreed.

"What about Pedro Zemog?" Joe went on. "Zemog took a gold horse. Carlos took a gold mask. Is there a connection?"

"We don't know enough about this guy Zemog," Biff commented.

Suddenly Frank sat up in his chair. He put his glass down so hastily that soda spilled over the rim on to the marble-topped table. "Zemog!" he exclaimed. "Zemog. I have an idea. Read it backwards!"

"G-o-m-e-z," Tony ticked off the letters.

"That's a popular Mexican name," Frank continued. "Maybe that's the real name of the man we're after. Come on, let's check the directory."

The boys went to a phone booth and Frank flipped the pages of the telephone book. He ran his finger down a column of names.

"Boy, Gomez is like Smith back home," he said. "And there are a lot of Pedros among them."

"We'll have to split up and take the names one at a time," Joe suggested.

Frank nodded and wrote two lists of names. He gave one to Biff, who would be accompanied by Chet and Tony. The Hardys took the second list.

They called on half a dozen men named Pedro Gomez. None was the person they were looking for. The seventh call took them to an apartment in the suburbs of Mexico City. Frank rang the bell. A man with grey hair opened the door. When he saw the

Hardys, he tried to shut the door quickly, but Frank blocked it by placing his foot on the sill. "Pedro Gomez," he said sternly, "we want to talk to you. May we come in?"

Gomez opened the door. "All right. You might as well. I am tired of running."

They went into the apartment. Apparently Gomez was alone. He was nervous and shifted uneasily from one foot to the other.

"You will not find what you came to get," he told them in an unfriendly tone.

Frank and Joe were startled by the words.

"You admit you had it?" Joe asked incredulously.

"Of course I had it. But I have it no longer. I sold it a few days ago."

"You sold the Scythian figurine?" Frank exclaimed.

Now it was Gomez's turn to look startled. "The what?"

"The day you visited the museum in New York you stole the figurine of a rearing horse and ran off with it!" Frank reminded him.

"Oh, no! I did not steal the piece!"

Frank stared at the Mexican. "Come on, Mr Gomez, we saw you running out of the place."

"Of course I ran. I was afraid for my life!"

"Why don't you tell us your version of the event?" Joe suggested.

The man nodded. "Yes. But I think you will not believe me."

"Try us."

Gomez said he had seen a tall blond man open the display case and take out the horse. When the man realized that Gomez had observed him, he hit the Mexican on the head and knocked him against the wall.

"When I got up, the blond man had left the room," Gomez said. "I ran out after him, but could not see him. Then I heard the guard shout and realized I would be the prime suspect. So I hurried out of the door and luckily got a taxi right away."

Frank and Joe looked at each other. "A tall blond man!" Frank said. "That fits in with the description the guard gave us."

"But, Mr Gomez," Joe said, "why do you travel under an alias?"

"I am a salesman of rare stamps. I must take every precaution when I travel."

"So that's what you had in your briefcase," Joe marvelled. "The bulge we thought was the Scythian horse was actually a package of stamps."

Gomez nodded. "Unique Ruritanian issues, two hundred years old. Priceless! I thought you were trying to steal them from me. That is why I told you just now that I sold them. I did not know you were referring to the Scythian horse."

"What about the letters A.P.?" Frank asked. "We found two telegrams addressed to Pedro Zemog, and signed with those initials."

"They stand for Associated Philatelists," Gomez explained. "I represent the company that sends me buyers' orders by telegram when I am on the road. The first one told me to take the Ruritanian consignment to Zurich, but the Swiss buyer backed out at the last minute. Then I was told to go to my hometown of Mexico City, where a deal went through."

"You ran from us in Zurich because you thought we were after your stamps?" Joe asked.

Gomez nodded.

"And you used the name Jones at the hotel because you knew we had seen you on the plane?"

"Correct."

"Incidentally, were you in Chapultepec Castle the other day?"

Gomez smiled. "Yes. I saw you, and I knew you saw me. So I left."

"Have you ever been to Wakefield?"

"What?"

Joe described the gold heist at the mint.

"My friend," Gomez protested, "you have suspected me of two crimes that I did not commit!"

"My apologies," Joe said.

"Now then, who are you?" Gomez demanded.

"We're Americans from Bayport, Frank and Joe Hardy. We're investigating the thefts we told you about."

While Joe was talking to Gomez, Frank tried to reconstruct the scene at the museum. The guard had said he saw the tall blond man emerge from the Animal Chamber and bury his cigarette in the sand bucket. Maybe the man had hidden the figurine instead!

"Mr Gomez," Frank said, "may I use your phone and call the Early Art Museum in New York? I'll pay you, of course."

"Go ahead."

Frank was connected with Orlov. Before he could say anything, the Russian curator gave a cry that Joe and Gomez could both hear.

"Finally you call!" he exclaimed. "Why have you not contacted me sooner?"

·17·

Hypnotized!

"WE didn't have news for you until now," Frank said.

"News? I hope good news!"

"Yes. Look for the missing figurine in the sand bucket in the hallway."

"What? But—" Orlov put down the phone in confusion. A few minutes later he came back on. "You were right! This is fantastic. How did you know?"

"We found Zemog."

"Remarkable. He hid it there?"

"No. The tall blond man did. When he saw the guard, he put the horse in the sand bucket because he was afraid he'd be caught."

"You mean Zemog is not the thief?"

"No. He was an innocent bystander who saw what happened. The blond man hit him and knocked him against the wall. That's why he ran out of the building."

"Amazing, absolutely amazing! I am very happy about it. Thanks to you, good international relations have not been endangered, and I shall report on your good work to my government."

Orlov hung up. Frank told Gomez and Joe about the discovery of the Scythian figurine.

"That is a relief to me," Gomez said. "It proves once

and for all that I am not the thief!"

"It sure does, Mr Gomez," Frank agreed.

"If we ever need rare stamps," Joe said, "we'll give you a buzz."

The Hardys went back to the Montezuma Hotel and waited in the lobby for their pals. Chet, Biff, and Tony straggled in, looking worn out. Chet flopped down into an easy chair and ran his fingers through his hair. "I'm bushed!" he said.

"I'm disappointed," Tony stated. "Every Pedro Gomez we talked to was a false lead."

"Don't worry," Frank said. "We found the right one!"

After telling his friends about the rare-stamp salesman, Frank led the way to the room where Fenton Hardy and John Armstrong were discussing strategy.

"Carlos Calderón is clean," Frank said. "We also found Zemog. His real name is Gomez and he sells stamps. And—the gold horse never left the museum in New York."

"What!" Mr Hardy exclaimed in surprise. "Tell us all about it."

When the boys had finished their account, Mr Hardy smiled. "Good detective work, boys. As far as the Mexican angle is concerned, I think we've exhausted it. We've been in touch with every conceivable agent dealing in gold, and nothing has turned up. I've also spoken with Johann Jung on the telephone just now, and he says the gold has not surfaced in Switzerland."

Armstrong put his head between his hands. "We're up against a stone wall!" he said in despair. "No leads whatsoever. But I still feel the solution lies here in Mexico."

"John, you can't go by a hunch. I vote we return to Wakefield and start from scratch."

Armstrong threw up his hands and sighed. "All right. At this point, I don't know what to do."

The group caught a jet for New York the next day. Chet, Biff, and Tony went back to Bayport, while the other four reached Wakefield in the evening. The Hardys checked into a motel, and Armstrong went home.

"I can't get this hypnosis business out of my mind," Joe confessed. "Who hypnotized Carlos? We know Murphy was in custody, and Gomez is on the level. Too bad Carlos couldn't remember anything."

Frank had an idea. "Wait a minute! That's what the guards at the mint said. They couldn't remember anything about the gold heist the night they were on duty. Maybe they were hypnotized, too!"

Mr Hardy nodded. "Good thinking, Frank. That would explain how they passed the lie-detector test. They could have let the thieves into the vault. And they could be telling the truth when they say they don't know a thing about it."

Frank and Joe were electrified by the theory.

"Then who hypnotized the guards?" Joe asked.

"The same guy who hypnotized Carlos," Frank replied. "We were shadowed all the way from Wakefield to Palango. Look! The gang leader used hypnosis to steal the gold. If he came down to the dig, he could have worked on Carlos, too!"

"That's an involved theory," Fenton Hardy said. "And if you're right, chances are the man followed us back to Wakefield. We'll keep the mint under surveillance all day tomorrow. Now let's get some sleep!"

The private investigator and his sons roomed together, but had separate beds. Mr Hardy was next to the window and Frank near the door, with Joe in between. Exhausted from their long journey, they fell asleep at once.

Frank woke suddenly in the middle of the night. He had an uncanny feeling that something was wrong. "Probably a nightmare," he thought. Then he heard a scuffing noise and raised his head.

A ghostly figure glided across the room through the darkness, opened the door, and went out. The door clicked shut.

Frank noticed a slight sickish-sweet odour in the room. It grew rapidly stronger. His head began to swim. His detective training warned him what was happening. He leaped out of bed, and opened the door wide. Joe, awakened by Frank's shout, threw all the windows up. Mr Hardy lay still.

Coughing and choking, the boys pulled their father from his bed and propped him up with his head out one of the windows. They leaned over the other one, gasping for fresh air. Mr Hardy began to breathe regularly again.

By the time he revived, the gas had dissipated. They sat down on their beds and talked over their close call.

"It seems as if Frank's theory has merit," Mr Hardy said. "Our enemy may have followed us back here, and now he wants to get us out of the way."

"But if the gold is already in Mexico or somewhere else, why would he get nervous because we're back in Wakefield?" Joe asked.

"He probably wouldn't. Which means, the gold must still be here!"

"He's sure determined to kill us," Frank said. "He's as dangerous as a rattlesnake!"

"I think one of us should keep watch for the rest of the night," Mr Hardy said. "I'll do it."

"We'll take turns," Frank suggested.

"Don't worry about it," his father said. "Most of the night is already gone. You two go back to sleep. Someone has to be bright and alert in the morning."

They bolted the door, but nothing more happened. After an early breakfast they took a circuitous route through the woods to the mint. Fenton Hardy left his sons near the front gate and concealed himself behind a clump of trees where he could watch the entrance without being seen. Frank and Joe slipped behind some bushes at the back of the building and kept vigil near the rear door and side exit.

Workers began arriving. They left their cars in the parking lot and entered the building. Then visitors streamed in.

"They don't know about the gold heist," Frank whispered.

"Armstrong has been keeping quiet about the theft," Joe observed.

Hours went by. The sun grew hot, and the Hardys felt cramped.

"I'm hungry," Frank said.

"I'll have a hot dog and a bottle of iced lemonade," said Joe.

"Make mine a hamburger," Frank joked, "and a side order of French fries. I'd like to be somewhere that sells food right now, Joe!"

"So would I," Joe said. "Surveillance is tough when you're hungry."

They took out some biscuits they had brought with them and had their mid-day meal. Evening came, and the boys strained their eyes towards the rear gate of the mint but saw nothing suspicious.

Suddenly dry leaves snapped in the bushes behind them! The Hardys whirled around and got ready for action as the sound approached.

"I'll tackle him!" Frank whispered. "You clamp your hand over his mouth."

The noise grew louder, then seemed to stop behind a bush nearby. The branches parted and a face peered through at them. It was that of a little black and white terrier!

The Hardys laughed and sat down in relief.

"A canine suspect," Joe chortled.

The dog advanced, wagging his tail. Frank stroked his back. Joe scratched his ears.

"Okay. Off you go," the boy said. The terrier rubbed his head against the young detective's arm and licked his hand. "Go home!" Frank commanded. Instead, the dog climbed into his lap, where he settled down.

The Hardys tried to push him away. Thinking they wanted to play, he rolled over and over, pawing the air in a friendly fashion.

"We must get rid of him" Frank muttered.

Joe found an extra biscuit in his pocket. "This should do the trick," he said, chucking the biscuit in a high arc over the bushes.

The terrier darted after the flying missile, and came back with the biscuit in his mouth! The Hardys groaned as he laid it at Joe's feet.

Eagerly the animal looked up at him, wagging his tail, obviously asking for another chance to fetch the biscuit. Getting no response, the dog began to whine.

Frank became alarmed. "If he starts barking, everybody in the mint will know we're here!"

Just then a small bearded man came through the back gate and headed in their direction. The Hardys were frantic with fear that the dog would give them away!

The bearded man came directly towards them, walking up to the bush they were hiding behind. The dog growled at him.

"That did it," Frank thought. "How are we going to explain?"

The man seemed to pay no attention, however. Instead of circling round the bush and confronting the boys, he veered to one side and walked into the woods without even looking at the dog.

"Joe! What do you make of that?" Frank asked, puzzled. "He didn't blink an eye!"

"I don't know," Joe said slowly, watching the man intently. "He—he's strolling along in a funny way, almost like a zombie!"

"Joe! Maybe he's been hypnotized. Let's follow him."

·18·

The Big Discovery

THE bearded man walked rapidly through the woods. It was dark enough for Frank and Joe to follow him at a close distance. They were relieved when the terrier dropped behind and then ran off.

"I hope he's headed for home," Frank thought.

The man they were shadowing never looked behind or to either side as he went. He kept his right hand plunged into the pocket of his jacket as if protecting something. Reaching the dirt road that Frank and Joe had scouted before, he avoided the road itself by moving through rough underbrush to the left.

"He doesn't want to be seen by anyone coming down the road," Frank murmured.

"I guess the guy who hypnotized that man told him to stay clear of it," Joe replied.

The stranger turned away from the road and walked on through the woods to the empty airstrip, which he crossed. A plane could easily land or take off on it.

"Somebody's keeping the place ready to use," Frank said in an undertone.

"A plane could even be parked in the underbrush," Joe replied. "I wonder if the bearded man is meeting the pilot here."

Their quarry did not stop, however. He walked across the airstrip into the woods on the opposite side. He and his two shadows continued past tall trees whose bare branches were etched in sharp outlines against the night sky.

Soon they came to an old unused dirt road. In spite of the darkness, the boys could see two parallel furrows. A vehicle had recently been driven up the road.

They followed the man until he came to a barbed-wire fence with a wooden gate. The Hardys ducked into the underbrush and watched the stranger advance to the gate. Another man approached from the other side, cradling a rifle over his arm.

"Give the password," he demanded.

"Golden moonlight."

The gate was opened and the bearded man went through, disappearing round a bend. The guard sat down on a stump and placed his weapon across his knees as he resumed his vigil.

Frank tapped Joe on the shoulder. He pointed along the fence, indicating that they should scout in that direction. Stealthily the two boys crept through the underbrush past the guard. They followed the fence until they noticed a light shining through the trees. Moving closer, they saw the outline of a cavernous barn on the opposite side. The light came from a window, its beam falling upon a dusty pick-up truck parked outside.

"We'd better investigate," Joe said, and he depressed the barbed wire with his foot. He put a hand on one of the fence posts and vaulted over. Frank followed, but his foot slipped and his jacket became entangled in the barbed wire!

"Joe!" he hissed. "I'm caught!"

His brother took off his own jacket, which he used to protect his hands as he pushed the barbed wire down. Frank pulled himself free and dropped down on the other side.

Slipping up to the area of the light, the Hardys hit the ground and crawled to the barn. Joe snaked his way round the pick-up truck and Frank followed him. Then they peered into the barn window, which was ajar.

They saw an enormous room. A floor of broad planks extended from wall to wall. Dark rafters loomed overhead, and on either side of the room rickety stairs led to the hayloft.

Each side of the building had a heavy reinforced wooden door fastened by a large bolt and chain. Peepholes had been cut in the doors so that anyone on the inside could identify visitors before admitting them.

Three men, playing cards, were seated at a table in the middle of the barn under a single overhead light bulb. They were a rough-looking threesome with two days' growth of beard on their faces. Two wore jeans and check shirts. The man who seemed to be their leader was dressed in slacks and in a turtleneck sweater.

Turtleneck dealt the cards. Each man picked up his hand and looked at it. One of the men wearing jeans started his bet and threw some chips into the pot.

As Frank and Joe surveyed the scene, their eyes focused in a corner that gave off a golden glow.

Gold bars lay stacked on top of one another!

"Maybe that's the gold from the Wakefield Mint!" Joe gasped.

Frank nodded as the betting at the table continued.

Turtleneck drew in the pot, adding a stack of chips to those he already had.

"I'm having lousy luck," one of his companions said. "I want a new deck of cards."

Turtleneck glared at him. "You accusing Jake Slobodky of cheating? You saying I just dealt from the bottom of the deck?"

"Naw," the man replied. "I'm just saying my luck might change with a new deck."

The game continued. Jake won again. He grinned as he raked in the chips.

The third man slammed his cards down in disgust.

"You complaining about how I deal, too?" Jake demanded.

"I'm complaining about this waiting," the man grumbled. "We've got the gold here. The plane's ready. Let's get this show on the road!"

"You calling the shots now?" Jake asked.

"No, but I got a stake in this operation. And if you want my opinion, I say—"

A loud knock on the door interrupted him. The three men jumped to their feet and tiptoed to the door, where the pair in jeans flattened themselves against the wall. Jake opened the peephole and looked out.

"Give the password!" he ordered.

"Golden moonlight."

"Okay. Come on in."

Jake unfastened the chain and shot back the bolt. The bearded man entered. His eyes were wide open and his face expressionless.

"He looks just the way Carlos did," Joe thought.

The bearded man still had his right hand deep in his pocket. He stopped inside the door as if rooted to the spot. The other three gathered round him expectantly.

Jake spoke loudly to him, emphasizing each word. "What is your mission?"

"I must deliver the message," the man said in a weird voice that seemed to come from a great distance.

"What is the message?"

"I do not know."

"Where is the message?"

"I have it here." He drew his hand out of his pocket. He was clutching a piece of paper in a very tight grasp.

"Give me the message," Jake ordered. "And then return to your home."

The man handed the paper to him, did an about face, went through the door, and walked down the road towards the gate. Jake locked the door. "The trance works," he chortled. "That guy'll be dead to the world till he wakes tomorrow morning. And he won't remember coming out here. Just like the guards who let us heist the gold from the vault."

"But this man was able to talk. I don't like it," one of the men in jeans objected.

"Nothing to worry about. He's programmed to answer just the questions I asked. If the Hardys catch him, he won't spill the beans." Jake held the paper up to the light under the table.

"Wow!" he exploded. "Tomorrow is D-Day! The plane arrives at midnight and we'll be airborne pretty soon and got to be ready to move. Hey, gang, we're gonna be rich!"

After the general excitement had died down, the men started another game of cards. Jake won again. "This is my lucky day!" he boasted.

Frank nudged Joe. "They know we're on their trail," he whispered.

"But they don't know how close we are," Joe replied. "Think we should go and let Dad know?"

"Not yet," Frank advised. "Jake and his pals are small-time crooks. Let's stay and see if we can find out who the ringleader is."

"Good idea."

The card game ended, and the players rose to their feet. Jake stretched and rubbed the back of his neck. "Might as well hit the hay," he announced.

"That's not so easy to do," the big loser grumbled. "The hayloft's full of hay and dust. What a place for us to be holed up!"

"We'll use the cots in the corner, as usual," Jake said, "and it'll be for the last time."

Click! A rifle bolt had suddenly slipped into place. Frank and Joe whirled round. They found themselves staring into the business end of a shotgun!

·19·

Captured!

THE guard who had been standing at the gate was looking through the sight of his rifle. The Hardys were caught! The man lowered his weapon and gave them a wolfish grin. "Okay, wise guys. We'll take care of you. We don't like snoopers around here. Get going and keep your hands where I can see them. Move!"

Frank and Joe started walking. The guard prodded them with his rifle. "Reach for the sky and hurry up. No funny business!"

He forced the boys round the corner of the barn to one of the doors and knocked three times in rapid succession. The peephole opened. Jake peered through suspiciously. "What's up?" he growled.

"We got visitors."

"Well, well. Bring them in!"

Jake opened the door, and the man with the gun forced the Hardys inside the barn.

"I found them eavesdropping at the window," he explained. "Figured you might want me to introduce them to you."

"You figured right!" Jake snapped. "How long have they been there?"

"Long enough!"

"Good going, Sam. If anybody else sneaks up to the barn, bring them in too. These guys may have confederates."

"Right." Sam left. Jake bolted the door.

The two men in check shirts were armed. They glowered at Frank and Joe while Jake started the interrogation.

"All right," he snarled. "What do you mean by sneaking around here?"

The Hardys tried to bluff their way through the predicament in which they found themselves.

"We were hiking through the woods near here," Frank said. "We didn't know about the barn until we saw the light through the trees."

"We were hungry," Joe added, "and came to see if we could scrounge a meal."

The three men laughed in a sinister manner. "Oh sure," Jake sneered. "You just happened to be spying on us through the window. You punks had better talk—and fast!"

Frank and Joe remained silent. They were playing for time. Their captors scowled at them.

"Talk won't do any good," one of the check-shirted men said. "We've got to do them in. They've seen the gold."

The other supported him. "They know too much. Let's deep six 'em, now!"

Amazement gripped Frank and Joe. Those were the words on the note Joe had found in the abandoned car at the airstrip!

The speaker misunderstood their reaction. "So, that scares you, does it? Well, it should. We mean business!" He moved towards Joe, and his companions walked up to Frank. The Hardys braced themselves.

Then Jake stopped. "We have to wait for Mr Big. Maybe he'll want to talk to them. Let's tie these guys up and sit tight until he gets here. It won't be long."

The men pushed the Hardys into a corner, made them sit down with their backs to the wall, produced rope, and tied their hands behind their backs.

The crooks returned to their card game. Frank and Joe sat side-by-side with the ropes chaffing their wrists and conversed in whispers.

"Joe, nobody knows we're here," Frank said. "Too bad we didn't have a chance to alert Dad before we followed the man with the beard."

"Right. We'll have to get out of this on our own," Joe replied.

Three quick knocks sounded on the door, followed by three slow ones, then the three fast ones were repeated. The men at the card table leaped to their feet.

"Mr Big!" Jake exclaimed. "That's his signal. Get ready, and don't talk out of turn."

He unbolted the door without looking through the peephole, and swung it open. Mr Big entered.

The Hardys gasped. *John Armstrong*, the administrative assistant of the Wakefield Mint walked into the room!

"Everything in order, Jake?" he asked.

"Sure thing, boss. Except a couple of prowlers came sneaking around the barn."

"Prowlers?" Armstrong sounded alarmed.

"Don't worry, boss. We caught 'em and we've got 'em."

"Where are they?"

"Over there." Jake pointed to the corner where the

two captives were tied up.

Armstrong threw up his hands in astonishment. "Don't you know who they are?" he demanded.

"Should I?" Jake queried.

"Well, maybe not. They're Frank and Joe Hardy!"

"Fenton Hardy's sons?" Jake squinted uneasily. "That means the detective is on to us."

Armstrong shook his head. "Hardy doesn't know anything about our operation. And these two don't matter any more." He advanced towards Frank and Joe. "Fooled you, didn't I?" he asked slyly.

"You sure did," Frank admitted. "First you steal the gold. Then you send us on a wild goose chase to Switzerland by spreading the rumour that the gold will be sold there."

"It would have been sufficient if my friend Rudolf Kling hadn't picked a loser like Pfeiffer to do the talking," Armstrong growled.

Frank nodded. "Pfeiffer was caught in a burglary. And when we left Zurich after that, you sent us to Mexico by dreaming up the clue of the aeroplane, then insisted on travelling to Palango with Dad to get us and him as far as possible from Wakefield. The gold was here all the time."

Armstrong agreed. "The guy I had hired to fly it out gave me trouble on the time schedule. That's why I had to keep you occupied in distant places. Then the idiot got himself arrested in Mexico City just before we came back. But I got a replacement for him, who'll do the job tonight and—"

Frank interrupted him. "Your pilot was arrested? Is his name Hank Corda?"

"Right. I didn't know about his connection with

Murphy. He had Corda's name and address on him, and when he was booked the cops found it. That was all I needed! But I fixed it. This is the final case for Frank and Joe Hardy. We're going to drop you into the sea from our plane and this time tomorrow you'll be playing with the fishes in the Caribbean!"

The ringleader turned towards his henchmen. "Forget about these boys," he said. "Our plane arrives around midnight. The pilot wants this to be a quick job. So do I."

"Everything is ready, boss."

Armstrong walked over to the gold bars, picked one off the top, and looked at it. It glittered in the glare of the overhead bulb.

"That's a beautiful sight," he said. "I haven't seen these since they were in the vault at the mint. I was at home when the theft took place, if you recall."

Jake grinned. "Best alibi anyone ever had."

Armstrong looked pleased. "I think so. Well, these bars have come a long way to get to this barn. From Siberia to Moscow to Zurich to Wakefield. Next stop—an uninhabited island in the Caribbean. We divide the loot there and go our separate ways. If we ever meet again, we don't know one another." Armstrong put the bar back on the pile. "Say, how have you fellows been killing time out here?"

"Playing cards," Jake replied.

"How about dealing me in?"

"Sure thing, boss."

Armstrong occupied the fourth chair at the table. Jake dealt the hands and the game began.

Frank gently tried to pull his wrists apart. He felt a slight give in the ropes. Tapping Joe's foot with his, he leaned towards his brother. "I may be able to untie myself," he whispered. "How about you?"

Joe tested his own bonds. "Not a chance."

Twisting his right wrist against his left, Frank felt the rope stretch. He explored with his fingers until they closed over the knot. Using his escape technique, he figured out how the knot had been tied and rubbed it between his thumb and finger. Gingerly he tugged at the shorter strand.

It moved. Little by little, in an agonizingly slow process, Frank drew the shorter strand loose. His hands were free! He sat still for a moment, watching the card game. All four players were intent on the betting as the pot grew larger and larger.

Frank pressed his shoulder against Joe's to hide his fingers, which were working on his brother's bonds. The second rope fell away and Joe was released.

"They may not notice us," Frank whispered, "if we sneak up in the hayloft, go out the window, and shin down the drainpipe."

"What about the guy at the gate?" Joe asked.

"We'll worry about him when we get there. The first thing is to get out. Come on!"

The Hardys rose slowly to their feet, never taking their eyes off the card game. They tiptoed over to the stairs. Frank led the way up step by step. As he placed his foot on the top rung, it creaked loudly.

The noise cut through the stillness of the huge barn, setting up echoes in the rafters. Startled, Armstrong swivelled in his chair and looked for its source. He spotted Joe's feet at the top of the stairs.

"The Hardys are loose!" he cried angrily. "After them! Don't let them get away!"

The other three men scrambled to their feet, tipping over the chairs in their haste. They pounded across the floor to the stairs.

Now that their escape had been discovered, Frank and Joe plunged forward into the hayloft. The atmosphere was hot, the air was dusty, and the hay was slippery. The boys leaped to the right behind a high pile of hay. Staying low, they ran towards the opposite end of the hayloft, slipping and sliding all the way.

Footsteps pounded up the stairs, and Jake and his two henchmen climbed into the loft.

"Where are they?" Jake bellowed.

Seeing no movement, he led the way to the left side, where clear boards offered easier footing. Frank and Joe saw them go past, and jumped into the middle of the hay, believing they could cross over and reach the stairs.

But Joe's feet shot out from under him. He skidded on the hay—right into Jake, who had doubled back. The unexpected collision caused Jake to tumble into a large pile of hay. He coughed, wheezed, and sneezed, then came up with wisps of dry weeds sticking from his hair. Before he could extricate himself, Frank and Joe ran down the left side while the other two pursuers came up on the right.

A tall pole near the stairs at the far end of the loft reached up to a crossbeam. Frank clambered up the pole on to the crossbeam, and Joe followed instantly. The brothers perched where they could look all the way across the hayloft.

"I hope they think we went downstairs," Frank muttered.

The three men gathered beneath them, panting,

swearing, and looking around furiously. "They got to be up here!" Jake snarled. "We don't go down till we find where they're hiding!"

"Which way?" said a check-shirted searcher. "Left or right?"

"Left, right, up, and down! Look everywhere."

The Hardys were sure to be discovered. Frank signalled Joe. Balancing themselves on the crossbeam, they hurtled down simultaneously, hitting the three men across the shoulders and knocking them down in a heap. Then the boys dived for the stairs, and jumped down three steps at a time. When they reached the bottom, however, they ran straight into the muzzle of a gun!

"Okay, wise guys," Armstrong said. "The game is up!"

·20·

In the Nick of Time

As Armstrong gave his command, the Hardys froze in their tracks and raised both hands over their heads. Footsteps pounded down the stairs behind them.

"Nice going, boss," Jake called out.

"Tie them up again," Armstrong ordered, "and this time see that they stay that way!"

Frank and Joe were hustled over to a corner and bound with ropes round their wrists and ankles. Jake tested the knots.

"Don't worry," he said. "These guys will stick around till we move them."

"Good," Armstrong said. "All we have to do is take them with us and unload them from the plane at five thousand feet. By the way, you'd better bolt the barn door again."

Jake walked to the entrance and reached for the bolt. *Wham!* The door burst open, the edge striking Jake and knocking him off his feet!

Fenton Hardy stepped into the barn, followed by the Wakefield chief of police and a number of officers. "Drop the gun, Armstrong!" the detective commanded.

Armstrong hesitated for a second, then the rifle clattered to the floor. The police disarmed his henchmen, who sullenly refused to say anything.

"We'd like to join the party," Joe called out, "but we're tied up."

Fenton Hardy walked over and unfastened the ropes. "Are you all right?" he asked.

"Fine," Frank replied. "But we wouldn't have been for long. These men were going to let us take a long-distance swallow dive into the Caribbean."

"You got here just in the nick of time," Joe said, relieved.

Armstrong swung round at the worlds. "Hardy," he grated, "how did you figure out my little scheme?"

"It hit me while I was keeping the front gate of the mint under surveillance. The guards at the mint had been hypnotized. And from the way my sons described Carlos Calderón, he, too, must have been in a trance."

"We wondered who did it," Frank put in, "but never guessed the truth."

"Neither did I, Frank," Mr Hardy said. "For the longest time I suspected a third person who might have tailed us to Mexico. Yet Armstrong had the opportunity to hypnotize both the guards and Carlos! Of course, the theory seemed ridiculous. The administrative assistant to the director robbing his own mint! Nevertheless, I decided to shadow him, and it paid off."

"Dad, why didn't you let us know?" Joe asked.

"By the time I realized all this, you two had left your post at the rear gate of the mint. I presume you had good reason?"

Frank described how they had seen the hypnotized man with the beard and decided to follow him.

"Good thinking," Mr Hardy said. "Anyway, I went

to a pay phone and called Chief Erikson, and he came on the run with his men to help me make this arrest."

"Glad to round them up, Fenton," Erikson replied. "I know how often you've been right about criminals."

Mr Hardy turned to Armstrong. "We saw you come out of the mint. You didn't know it, but you had a police escort every step of the way through the woods to the barn."

"We collared the man with the rifle at the gate," the chief took up the story. "Then we came up the road and watched the action in the barn for a while."

"You took a chance, Erikson," Armstrong declared. "As Hardy just said, the hypnotism theory was just a hunch. If you had made a mistake, I could have had your badge."

Erikson shook his head. "Not really. You see, I come from Chicago, and I remember a stage hypnotist who called himself the Great Gordino. His act was to call for volunteers from the audience. He'd put them in a trance and make them perform odd antics, like playing leapfrog on stage, and so on. The Great Gordino got into trouble. He bet on the horses, lost heavily, and disappeared from the Windy City one jump ahead of the sheriff."

"What was his real name?" Joe asked.

"John Armstrong! I never connected Gordino with the Wakefield Armstrong until your father told me he suspected this man of being a hypnotist. Then I was sure. I felt we should go all out after this suspect."

Armstrong caved in. "Sure, I was Gordino in Chicago before I arrived in Wakefield and got a job at the mint. And I had debts. Then I became greedy and wanted some of this gold."

"So you figured out a way to rob the mint?" Frank prodded him.

"I took a holiday in the Caribbean last winter. When I met Hank Corda, I made a deal with him. He put me in touch with Jake, who, with his men, cut the airstrip in the woods."

Jake glared at Armstrong, but did not deny the charges.

"Then you hypnotized the mint guards, told them to turn off the alarm system and the cameras, and to let Jake in," Frank deduced.

Armstrong nodded. "It worked like a charm. I'm still a pretty good hypnotist."

"You're a pretty good actor, too," Fenton Hardy said. "You fooled me completely when you engaged me to handle the case. And here you were simply using me to divert suspicion from yourself."

"Of course. If anyone asked me what I was doing about the gold heist, I could say I hired the famous private investigator from Bayport to run down the clues. But you ran down too many, Hardy!"

"Why did you have our father kidnapped?" Joe asked.

"Because he brought you into the act. That spoiled my plans because with that many people working on the case, it became too dangerous. So we wanted to get him out of the way before he could tell you anything he might have found out."

"But when he escaped," Frank said, "you left the note instructing your men to deep six F.H. in the glove compartment of the car used to transport the gold to the barn. You were giving Jake his orders."

Armstrong nodded. "Jake didn't like this, so I tried

to keep you all away until the gold was safely out of this country."

Joe turned to his father. "He sent us to Zurich and had the rumour spread about the Wakefield gold being sold there," he said. "When that didn't keep us there long enough, he dreamed up the clue about the plane with 'Mexico City' on it."

Mr Hardy chuckled. "It must have been a surprise for you, John, when we actually found such a plane."

"It fitted right into his plans," Frank put in.

"So you hypnotized Carlos Calderón in Palango to have another suspect who would take up our time," Mr Hardy said to Armstrong. "And when we came back to Wakefield earlier than it suited you, you gassed us in the motel. It was all part of your plot!"

Armstrong became angry. "Nothing would have happened to you if you had listened to me! Why wouldn't you stay in Mexico? When you refused, I had no alternative!"

Frank chuckled. "You probably figured you had everything under control when you came out to the barn tonight. You must have been surprised to see Joe and me trussed up like a couple of chickens ready for the spit!"

"Armstrong, your pilot will get a surprise, too," Fenton Hardy said. "The police will have a welcoming committee waiting for him when he lands at the airstrip."

"The getaway plane is due very soon," Frank reported. "We heard Armstrong say about midnight."

"Put a stake out at the airstrip at once," Erikson directed his lieutenant. "Impound the plane, bring in the pilot, and have these prisoners taken away."

"Would you also call the Zurich police and have them arrest a man named Rudolf Kling," Frank added. "He was Armstrong's accomplice, who hired Pfeiffer to spread the rumour about the gold being sold in Switzerland."

Armstrong, Jake, and their two henchmen were led out in handcuffs. Mr Hardy and Erikson walked over to the corner where the gold was stacked. The boys joined them. The bright shimmer of the bars dazzled them, and the hammer and sickle imprint was clearly visible.

"I've always wanted to know what a million in gold looked like," the police chief confided. "Now I do."

"If Armstrong's plan had succeeded, it would have been one of the century's most notorious crimes," Fenton Hardy observed.

"But it failed, thanks to you Hardys," Erikson pointed out. "By the way, Director Wadsworth of the mint returned from his holiday today. He's upset about the whole thing and will be relieved to hear that you've solved the case."

"I'll bet he won't be pleased to hear who the culprit is," Frank said.

"True. On the other hand, the three guards who were arrested are vindicated now and will be back at their jobs soon."

The gold bars were loaded into the pick-up truck, and two officers guarded them while a third took the wheel. Chief Erikson gave the Hardys a lift to their motel.

The following morning Mr Hardy spoke to Director Wadsworth on the telephone. He confirmed that the pilot had been arrested and thanked Mr Hardy profusely for his help.

"I would never have suspected John Armstrong," the director said with a sigh. "I trusted him completely. Well, I'm glad he hired *you* to recover the gold."

The Hardys packed their bags and were soon on their way to Bayport. Frank felt a little disappointed, as he usually did when they wound up a case and the excitement was over. He did not anticipate their next thrilling adventure, *The Firebird Rocket*.

When they arrived home, they were greeted anxiously by Mrs Hardy and Aunt Gertrude.

"I'm so glad to see you," Mrs Hardy said. "Is everything all right?"

"Everything is great!" Joe replied with a grin.

"I'm sure it was dangerous," Aunt Gertrude put in.

"Oh no, Aunty, it was no trouble at all. By the way, we brought you a souvenir."

"Yes? What is it?"

"You have a choice. Either a jaguar god or a feathered serpent!"

The Firebird Rocket

First published in a single volume in hardback in 1978 by
William Collins Sons & Co Ltd.
First published in paperback in 1989 in Armada

·1·

A Frantic Warning

FRANK and Joe Hardy were performing a chemical test in the laboratory above their garage. The boys were checking out a clue for their father, the famous private detective Fenton Hardy.

Frank held a test tube up to the light. In it was a dark-coloured solution soaked from a torn piece of cloth Mr Hardy had sent from the Space Flight Centre in Florida, where he was working on a new top-secret case.

"If Dad's hunch is right," said Frank, "that cloth was stained with the invisible dye he uses to trap suspects."

Joe nodded. "The methyl test will tell us."

He picked up a plastic bottle labelled METHYL YEL-LOW. Unscrewing the cap, he tilted the bottle until a trickle fell into the solution.

Pufff! A burst of acrid vapour shot up into the boys' faces. They staggered back, clutching their throats! Frank dropped the test tube, which smashed, and the bottle fell from Joe's nerveless fingers, clattering on to the wooden floor! The two boys rubbed their eyes, fought for breath, and felt giddy.

"The bottle!" Joe croaked. "It contains the wrong chemical!"

Desperately Frank groped about on the floor till his fingers closed over the plastic container, which was still oozing a wisp of vapour. He managed to screw the cap back on. Joe opened the window, and they collapsed on the window-sill.

Fresh air poured into the lab, dispersing the fumes and clearing their heads.

"That stuff was liquid tear gas, or I'm a monkey's uncle!" Joe exclaimed.

Frank examined the bottle. "It's supposed to be methyl yellow," he declared. "That's what the label says."

"Somebody switched it!"

"That's possible. But who? And why?"

"Let's talk to the guy at the chemistry shop who sold us the bottle," Joe suggested, always eager for a mystery.

Joe Hardy was blond and seventeen. His dark-haired brother, Frank, was a year older.

As they were clearing up the mess from the broken test tube, the Hardys heard the doorbell, which was wired to ring in the garage as well as the house.

Hurrying out of the garage, they went through the house and opened the front door. The caller was a well-dressed, portly man, clutching an ivory-headed cane. He peered at the boys through gold-rimmed pince-nez, which he held in place on his nose with thumb and forefinger.

His gesture called their attention to the ring he was wearing. It was set with a huge red ruby.

"Is this the Hardy house?" he inquired in a deep, booming voice.

"Yes, sir," Frank replied.

"I'm Oliver Ponsley," the man announced. "I would like to consult Fenton Hardy on an urgent matter."

"Dad's away on a case right now, but would you care to come in and tell us about it?" Frank said politely. "As soon as we hear from him, we can give him your message."

"Thank you. I would appreciate a chance to explain my problem."

Frank led the way into the living-room. Their visitor settled himself on the sofa, which groaned under his weight, and clasped his hands over his ivory-headed cane. Frank and Joe sat down in easy chairs and waited for him to speak.

"You boys often assist your father on his cases, do you not?" Ponsley inquired, sizing them up with a shrewd glance.

"That's right, sir," Frank replied.

"And we've solved a few mysteries on our own, Joe added, grinning modestly.

"So I've heard. Well, then, perhaps you can help me with this one, at least until your father returns."

"We'll be glad to do whatever we can, sir."

"Fine! My problem is this—a young man named Michael Moran has disappeared, and he must be found. Quickly!"

"Have you notified the police, Mr Ponsley?" Frank asked. "They should be able to help you on a missing persons case."

"Not on this one," Ponsley retorted sharply. "We can't risk the publicity. Michael Moran is the son of Senator Jeff Moran!"

He reached into his pocket and produced an old snapshot, which he handed to Frank. The Hardys saw a clean-cut youth, not much older than Frank, holding a baseball bat on his shoulder.

"That's the last photograph of Michael before he left home," Ponsley told them. "He's been gone for over a year now."

"A *year*? Good grief! Hasn't his family tried to locate him at all?" Joe asked.

"No. They felt he wanted to go away and think things out for himself, and that he'd come back when he was ready."

"Then why are they looking for him now?"

"Michael used to work for the Mid-County Bank. As you may have heard, the bank was recently broken into and robbed."

"Gosh, yes. I remember hearing about that on the news!" Joe exclaimed.

"The next day, the police caught the two crooks who pulled the job," Frank recalled.

"That's right." Ponsley nodded. "What you may not know is that the culprits are now trying to incriminate Mike Moran."

"How come?"

"The bank's alarm system was tampered with, which convinced the FBI that the robbers had inside help. So now those two scoundrels are saying it was Mike who gave them information on the alarm system."

"Is there anything to support their accusation?" Frank asked.

"Mike studied electrical engineering before he left college to work at the bank. And a bank employee named Thurbow remembered that Mike showed some interest in the alarm system while he was there."

"That doesn't prove anything," Joe said.

"Certainly not!" Oliver Ponsley boomed. "So far, the FBI has made no official charge against Mike, but his family is very upset, especially since Senator Moran is running for re-election. A scandal could wreck his political campaign. He's sure Mike is innocent, and wants him to come home and clear his name."

"Mr Ponsley, how are you involved?" Joe asked.

"I'm on Senator Moran's staff and a friend of the family's. I want to prevent any bad publicity before the news leaks out. That's why I came to see your father."

"Tell me," Frank said, "when and where was Mike last seen?"

"Leaving the bank one day last February. But he never arrived home that day."

"Has he written?"

"Yes, a number of postcards from Chicago. The last one came about three months ago, saying he was leaving the country. After that—silence."

"Any other clues?" Joe asked.

"Just one." Ponsley slipped the ring from his finger and held it up to the light so the boys could see it better. Sunshine slanting in through the window seemed to bathe the room in the gem's lustrous red glow.

"Michael always admired this stone," Ponsley said. "He was fascinated by rubies, so his parents bought him one as big as mine and had it mounted in the same kind of setting. Find a ring like this, and you'll find Mike Moran."

The Hardy boys examined the gem and felt sure they could easily spot a duplicate.

"Now then," said Ponsley, slipping the ring back on his finger, "I want you to get on the case right away. Fly to Chicago tomorrow and see if you can pick up

Michael Moran's trail. Make your first report to me by the end of next week. Speed is essential!"

"But we can't leave town right now," Frank said. "We're waiting for a phone call from our father. He may need us to help him with his own case."

"We'll let you know as soon as we're in touch with him," Joe added.

"Hmph." Frowning, Ponsley rose to his feet and adjusted his pince-nez. "Very well. If that's the best you can do, I'll just have to wait. You can call me at this number."

He handed Frank his business card and the boys escorted him to the door. They watched him lumber down the steps, squeeze behind the wheel of an expensive car, and drive off.

Frank and Joe returned to the living-room.

"How about that ruby?" Frank enthused.

"Big as a pigeon's egg!" Joe said. "Boy, that stone must be worth a bundle!"

"Say, could thieves have gotten to Mike Moran?" Frank said suddenly. "Maybe they did him in for his ring!"

The two boys exchanged worried looks. Joe felt cold chills prickle up and down his spine.

"A ruby that size would sure attract crooks!" he agreed. "I wonder——"

He broke off at the sound of brakes screeching out in the street. Tyres grated harshly against the kerb in front of their house, and a car jolted to a stop. Its door opened and slammed shut. Someone raced up the steps and pounded on the door.

"Open up!" a man's voice shouted. "You Hardy boys are in danger! You may be killed!"

·2·

The Runaway Rocket

"WHO the dickens is that?" Joe blurted.

"Search me, but he sounds pretty worked up!"

The doorknob rattled violently, and the thumping continued. Then their caller began ringing the bell.

"Take it easy! We're coming!" Frank yelled.

He yanked open the door. The man outside tumbled in and had some trouble regaining his balance.

"It's Mr Oakes from the chemistry shop!" Joe exclaimed, recognizing his face.

The man was gasping. He stuck his hand into his pocket and pulled out a long plastic bottle. The label read METHYL YELLOW.

"My assistant made a terrible mistake," Oakes said, panting. "He put the wrong label on a bottle of liquid tear gas and sold it to you as methyl yellow. This is what he should have given you. If you use that other stuff in the wrong kind of chemical experiment, it could even blow up in your faces!"

"We know. We found out the hard way," said Frank. "We already had an accident."

"Great Scott! Was anyone hurt?" Oakes inquired anxiously.

"No, luckily we reacted as soon as we inhaled the fumes, and Joe got a window open fast."

"Thank goodness!" The man sighed with relief. "My phone is out of order, so I hopped in the car and drove here the minute I discovered what Bob had done. You both have my deepest apologies. I'm really terribly sorry."

"That's all right, Mr Oakes," Joe said. "We were just about to come back to your place and find out what happened."

"A mistake—a dreadful mistake! Would you please give me that wrong bottle now?"

"Sure," Joe said. "I'll go get it." He took the methyl yellow out to the laboratory above the garage and returned with the liquid tear gas.

"We supply this stuff to various security guards around town," Oakes explained. "In fact, one of them came in to get some just before I told Bob to fill your order. I can only suppose that's how the mix-up occurred."

After repeating his apology, the manager of the shop left with the dangerous chemical.

"Well, that solves one mystery," Frank said as he shut the front door. "Now we can concentrate on the Mike Moran case."

"Unless Dad needs us," Joe reminded him. "But listen. Suppose we do get a chance to look for that guy. How would we trace him in Chicago?"

"Good question. For one thing, we'd have to find out more about him—what his interests are, how he spends his spare time—stuff like that."

Frank broke off as the telephone rang. Joe hurried to pick it up, heard his father's voice, and gestured to Frank to come and listen in.

"Dad, where are you calling from?" he asked.

"The Space Flight Centre in Florida," Fenton Hardy replied. "This case is turning out to be even tougher than I feared."

"Can you tell us anything about it?" Frank put in.

"Not on the phone. The investigation's being conducted under airtight security."

"We goofed on testing that scrap of cloth you sent us," Joe said. He told his father about the accident in the lab.

"That's all right. No harm done," said Mr Hardy. "I identified the wearer by means of a polygraph test. I had him figured as a prime suspect in this case, but he cleared himself. Now I've got another job for you, at Princeton."

"You mean Princeton University?" Frank queried. "In New Jersey?"

"Yes. I want you and Joe to go there tomorrow morning. Talk to Professor Arthur Young at the Aerospace Laboratory. He'll clue you in on the case, and I hope he'll give you a lead to work on. Report to me after you see Professor Young."

"Dad, how do we get in touch with you?"

"You can reach me through a hot line to the Space Flight Centre. The number is the Centre's initials followed by the first four digits—SFC-1234. Got it?"

"Got it," Frank said.

Mr Hardy's voice became tense. "Be careful," he warned. "This job is too important for any slips. NASA is involved. An international incident could be in the making."

"We'll be careful," his sons promised, then Frank told his father about the visit by Oliver Ponsley.

"He wants us to find Mike Moran."

"My case has priority," Mr Hardy replied. "After we've cracked it, you can look for young Moran. So long." He hung up.

Joe replaced the phone and the boys began to talk about their trip to Princeton.

"The home of the Princeton tiger!" Joe said with enthusiasm. "Wow! Maybe we'll get a chance to see some of their athletic teams work out."

"I think we'd better just stick to the Aerospace Lab," Frank said. "We're on a case, remember? I wonder what Professor Young knows about Dad's investigation. Maybe somebody stole a missile!"

"Yeah, sure." Joe grinned. "Like maybe a crook slipped an interplanetary rocket up his sleeve and walked out unnoticed. If you ask me—"

He was interrupted by a series of loud reports in the street. A clanking sound drew near.

Frank grinned. "Chet Morton's coming."

Joe peered out the window at the approaching jalopy. "Looks like he's got the whole gang with him. Let's go see what they're up to!"

As the Hardys grabbed their jackets and ran outside, Chet's fire-engine-red car pulled up to the kerb. Its roly-poly, freckle-faced driver applied the squeaky brakes and brought his car to a jolting halt that threw his passengers forward, then bounced them back in their seats.

"Should we call a doctor?" Joe inquired. "Or are all of you still in one piece?"

"Wait'll we check," said Biff Hooper, a husky six-footer. He was crowded into the back seat with Chet's pretty sister Iola and Tony Prito.

"No broken bones—yet," Tony reported. "The

question is, will we be able to walk away from this moving wreck?"

"What I'm worried about is my back," groaned Phil Cohen, who was sitting up front beside Chet. "I think I slipped a disc when we stopped."

Frank laughed at the driver's indignant look. "What's that you were telling us, Chet, about your rebuilt shock-absorbers and the smooth suspension you were engineering on this job?"

"So it's got a few bugs." The stout youth shrugged. "I notice that doesn't stop these wise guys from thumbing a ride in my racer whenever they need a lift. You'll have to admit it's really sharp looking!"

"People call it the *Red Menace*," Phil wisecracked.

The car's body metal had a worn, battered look but gleamed with a fresh coat of paint.

"Not bad for an old heap," Joe said, grinning. "When are you going to install a refrigerator?"

"Hey, that's an idea!" Chet said, snapping his fingers.

The Hardys' plump pal had helped them on many investigations. Even though he preferred food to danger, Chet never let Frank and Joe down when they were in a tight spot.

"Hop in, you two. We're wasting time!" he went on. "We can talk about food supplies later. Right now we're on our way to Bayport Meadow."

"What's going on there?" Frank asked.

"The most exciting scientific event of the century!" Chet exclaimed loudly. "Up, up, and away! Don't miss it."

"Chet just finished his rocket," Iola confided. "He can't wait to try it out. It's in the trunk."

Laughing, Frank and Joe crowded into the car, practically sitting on their friends' laps. By now they were used to Chet's mania for new hobbies. His latest was rockets, and he had been working on one in his basement for weeks. He intended to enter it in a national high-school science contest.

The jalopy sagged under the extra weight but began to move. Chet drove it noisily through Bayport and headed for the meadow outside of town, while the others chatted and joked about the contest.

Joe had managed to squeeze into a place next to Iola. He usually dated her when the gang went to picnics or dances.

"Chet just might win," Iola told him. "He's really worked hard on this project."

"We'll all be cheering him on," Joe promised.

In a few minutes they reached the meadow, a large open area covered with dry brown grass. The soil was still slightly frozen from the winter's cold.

Chet parked and they all got out and checked the area to make sure no one was in the way of the test.

"Looks like you've got a clear firing range," Tony observed.

"As long as he aims straight," said Frank.

"Don't worry," Chet boasted confidently. "I've designed a foolproof steering system."

He opened the car trunk and lifted out his rocket. It was a two-foot-long cylinder with a pointed nose and tail fins. For a launching pad, Chet stuck two pipes in the ground, mounted a cradle on them, and placed the rocket in it. The missile tilted at an angle with its upper end pointing skywards. Then Chet attached a control wire with a switch at one end.

At last the tubby teenager stepped back proudly to survey his handiwork. "Ah! Ready for the countdown!"

"Man, that looks like a space probe to the planet Mars!" Frank joked admiringly.

"Powerful enough to carry an astronaut to the moon," Joe suggested.

"Any astronaut but Chet," said Biff. "With a payload that heavy, even a Saturn rocket would never get into orbit."

"Quiet, you guys!" Chet commanded. "The Morton Moon Grazer is about to be launched. My electrical igniter will do the trick. Here goes!"

He pressed a remote-control switch. There was a flash and loud report, followed by a burst of smoke. The rocket shuddered, left its cradle, and shot high in the air. Chet's friends were impressed and burst into applause.

Chet bowed. "It'll land at the far end of the meadow," he predicted.

They all shaded their eyes and watched. Suddenly the missile began to wobble and veer off course.

"Oh, oh! It's looping over to the right!" Joe blurted.

The rocket appeared to be zooming down beyond the strip of woods fringing the meadowlands.

"There are farms on the other side of those trees!" cried Biff.

"What happened to your foolproof steering system?" Frank inquired.

Chet gulped and turned pale. "S-S-Something must have gone wrong!"

"No argument there. Come on! We'd better find out where your Moon Grazer lands!"

The boys and Iola ran round the edge of the meadow

and headed through the stand of trees.

"Must've come down on Old Man Jessup's farm!" Phil guessed. "Boy, that guy's a real crab!"

Chet shuddered. It took them several minutes to cover the distance, and he was puffing and panting anxiously by the time they approached Jessup's farm-yard. He turned even paler as the loud squawks of frightened chickens with an angry bellowing voice reached their ears from the other side of the barn.

"Oh gosh!" Chet exclaimed. "Sounds like we're in real trouble!"

"What do you mean *we?*" said Biff.

The words were hardly out of his mouth when the barnyard noises were drowned by the shrill wailing of an approaching police siren!

·3·

The Blow-Up

A SCENE of wild confusion greeted the teenagers' eyes as they rounded the barn. Feathers were flying as several species of domestic fowl, white Leghorns and Rhode Island reds, hopped, cackled, and fluttered about the yard. Chet's rocket had smashed their chicken coop.

Enoch Jessup, a gaunt, bushy-browed man in overalls, was shouting orders to his farmhand, who was trying to round up the frightened fowls and calm them down by scattering feed.

Just as Jessup's glance fell on the young people, a police car with flashing lights screeched to a halt near the farmhouse. A burly man in a brass-buttoned uniform jumped out and strode towards the scene of the disaster.

"Oh, brother! It's Police Chief Collig himself!" muttered Tony Prito.

"What's going on here?" Collig demanded.

"You've got eyes! What does it look like?" Jessup retorted. "These young scamps just wrecked my chicken coop with their blame-fool contraption! Scared the wits out of my best laying hens!"

Turning to the boys, he growled, "Which one of you

171

young idiots is responsible for this outrage?"

"W-W-We weren't aiming at your chicken coop, Mr Jessup," Chet stammered. "It was j-j-just an accident. . . . I mean, that is . . . well, I—I guess *I'm* sort of responsible."

"*Sort* of responsible, my foot! Your nitwit contraption smashed my henhouse, didn't it?" Shaking his finger in Chet's face, Enoch Jessup proceeded to bawl out the trembling youth.

"All right. All right! Take it easy," Chief Collig cut in. "We got a call from some motorist who saw you kids about to fire a rocket. Good thing I grabbed a squad car and came myself. I might've known you'd be at the bottom of this mess, Chet Morton. You and your harebrained hobbies!"

"Actually, Chet made the rocket for a high-school science competition, Chief," Frank Hardy spoke up. "I know the test went wrong, but he's worked hard on this project. I think he deserves credit for making a model that flew as well as this one did. After all, our country *needs* rocket engineers, and they have to start somewhere."

"Tell you what, sir," Joe added. "If Mr Jessup won't press charges, we'll all pitch in and repair his chicken coop. We'll even help out with a few chores."

"Sounds fair enough," Collig agreed. "What do you say, Enoch?"

The farmer's scowl relaxed. "Why not? Makes more sense than wasting time in court."

Biff Hooper borrowed Chet's car keys and hurried off to get some fresh timber, while the others cleaned up the debris from the wrecked coop. Luckily the coop had broken the missile's fall, so that the rocket itself was not much damaged and would probably fly again.

"Boy, you Hardys really saved my neck," Chet said as they drove back to Bayport.

"Forget it. It was fun," Joe said.

"Think you can still enter your rocket in the competition?" Frank asked their chubby pal.

"Sure. I can make repairs tonight and turn it in tomorrow morning."

Although spring holiday had started, Mr Palmer, the science teacher, had promised to be on hand at the high school to receive last-minute entries.

Frank and Joe found their mother and aunt just back from the supermarket. Aunt Gertrude was their father's sister.

"Where have you boys been?" she demanded tartly.

"Watching an unidentified flying object, Aunt Gertrude," Joe told her with a grin.

"What's *that* supposed to mean, young man?" Her eyes flickered suspiciously as she looked at her two nephews.

The tall, sharp-tongued spinster was extremely fond of Frank and Joe and secretly longed to take a hand in their detective work, although she could seldom bring herself to admit it openly.

"Chet fired a home-made rocket," Frank said, and he described the crash landing.

"Good heavens! I'm glad no one was hurt," Mrs Hardy exclaimed.

Aunt Gertrude sniffed. "That boy Chet needs a firm hand."

"Someone like you to help fire his rockets?" Joe teased.

"He could do worse," Gertrude Hardy snapped.

"Apparently you two didn't help him steer it right."

The boys laughed, and Frank said, "Score one for Aunt G.!"

He told them about Oliver Ponsley's visit and their father's call. "We have to go to Princeton first thing in the morning," Frank added.

"Oh dear," his mother said. "I hope you're not going to get involved in anything dangerous." Mrs Hardy, an attractive woman, worried whenever her husband and sons took a new case.

"Well, what's dangerous about going to a university?" Aunt Gertrude scoffed. "Might learn a thing or two there at Princeton, as long as they don't start playing any foolish college pranks."

"We won't," Joe promised, chuckling.

"You're going alone?" Mrs Hardy asked, still a bit concerned.

"We were," Frank replied, "but now that you mention it, we might ask Chet to come along."

"Hey, good idea!" Joe said.

He rushed to the phone and called their overweight buddy. Chet was delighted at the suggestion and agreed at once to accompany them.

"Pack an overnight bag," Joe advised. "We may have to stay a day or two."

"That's okay with me," Chet said. "I was just thinking it might be a good idea to stay out of sight the next few days. Chief Collig will probably have every cop in town breathing down my neck for a while."

Joe then called Mr Ponsley and told him that they could not start searching for Mike Moran until they knew more about what was expected from them in their father's case. Ponsley agreed to the delay. "Call me as soon as you know more," he added.

Early next morning, the Hardys got into their sleek yellow sports coupé and picked up Chet Morton. Then they headed for Princeton. Threading their way through traffic, they reached the highway, where Frank put his foot down and kept the car whizzing along at the speed limit. Once the rush hour was over, they made good time under the brilliant sunshine.

"Get your rocket fixed, Chet?" Joe inquired.

"You bet. Handed it in just in time. I think I've really got a chance to win."

"I sure hope so. We'll keep our fingers crossed."

At a fork in the road, Frank turned on to Route 206 and soon they saw signs indicating that Princeton lay straight ahead. When they ran into Nassau Street, they knew they were at their destination. Shops lined one side of the famous Princeton thoroughfare, and university buildings occupied the opposite side.

"Now I know why it's called Ivy League," Chet quipped. "Look at the ivy on the dorms!"

"I wonder where the Aerospace Lab is," Frank said. He stopped for a red light near a couple of high stone gates flanked by iron railings. Beyond the lawn they could see Nassau Hall, the main building of the campus. Its slender tower rose towards the sky and was topped by a weather-vane.

A student carrying a couple of books under his arm started to cross the street. Joe leaned out of the window and asked him the way to the Aerospace Lab.

"Go down Nassau Street and turn right on to Washington Road," was the reply. "The lab is near the football stadium."

Frank followed the directions. They passed the

psychology and biology departments, and arrived at a science complex, where Chet spotted a sign reading: PRINCETON AEROSPACE LABORATORY. Frank parked and the young detectives went in.

They found themselves in a rotunda, where a model of a Saturn rocket stood upright in the middle of the floor. Round the walls behind glass were exhibits of dramatic moments in the history of space exploration.

Chet pointed to one of them. "The astronauts on the moon!" he said.

"And there's Skylab in orbit!" Joe exclaimed.

"And Telstar!" Frank marvelled. "They bounce signals off it out in space, and the signals are picked up by TV systems around the world!"

A guard approached and inquired what they wanted. When Frank explained their mission, he escorted them down the hall to a door bearing the nameplate: PROFESSOR ARTHUR YOUNG. The guard knocked and went in. A moment later he returned and announced that Professor Young would see them.

They entered a study lined with books, graphs, mathematical equations, and blow-ups of major rocket launchings. The professor rose from his swivel chair and shook hands with the visitors. After introductions were made, he made a motion indicating that they take three chairs near his desk, and sat down again. He was tall, thin, and slightly bald. He looked intently at the boys as he filled his pipe with tobacco and lit it.

"Your father phoned me and told me you were on your way," he said with a smile. "I'm very glad to see you and your friend. We need fast action."

"Professor, what is the problem?" Frank asked in a puzzled tone

"How much do you know about the case that has developed here at the lab?" Young countered.

"Nothing," Joe admitted.

"Well, I'll give you all the information I have. First let me show you round the place, so you get an idea of what we're doing. Then you'll see what we're up against and why we need your assistance."

He led them out of his office and through the building. "Everyone here is devoted to the exploration of space," Young commented. "This lab is one of the best in the world when it comes to interplanetary probes and the study of the solar system."

They passed a lecture hall, a library, two seminar rooms, and several offices belonging to famous scientists. Then they arrived at the lab itself, a maze of rooms in which experts were carrying out experiments on everything from liquid fuels to the problems of weightlessness in outer space.

"Boy, this sure beats Bayport High!" Chet exclaimed. "I could make myself a real rocket here. Maybe I'll apply for a job after I win the state science competition."

Young laughed. "Glad to have you aboard, Chet. Just be sure you get clearance from the Space Flight Centre when the time comes. You'll have to be okayed down there because we work for NASA. What we discover goes on the drawing-boards at the Centre."

"No wonder Dad said the case was hush-hush," Frank put in. "This lab must be filled with top-secret stuff."

Young became solemn. "That's the whole point of the investigation you're undertaking."

They arrived at a room where a youth was working at

a modified atomic reactor. Young introduced him as Smoky Rinaldo, a senior at Princeton University.

"Smoky can show you round from here on," the professor said. "When you've seen enough of the lab, meet me back at my office and we'll discuss your assignment."

He walked off and Smoky informed the visitors that he was doing research for a term paper.

"I'm into rockets, myself," Chet spoke up. "Fact is, I've got my own missile."

Frank chuckled. "You almost didn't. It flew straight—straight to earth."

"What are you talking about?" Smoky asked.

"Oh, nothing," Chet said hastily. "Why don't you show us the rest of the lab? I can't wait to see it."

The young people wandered through the last row of rooms, which were assigned to scientists experimenting with the shapes of nose cones and tail fins for partly developed rockets.

Suddenly a movement caught Frank's attention. Looking out of the corner of his eye, he noticed a man behind them. He was tall and lanky and wore a black beard and tinted glasses.

Frank paused before a blow-up of a Saturn rocket. Joe and Chet joined him. The man stopped at a work-bench and furtively glanced at them.

"I think we've got a shadow," the older Hardy informed Joe and Chet in an undertone.

Joe traced the curved line of a nose cone with his finger, pretending to be interested in it. "Are you sure?" he asked.

"No. It could be a coincidence. Let's go on and keep an eye on him."

Joe turned as they walked farther, catching a glimpse of the man. "Beard with glasses?" he asked.

"Right."

Smoky was slightly ahead of the group, explaining the interesting features of the lab. When they left the last room and walked back to where they had started, Chet asked, "Who's that guy with the beard over there?"

Smoky turned round to look. "I've no idea. Matter of fact, I've never seen him before."

The man obviously realized that the boys had noticed him, and instead of following them farther, he entered a door with the sign OFFICIAL PERSONNEL ONLY.

"He must be on the staff here," Smoky went on. "Would you like to see the reactor I'm working on? The interior is hot enough to handle uranium."

They walked over to the instrument. "We can't see the interior," Joe pointed out.

"That's because it's running," Smoky said. "Just follow me, and you'll find out what's in there." He led the way to a diagram on the wall representing a slice through the reactor from top to bottom.

"This is how the machine is put together," the student explained. "The core in the centre marked A is where the uranium goes. The letter B stands for the pressure vessel, and C is the casing. These tubes extending from the core to the top are the fuel—"

A loud sputtering noise broke out. Red sparks flashed through the air around them. Chet turned pale and shouted, "The reactor's going to explode!"

·4·

A Strange Disappearance

CHET dived to the floor, crawled under a workbench, turned round on his hands and knees, and stared at the other three. Frank, Joe, and Smoky remained standing.

"You guys want to get blown up?" Chet quavered.

"False alarm, Chet," Smoky said.

"How do you know?" Chet demanded.

"Because that wasn't the atomic reactor," Smoky explained. "It has a fail-safe protection. If anything goes wrong, the motor shuts off automatically. And besides, this is a modified reactor. It doesn't have enough power for an atomic explosion."

A man in overalls came over. He was wearing a plastic eyeshield and carrying a blowtorch. "Sorry about that," he apologized. "I'm working on a wire coil with this torch. The coil's too soft for the flame, and that's the reason for the noise and sparks."

"That's okay," Smoky said. "Don't worry about it."

As the man walked off again, Chet crawled out from under the workbench and got to his feet. He looked embarrassed. "Guess I over-reacted," he said sheepishly.

Frank soothed his feelings. "It's better than taking chances. Well, we've seen the lab. Let's report to Professor Young and find out about our assignment."

The Bayport youths left Smoky Rinaldo tinkering with the heat shields on the atomic reactor. They rejoined the professor, who shuffled some papers, placed them on the desk, and leaned back in his swivel chair.

"How do you like the Aerospace Lab?" he inquired genially.

"We like it fine, Professor," Frank declared, "except for one thing."

"What's that?"

"We were being followed." Frank told him about the man who seemed to be shadowing them through the lab.

Young frowned. "I've never seen anyone who matches that description, but I'll try to find out who he is. The lab is strictly off limits to unauthorized personnel."

Through the intercom he ordered an immediate search of the premises. Then he turned back to his visitors. "Now," he said, "let me tell you about the mystery."

The boys leaned forward in their chairs, eager to hear every word.

"It concerns Dr Adrian Jenson," Young went on. "You may have heard of him."

"The rocket scientist," Joe said. "He's been working on space probes ever since the astronauts landed on the moon."

"And he won a prize for his mathematics on trajectories," Frank added. "The path of re-entry from outer space into the earth's atmosphere."

Young smiled. "You know your rocketry," he complimented them. "Well, Dr Jenson and I have been working on a revolutionary new engine powered by nuclear energy. We call it the Firebird, and it's due for a test flight in a couple of weeks. Dr Jenson flew to Australia three days ago to follow the flight of the Firebird at the Woomera Monitoring Station."

"Australia?" Chet spoke up. "Why there?"

"When a rocket is fired into orbit from our Space Flight Centre, its path over the Southern Hemisphere is followed at tracking stations south of the equator. Woomera is one of the best of these installations. We are co-operating closely with the Australian government in monitoring our missiles, and our people go there frequently."

"But why the mystery?" Joe asked.

"Dr Jenson never got to Woomera. He hasn't been heard of since he left Princeton!"

Frank let out a low whistle. "Did he actually get on the plane?"

"Yes. We checked with the airlines. He arrived in Sydney and picked up his luggage. There the trail ends. We also searched his desk for clues, but found nothing."

"And you've notified the Australian police?" Joe asked.

"We did that immediately and they've been working on it ever since. However, both we and NASA wanted a top-flight investigator assigned to the case at this end—especially since there were indications that the plotters had been after him in this country. Our project's top-secret, so the investigation has had to be kept under wraps, and your father seems the ideal man to handle it. But so far we have no real clue to Dr Jenson's whereabouts. It really is most mysterious."

"Maybe some enemy agents kidnapped him!" Chet exploded. "Maybe they're brainwashing him!"

"That's possible," Young admitted. "The Firebird Rocket is classified. Dr Jenson and I are the only scientists who know the secret of the nuclear engine. If enemy agents kidnapped him, he may have revealed the secret. A foreign power could be building a Firebird right now!"

Frank said, "You mentioned that someone had been after Dr Jenson in this country."

Professor Young nodded. "A neighbour noticed a car with Florida plates parked outside his house after he left. And the police discovered that his home had been broken into and ransacked. Also, telephone company records show that a call was made from there that same night to a pay phone in Florida near the Space Flight Centre."

"So that's why Dad's been concentrating on the case down in Florida!" Joe said.

"Exactly. But he wanted all aspects of the case covered and decided his sons could handle the investigation here at the Aerospace Lab. So here you are."

"And we've brought Chet," Frank said. "He's helped us many times before and is reliable."

"That's fine by me," Young said. "I trust your judgement."

Chet grinned and said he would do his best to help the Hardys crack the case.

The professor continued. "Your task is to investigate all possible leads at the lab and see if you can find the clue you need to solve the mystery while your father does the same at the Space Flight Centre. I have some information that might help you."

"Oh?" Frank asked. "What is it?"

Young's answer surprised him. "Jenson and I received a warning letter and threatening phone calls. Here, I'll show you."

He reached into a drawer and took out an envelope. Removing the letter, he handed it to Frank. Joe and Chet craned their necks to see it. The message was crudely pieced together from words out of a newspaper.

It said: *Kill the Firebird or else!*

"Someone's trying to sabotage your rocket!" Joe exclaimed. "They don't want it to be launched."

"That's right, and whoever wrote the letter means business."

"Professor," Frank said, "do you realize that you may be in great danger yourself?"

"Everyone here is aware of that. I have been assigned a personal bodyguard, without whom I do not leave the building. I don't want you to worry about me. Just find Dr Jenson!"

Frank was about to say something when he heard a noise outside the door.

"An eavesdropper!" Frank thought. Leaping out of his chair, he strode to the door and swung it wide open.

Smoky Rinaldo was standing there!

"Hi," Frank said. "Are you interested in our conference?"

Smoky looked surprised. "I didn't know a conference was going on in Professor Young's office. When I heard voices, I stopped momentarily to see if I should come in or not." Glancing past Frank, he addressed Young. "I can't tell if the fuel is getting hot enough. Would you mind checking it when you have a chance?"

"I'll be right along, Smoky," the professor promised. Then he said to the boys, "I'll phone the Nassau Club and make arrangements for you to stay there while you're in Princeton. It's on Mercer Street."

Young made the reservations, then went with Smoky to the atomic reactor while Frank, Joe and Chet drove to the Nassau Club. The driveway curved in a semi-circle past the steps leading up to the front door of the stately building.

Frank parked the car. "Do you think Smoky was eavesdropping?" he asked as the boys got out.

"I'm inclined to think he's honest," Joe said. "But we'll keep an eye on him."

The boys entered the building and went to the front office to see about their room. Frank inquired while Joe and Chet looked around.

A hallway led through the first floor to a cloakroom at the rear. Members of the club were seated in the reading room to the left, scanning the latest newspapers and magazines. Two portraits hung on the opposite wall, flanking the entrance to the main dining-room.

"I wonder who those old geezers are," Chet whispered to Joe.

The younger Hardy walked closer, surveyed the inscriptions under the portraits, and came back. "They're two presidents of the United States," he said. "Woodrow Wilson and Grover Cleveland."

Frank strode out of the office and announced that they were set for the night. The three drove to the rear of the club and left the car in the parking lot. Walking towards the back door, they examined the building, which had plenty of corners and angles, tilting roofs and high eaves.

"The club would make a good haunted house," Joe suggested. "All we need is a spooky face at the window. Frank! There he is!"

"Who?" Frank asked, glancing in the direction his brother had indicated.

"The guy from the lab!" Joe gasped. "He was right there, looking out that window. The fellow with the tinted glasses!"

"I don't see him now," Frank stated, "but let's go inside and see if we can catch him!"

The boys hurried up the wooden steps and through the cloakroom door. Seeing nobody, they hastened down the hallway into the reading room, through the dining-room, and to the front door.

A footfall on the carpet made them whirl. Their shadow was trying to tiptoe down the stairs to the basement!

The boys rushed after him. As they reached the bottom of the stairs, they saw him run into the bar. By the time they got there, he was exiting by another door.

The pursuers went pell-mell up the stairs to the second floor, and then to the third floor, where Chet was too exhausted to go any farther. He sat on the top step and watched the Hardys race along the corridor to where the man was climbing out of the window. The fugitive slid down the fire escape to an alley at the bottom, and hurried round the corner into Nassau Street.

When Frank and Joe reached the spot, the man had vanished!

·5·

Night Visitor

"NO SIGN of him," Joe said, looking up and down the street. "He could be anywhere by now."

Frank nodded glumly. "You're right. We lost him."

The boys returned to the club and picked up Chet, then went to their room. It overlooked the alley and had a fire escape under the window.

"Good," Chet declared when he noticed the exit. "We can get out of here in a hurry if we're cornered by crooks. Say, how about chow? I haven't eaten since breakfast. I might faint."

"If you do, you'll shake up the club," Joe quipped. "It wasn't built for your weight."

Chet looked pained, but Frank came to his rescue. "I'm with you, Chet. It's dinner-time anyway."

The boys freshened up a bit, then went to the dining-room. After giving the waiter their order, Chet leaned back in his chair. "Well, Hardys," he grinned, "do you have a plan for solving the big mystery yet?"

"We're working on it," Joe said, sipping water from his glass.

"I think Jenson was kidnapped by a foreign power," Chet declared.

"Maybe he *worked* for a foreign power and left on his

own," Joe put in. "That's a possibility."

"You mean as a spy?" Chet asked.

Joe nodded. "Perhaps he developed the Firebird Rocket and sold the secret to someone else."

Frank shook his head. "But why would he wait until the United States finished building the missile? I think he would have given away the secret earlier and stolen the plans in order to prevent us from completing the project."

Chet nodded. "I'm with Frank. The spy angle doesn't seem to fit in this case. Jenson was probably kidnapped."

"So where do we start with our work?" Joe wanted to know.

"We interview all the people at the lab," Frank said. "Let's hope somebody there will be able to give us a line on that bearded creep."

The boys discussed their strategy during dinner, and after they had dessert, Chet suggested that they go for a walk to clear their heads.

"I have a better idea," Joe said. "I noticed a sign saying that there's dancing after dinner. Why don't we listen to the music for a while?"

"Oh, good," Chet said. "I'm all for it."

A group was playing in the lounge, and couples edged on to the dance floor. The boys sat down and before long Joe noticed three attractive girls standing nearby.

"Hey, what say we meet those young ladies over there?" he said.

"Sounds great," Frank agreed. "I'll invite them to our table." He got up and soon returned with the girls in tow.

"Hi," said the pretty blonde right behind Frank. "I'm Hedy Hollweg. My friends are Pat Morrison and Jane Linski."

The boys introduced themselves and asked the girls to dance. Frank paired off with Hedy, Joe with Pat, and Chet asked Jane. After a while, they went back to the table, and animated conversation followed.

"We're freshmen at Princeton," Hedy said, "and are studying American literature. What are you doing here? I haven't noticed you on campus."

"Detective work!" Chet boomed. "I've solved a lot of cases with the help of the Hardys!"

Frank and Joe grinned. They were used to having Chet brag a little, especially in front of girls.

The girls were intrigued. They bombarded the boys with questions about crime investigation.

"You must be here on an important case," Jane surmised.

Chet opened his mouth but Frank kicked his foot under the table as a signal to keep quiet about Dr Jenson. Joe changed the subject. "How do you girls like Princeton?"

"It's great!" Hedy said. "I'm glad they let women in."

Pat nodded vigorously. "This is one thing Women's Lib did for us. Princeton used to be for men only. But no more!"

"Personally, I wouldn't want to go to a school that excludes girls," Chet said, eyeing Jane appreciatively. He smiled at her. "Would you like to dance?"

The young people had a fun-filled evening, and when they finally said goodbye to each other, the Bayporters thanked the girls for their pleasant company. Then

Hedy, Pat and Jane went to their dormitory while the Hardys and Chet walked up to their room. Soon they were fast asleep.

A sudden noise woke Joe in the middle of the night. It came from the alley below their room. Throwing off his blanket, he got out of bed and padded silently to the window.

A pebble landed squarely on the pane. Joe peered over the sill into the darkness. He could barely see a figure on the ground below, throwing another pebble, and another.

Joe pushed the window open. "Hey, what do you want?" he whispered loudly.

"Joe! It's me, Smoky. I've got something for you!" was the reply.

"Okay, come up the fire escape," Joe said.

As Smoky climbed up the rungs of the ladder, Joe roused Frank and Chet. "We have a visitor," he told them. "It's Smoky."

"At this time of night?" mumbled Chet, who was still foggy with sleep.

"Strange time for a visit, all right," Joe agreed.

Smoky clambered in through the open window.

"What's wrong with the front door?" Frank grumbled.

"They lock the place up at night," Smoky explained, "and I didn't want to cause a disturbance."

"There's also the telephone," Chet pointed out.

"I know. But I didn't want to call because I have something to show you. I——"

"How did you know this was our room?" Frank interrupted.

"It was the only vacant one before you came,"

Smoky answered. "There was no other place for them to put you in."

"Smoky, I think you're crazy. Do you know what time it is?" Joe asked.

"Hey, don't get mad. I'm trying to help you!"

"Why couldn't it wait till morning?"

"Because I've got to get some sleep. I've worked in the lab till now and I have an exam at noon. By the time I would be able to call you, you'd be gone."

"All right. What have you got?" Frank asked.

Smoky withdrew a sheet from his pocket and held it up for them to read. "Look at this!" he said.

A row of words had been cut out of a magazine and glued on to the paper, just as in the threatening note Professor Young had received. It read: *The Firebird will never fly!*

Frank, Joe and Chet were flabbergasted by the message, which seemed to leap at them from the paper.

"Where did you get this?" Frank asked Smoky.

"It was under the blotter on Dr Jenson's desk," the boy replied. "He keeps memos there. As I told you, I worked late on the reactor, and I needed to clear up a problem about the power transmission. I thought Dr Jenson might have left a memo on it, since we talked about it recently. So I looked under the blotter and found this paper instead."

"Any idea how it got there?" Frank inquired.

"None. But I know that Dr Jenson's missing and figured you're investigating. I couldn't help hearing that much when you thought I was eavesdropping in the corridor. I decided I'd better get this message to you pronto. I'll let Professor Young know about it in the morning."

"Thanks for your trouble," said Frank. "This could be important."

"Professor Young told us Jenson's desk was searched for clues when he disappeared," Joe said. "How come it didn't turn up then?"

"Must've been put under his blotter after that," Frank guessed. He shot a questioning glance at their visitor, waiting to hear his comment.

Smoky shrugged. "It could easily have been overlooked, because it was between a couple of memos. Well, I'd better be going. I have to get some rest or I'll flunk my exam tomorrow."

The boy jumped on the window-sill and swivelled his legs on to the fire escape. He climbed down into the alley and seconds later vanished behind the buildings.

Frank placed the puzzling message on the table under the light of the lamp and the boys studied the warning.

"What do you make of it?" Frank asked his two companions.

"The way it reads," Chet declared, "this could be a threat or just a straight message."

"Why cut out words to send someone a message?" Frank objected. "Why not just write it?"

"To avoid having your own writing recognized."

"Sure, but *whose* own writing?" said Frank. "Are you saying Jenson himself is a phony or a traitor?"

"Well, he must be," Chet argued, "if this is his work."

"Yeah. If! That's the question," said Joe.

"There's no way to tell. If you ask me, our first problem is, how did this get under Jenson's blotter after he disappeared?"

Frank glanced at his brother. "You think Smoky's lying?"

"Let's just say we have no reason to trust him so far."

"Maybe not. On the other hand, the message could have been overlooked, as he says."

"That's right," Chet added. "Jenson may have put it under his blotter and forgotten about it. Perhaps he didn't take the warning seriously."

"Boy, the situation looks serious now," Chet said. "If NASA goes ahead with the Firebird launching, it may be curtains for both Young and Jenson."

"For all we know," Joe warned, "it may have been curtains for Dr Jenson already!"

·6·

A Ghostly Hand

CHET gulped. There was silence for a moment.

Then Frank said, "We don't have much time to solve this case. Professor Young said the Firebird will be launched in a couple of weeks."

"From the Space Flight Centre," Joe added. "Maybe Dad's on to something down there. Let's call him in the morning and find out."

The boys went back to sleep and were up bright and early. After breakfast they found the maid cleaning their room, which prevented them from using the phone. They decided to use the club phone in the basement.

Frank and Joe squeezed into the booth and shut the door, while Chet stood guard outside in case any suspicious character tried to listen in. Joe dialled SFC-1234, the hot-line number Mr Hardy had given them for top-secret phone calls.

A woman's voice answered. "This is Space Flight Centre Control," she said crisply. "Please identify yourself and the party you wish to speak to."

"Frank and Joe Hardy," Joe said. "We'd like to speak to Fenton Hardy."

"Oh, yes. I've been alerted that you have clearance.

But Mr Hardy isn't here at the moment."

"Can you tell us when he'll be back?" Joe asked.

"Sorry, but I don't know. Mr Hardy wasn't in yesterday, either, and he hasn't phoned. Would you like to leave a message for him?"

"Yes. Please tell him to call us at the Aerospace Lab or at the Nassau Club in Princeton as soon as possible."

Leaving the phone booth, the Hardys told Chet they had failed to reach Mr Hardy.

"Where do you suppose he's gone?" said Chet.

Frank shrugged. "He may be following up an outside clue or keeping someone under surveillance. Maybe that's why he hasn't had a chance to phone."

"So what do we do now?" Chet asked.

"Let's go over to the lab and start talking to people," Joe said.

"Okay, but how about stopping at the library on the way?" Frank suggested. "I'd like to bone up a little on Australia. When Professor Young was telling us about Woomera yesterday, I realized how little I know about that whole continent."

"Same here," said Joe. "I guess we could all do with a quick fill-in on the scene down under. Who knows, it might even suggest another angle on the case to us!"

The three set out across the campus, passing students and professors on the way.

The university library was a multi-storey stone building, three storeys high. At the desk inside, Frank asked where they could find books about Australia. "On C Floor," an assistant told him. "Three storeys down. You can take the stairs or the elevator."

"I don't know about you," Chet declared, "but I'll ride."

The Hardys followed him into the elevator, and Frank pressed the button. The doors closed, and they descended to C Floor, where a wall chart guided them to the left. Following the numbers that marked the shelves, they came to the section on Australia.

Each of the boys grabbed an armful of books, which he carried to a large circular table. They sat down and began to turn the pages, flipping through to the chapters and illustrations that interested them. Frank concentrated on geography and history, Joe and Chet on the people.

"I'm going to see if I can find something specific on Woomera," Joe said finally and stood up. He returned his stack of books to their places. Then he scanned those on the shelf beneath. As he reached for one, a ghostly hand appeared from the opposite side! It clamped around Joe's wrist and held tight!

Startled, the younger Hardy boy pushed a big volume out of the way with his free hand and looked through the opening. A young man grinned at him.

"Smoky Rinaldo!" Joe exploded.

"I couldn't resist it," Smoky said. "I'm a great practical joker, you know."

"Some joke," Joe grumbled. "You scared me half to death."

"I didn't mean to," Smoky said. "Sorry."

"What are you doing here anyway?" Joe asked. "I thought you wanted to get enough sleep to be fresh for your exam?"

"I woke up early so I came here to do some research. By the way, you're being watched."

"What?"

Smoky jerked a thumb in the direction behind Joe,

who whirled round in time to spot an indistinct figure sneaking furtively between the shelves.

"I didn't get a good look at him," Smoky said, "but he seemed to be eavesdropping on you before, when you all sat at the table."

"I'm going after him!" Joe decided. "Want to come?"

"Sure thing."

Smoky and Joe met at the end of the stack. There was no time to alert Frank and Chet, since the man was hastening towards the exit.

Joe saw a ray of light reflected by tinted glasses. It was the man who had been shadowing them at the lab! He darted into the elevator and pushed the button. Joe and Smoky ran after him. He glowered savagely as they drew near, and then the elevator doors closed in their faces. The boys ran round to the stairs and took two steps at a time to the main floor, where they almost bumped into Professor Young!

"It's lucky you're here, professor," Joe blurted, and quickly described their pursuit of the bearded man with the tinted glasses.

"I saw him!" Young declared. "He got out of the elevator and went up to the next floor. You may be able to catch him!"

The boys rushed up, found no one on the floor above, and continued to the top. There was no sign of the man anywhere! Joe and Smoky asked a group of students if they had seen him. No one had.

"He must have gone down the back stairs," said a girl.

The boys returned to the main floor. Young was still there and told them he had been watching the main staircase. "I was ready to call for help if the man appeared, but he didn't."

"He probably took the back staircase," Joe said.

"Too bad," Young said. "Well, I hope you catch him next time. I'll keep an eye open and have him arrested if he shows up at the lab again. By the way, he apparently got in yesterday by flashing someone else's pass. An employee reported that his was stolen. But now that everyone's alerted, the fellow won't be able to pull the same trick twice."

Young walked off to work in the card-index file, and Smoky said he had to get going, too. He returned to the bookstack he had been examining before, while Joe went to question the attendant at the door.

"A man with tinted glasses and a beard?" the fellow said. "Yes, he walked out a few minutes ago."

"Thank you," Joe said. Disappointed, he joined Frank and Chet and told them about his unsuccessful pursuit.

"Don't worry. I'm sure we'll see our shadow again," Frank muttered. "Meanwhile we looked at all the books, including the one you pulled halfway off the shelf. We didn't find anything interesting on Woomera, so let's get over to the lab and start working."

The trio spent the rest of the week questioning employees and students at the lab, searching files and records, and investigating Dr Jenson's background and family. Not a single clue turned up.

As they were painstakingly searching the scientist's desk, Frank noticed a lightning bolt engraved on one side. He asked Professor Young about it.

"That's Adrian's unofficial trademark," Young told them. "The staff claims he solves problems with lightning speed, and one of the fellows marked his desk one day after Adrian helped him out on a critical project."

On Sunday night the phone rang as the boys were getting ready for bed. Frank lifted the receiver. "It's Dad," he called out. Joe and Chet joined him at the instrument and filled the elder Hardy in on what they had done in Princeton.

"I'm still investigating people at the Space Flight Centre," Fenton Hardy said. "Director Henry Mason is afraid that an attempt may be made to destroy the rocket on its pad. I joined the work crew in disguise and spent two days at the launch site. However, so far I'm up against a stone wall."

"Will you stay there until the launching?" Frank asked.

"Yes, I think so. It will take a lot more leg work to uncover a lead. Also, I'm setting up a brand-new security system for the launching. It's of vital importance that nothing goes wrong."

"What do you suggest we do?" Frank asked. "We've talked to everyone in the lab and nothing has turned up."

His father was thoughtful for a moment, then said, "I think your best bet is to go to Australia!"

·7·

Radioactive Evidence

"AUSTRALIA!" Frank exclaimed.

"Yes. Tell Professor Young I want you to try to pick up Jenson's trail in Sydney. A room was booked for him at the Australian Arms Hotel, but apparently he never checked in."

"Okay, Dad. We'll go as soon as we can."

"And another thing. Try to shake your shadow. He worries me. He obviously knows you're investigating the case and follows you wherever you go."

"We'll get rid of him on the way home," Frank promised and hung up.

"Do you think Young will let me go along?" Chet asked apprehensively.

"We'll ask him," Frank said and called the professor's home. He told Young about the conversation with his father and the detective's suggestion.

"That's a good idea," Young agreed. "Your father is right. You're being watched here. So far I haven't been able to find out anything about your shadow, and it's probably best if you leave Princeton without returning to the lab. Take a round-about route and make sure you're not being tailed."

"Will do," Frank said. "If I can't get plane reservations for tomorrow or Tuesday, I'll call you back. Can we take Chet with us?"

Young hesitated. "I'm responsible for the expenses in this case, Frank. I can't really make a requisition for three people without a pressing reason."

"I understand," Frank said, disappointed.

Chet, who had overheard the conversation, looked crestfallen. After Frank hung up, he patted his friend on the back. "Don't feel bad, Chet. We might be back sooner than you think."

"Feel bad!" Chet said. "I feel worse! I would love to see the kangaroos and the Great Barrier Reef. Just think of skin diving off the coral reef, more than a thousand miles of it! And fish in all colours of the rainbow——"

Frank and Joe booked a flight to Sydney on Tuesday. Early Monday morning the boys left the Nassau Club and drove home, making sure they were not followed.

"The coast is clear," Joe said. "No one is behind us."

They were not far out of Princeton, however, when Chet noticed a black limousine that seemed to keep them in sight. When Frank accelerated, the driver of the limousine followed suit.

"You'll have to get off this road to lose him," Joe said to his brother. But before Frank had a chance to do this, the limousine pulled nearly abreast of them. The driver honked his horn and motioned for them to pull to the side.

"Make a run for it!" Joe advised and Frank pressed the accelerator to the floor.

Another car drove between the limousine and the Hardys. Their pursuer swerved to the left, increased the speed of his powerful V-8 engine, and passed the second vehicle. He inched up to the Hardys and proceeded to cut them off!

Frank noticed the legend on the limousine's side, *Princeton Aerospace Laboratory*, as he wrenched the wheel desperately to avoid a crash. With split-second timing he turned to the right, past the front bumper of the limousine, careered off the highway into a rest area, and skidded halfway round before coming to a stop in a cloud of dust.

The limousine jolted after him and its driver braked to a halt. He bent his head and seemed to be searching for something in the seat beside him. Neither Frank nor Joe got a good look at him, but they wasted no time. They leaped from their car and wrenched open the door of the limousine. In a split second they collared the man and wrestled him out.

"Hey, fellows, wait a minute!" the driver pleaded. *He was Smoky Rinaldo!*

Frank dropped Smoky's arm. "You nearly caused a pile-up!" he said angrily.

"Is this another one of your practical jokes?" Joe almost shouted.

"Of course not," Smoky said. "But I had to catch you, and you ignored the horn when I tried to flag you down. You wouldn't stop, so I had to make you!"

"We thought you were the guy who followed us all over Princeton," Joe said, his anger cooling.

"I assumed you'd recognize me."

"With that goofy cap pulled down over your face?"

"Anyway, I didn't mean to cause an accident," Smoky went on. "I thought I could force you into the rest area by cutting you off."

"What did you want to stop us for?" asked Chet, who

had come up to join the three boys.

Smoky held up his hand and revealed a metal flask with Dr Jenson's name on it. "Here, look at this!"

"What about it?" Frank asked.

"It's radioactive!" Smoky asserted.

Chet retreated hurriedly. "It might explode!"

"Radioactive material doesn't just explode," Frank calmed him. "It takes a triggering device to start a chain reaction."

Smoky swung his flask by its heavy top. "No fear of that. It's not even radioactive enough to kill a cockroach."

Frank was getting irritated. "Did you chase us all the way from Princeton to tell us that?"

"No. I wanted you to know that I think Dr Jenson was up to something."

"Why?"

"Because I found this flask in one of the file cabinets. I was digging in some records and ran across the flask in the back of the bottom drawer. It's against regulations for anyone to take anything radioactive out of the lab."

Smoky explained that the steel flasks were used to hold nuclear materials during experiments. When the experiment ended, the scientist conducting it was supposed to send his flasks to a store-room lined with lead, where they would be decontaminated.

"Dr Jenson took this one and hid it in the file," Smoky concluded. "He shouldn't have done that."

"Did he ever break the rules before?" Joe asked.

"I have no idea."

"Did you tell Professor Young about it?"

"Sure. Right away."

"What did he say?"

"He found it very odd and called you at the Nassau Club. He was informed that you had just left. Since he didn't know what arrangements you had made and whether you would go home before you left for Australia, he asked me to try to catch up with you. He also gave me a photo of Jenson for you. So I drove in the direction of Bayport. I figured I'd go down the highway for a while, and sure enough, I saw your car."

Frank was thoughtful. "This is odd. I'm glad you caught us, Smoky."

"One thing bothers me," Joe said. "We searched all the files in his office and the flask was not there then."

"It wasn't in his office. It was in the records room." Smoky said. "In one of the general files that a number of people use. But it was Jenson's flask, all right, none of the others have any occasion to handle radioactive materials." He looked at the three boys. "Now you're not mad any more that I cut you off?"

"Of course not. You had no choice," Frank told him.

"Okay. I'll head back then. And good luck to you. I hope you find Dr Jenson!" Smoky got into the limousine and drove off.

Frank, Joe and Chet resumed their trip to Bayport and discussed the latest development.

"How about that!" Chet said. "I wonder why Jenson hid that radioactive flask in the general file?"

"Maybe he was going to smuggle it out of the lab," Joe suggested, "to hand it over to someone on the outside. The more I think about it, the more I'm convinced that he wasn't kidnapped by foreign agents after all. He made a deal with them!"

Frank was doubtful. "What could anybody do with a

radioactive flask? It doesn't seem worth stealing."

"I don't know. They might analyse the atomic formula from the stuff in the flask," Joe guessed.

"Okay," Frank gave in. "But where does that leave the warning message Smoky found under the blotter on Jenson's desk?"

"Jenson himself might have planted it there to throw people off his trail," Chet said.

"I don't know," Frank mused. "Suppose his kidnappers did it to mislead us after they grabbed him? And, frankly, I have my doubts about Smoky. He found the note and the bottle. Yet, Young assured us that Jenson's desk was searched. How do we know that Smoky didn't plant the stuff?"

"Aw, Frank," Chet said impulsively, "Smoky's a nice guy. He wouldn't do anything like that."

"Frank's right," Joe said. "We can't take anything for granted, not even that Smoky is a nice guy."

Chet sighed. "I don't know what to think any more. I give up."

"Let's call Dad before we leave and ask him to check out Smoky," Joe said. "And we'll call Professor Young to make sure he sent Smoky after us."

Some time later the trio rolled into Bayport. The Hardys dropped Chet at the Morton farm on the outskirts of town, then continued to their house, where they were welcomed by their mother and aunt.

"I'm glad you're back!" Mrs Hardy said, giving them each a hug.

"Not for long," Frank told her.

"What do you mean?"

"We're leaving for Australia tomorrow!"

"Australia? Hmph, next thing you'll be taking off for

Mars," Aunt Gertrude grumbled. "Now tell us what this is all about."

The boys did, and Gertrude Hardy frowned. "Do you suppose this missing scientist could have been captured by headhunters?"

"I doubt it," said Frank, keeping a straight face. "The Australian aborigines aren't headhunters, Aunty, and they don't run wild in Sydney."

"I know that," Miss Hardy snapped. "You didn't say he disappeared in Sydney."

"Well, that's where his trail ends, anyhow." Frank grinned and turned to his brother. "I'm going to call Professor Young."

"Good idea," Joe said. "I'll come with you."

They called Princeton, and the professor verified what Smoky had told them. "We didn't check that file because Dr Jenson seldom used it," he said. "I'm sure it was his flask, though, because he wrote his name on it, and I know his handwriting. When are you leaving?"

"Tomorrow," Frank said. "We'll get in touch with you when we find a lead."

When Frank put the receiver back into the cradle, Joe said, "While you're at it, would you call Mr Ponsley? We'll have to tell him that we can't work for him."

"Sure." Frank dialled the man's number. "This is Frank Hardy," he said a few seconds later. "I'm sorry we can't take the Moran assignment, but we're involved in our father's case and have to leave the country."

Ponsley was unhappy. "That is disappointing news. I was counting on you to locate Michael," he said. "Well, I'll have to get another detective. I need one now more than ever, because I have a new clue!"

·8·

Danger in the Surf

FRANK started to ask what the new clue was, but a loud click at the other end of the line told him that the man had hung up.

"Mr Ponsley says he has a new lead on Mike Moran," Frank said to Joe.

"What is it?"

"Don't know. He didn't tell me. Anyhow, it doesn't matter. We're tied up with the Jenson investigation. Somebody else will have to find Mike, wherever he is."

Early next morning the boys packed their bags and were just about ready to depart for the airport, when Chet arrived in his jalopy.

"Guess what!" he called out, bubbling over with excitement.

"What?" Frank asked.

"I won first prize in my category of the science competition, fifteen hundred dollars in cash!"

"Wow, that's great, Chet!" Joe exclaimed. "Have you decided what to do with it yet?"

"Sure! I'll go to Australia with you guys, of course!" Chet said. "I already called the airline. They had a vacant seat on your plane, so I packed my bags and came over here pronto!"

"That's terrific!" Frank said. "I'm glad you can come with us."

"So am I," Joe added. "And now we'd better leave so we don't miss our flight."

The boys said goodbye to Mrs Hardy and Aunt Gertrude and drove to the Bayport airfield, where they parked their car in an overnight lot. They took a plane to New York and transferred at Kennedy Airport to a jumbo jet for Sydney, Australia.

Soon they had settled into their seats at the rear of the plane. Chet sat at the window, Frank in the middle, and Joe on the aisle. Frank took a map of the Pacific from a folder provided by the airline and began to plot their route.

"We'll touch down at Los Angeles and Honolulu," he said. "From there it's non-stop to Sydney."

The plane took off. Suddenly a flash of red caught Joe's eye. A stout man was napping on the other side of the aisle, a few rows in front of the boys. The colour came from a large ruby ring he wore.

Joe stood up to see better. "That's Ponsley!" he exclaimed.

Frank picked up the map spread across his knees and got up, too. He looked across to where his brother was pointing. "It sure is, Joe. What's he doing here?"

"Maybe he's tailing us," Chet guessed.

"Well, if he is, he's not very good at it," Joe replied. "He's asleep, and that giant ruby is a dead give-away. Let's wake him up."

"Not me," Chet said hastily. "I'll stay in this seat until we land!"

Leaving their friend, Frank and Joe walked up the aisle. Joe nudged their acquaintance with his elbow.

Ponsley stirred, yawned, opened his eyes, and stared at the Hardys. He looked startled as he recognized them.

"Are you following us?" Joe demanded.

"Of course not," Ponsley replied.

"How come you're on this plane, then?" Frank asked.

"Senator Moran had a tip from a friend who just returned from abroad," Ponsley explained. "The man said he recognized Michael in a newspaper photograph of a soccer game in Sydney. The senator didn't give me time to find another detective. He told me to go to Australia myself, so I caught this plane and here I am."

"Quite a coincidence," Frank commented.

"That's right," Ponsley challenged. "What are *you* doing on this plane?"

"I told you we had to leave the country," Frank pointed out. "Our investigation led us to Sydney."

Ponsley beamed and gestured with his hand, causing his ruby ring to throw off rays of deep red. "Wonderful!" he exclaimed. "Both investigations will take place in Sydney. You can work on them at the same time!"

The Hardys talked it over and concurred that they might handle the two cases while they were in Australia.

"That's okay," Frank told Ponsley, "but our assignment comes first. We can't let the search for Mike Moran get in the way of that."

"All right," Ponsley said. "I'm glad you'll help me. After all, I am not really a detective!"

The Hardys returned to their seats and informed Chet about their conversation with Ponsley. Then they settled back for the rest of the flight to Los Angeles, where some passengers got off, others got on, and the jet became airborne again. The boys napped as it crossed the California coastline and headed out over the Pacific. Finally the Hawaiian Islands came into view, and soon they landed in Honolulu.

The captain's voice came over the intercom. "Please disembark. There will be a delay because of a technical problem."

Everybody went down the steps and into the terminal, where a stewardess informed them that the delay would last overnight. "A bus is ready to take you all to a hotel on Waikiki Beach," she said. "We'll continue the flight in the morning."

The boys and Ponsley boarded the bus with the other passengers and an hour later they had checked in at a luxurious hotel. From their window, the three Bayporters could see the broad band of white sand where the waters of the Pacific lapped ashore. White foam formed where the breakers rolled in. Surfboard riders tried to keep their footing on huge swells that carried them forward at express-train speeds, and most fell into the water. The rest glided triumphantly to the beach.

"What say we try it, too?" Joe asked.

"Affirmative," Frank replied.

"I'll show you how to ride a surfboard!" Chet boasted. "Lead me to it!"

They called Ponsley and asked him if he wanted to join them.

"No thanks," he replied. "I'll take a walk instead."

Leaving him in the hotel, the boys went to the bathhouse, rented swim trunks, and surfboards. Carrying their surfboards they pushed through the shallow waves and reached the point far out where the breakers suitable for surfing began to form.

"Last one in gets the booby prize!" Chet shouted gleefully, as he climbed up and balanced himself with his arms stretched out. A breaker caught hold of his board and sent it flying towards the beach.

Frank and Joe followed on either side. The three made long curves up and down over the ocean swells, and they leaned to one side or the other to compensate for the tilt of their boards. Sunlight gleamed off the water and the wind blew spray into their faces.

Chet had a lead at the start, but Frank and Joe skilfully manoeuvred over the turbulent breakers until they were zooming along just behind him.

Then a wave cutting across the breakers at an angle struck Chet's surfboard, knocking it round. The heavy impact caused him to lose his footing and he tumbled into the water. His crazily floating board whacked him on the side of the head and he sank out of sight!

Frank dived from his own board into the water in Chet's direction, and Joe came headlong after him. They groped underwater as long as they could hold their breath. Forced to surface, the Hardys gulped air and looked around frantically. Chet's head bobbed up near Joe. His eyes were closed, and his body limp. Presently he slipped below the surface again!

"He's out cold!" Frank yelled. "Grab him before he disappears!"

Joe did a seal flip that took him arching from the surface down into the depths, where he spotted Chet being dragged towards the open sea by a strong under-current. Using the breaststroke and kicking his feet hard, Joe reached his friend and pushed him to the surface. Frank splashed over, crooked an elbow under

Chet's chin, and swam on his back in the direction of the shore. Joe, who surfaced beside them, gave Frank a hand with his burden. As they touched the sand in the shallow water, Chet came to. The three stumbled on to the beach and sat down, gasping for breath.

A lifeguard jogged across the sand. "That was a great rescue," he complimented the Hardys. "I didn't come in because I could see you had the situation under control." He turned to Chet. "How do you feel?"

Chet rubbed his head. "Okay, I guess," he mumbled. "But I sure have a powerful headache. I'm going back to the hotel. Besides, I'm nauseated from swallowing half the Pacific."

He got to his feet and walked off. Frank and Joe went with him. They insisted that he see the hotel doctor, whose prognosis was that Chet would be fit again after a night's sleep. The diagnosis was correct. Chet woke up in the morning with nothing more than tenderness on the side of his head.

After breakfast the bus took all the passengers back to the airport, and soon they were on their way again. They flew south-west across what seemed to be an endless expanse of ocean before Samoa came into view. The boys talked to Ponsley for a while, then went back to their seats to read.

They stopped when the stewardess served their meals. Chet dug ravenously into everything that was put in front of him. Chet was never happier than when he was eating.

"Chet, there's nothing like chow to bring you back to normal," Frank declared.

"Lucky the airline doesn't have to feed you every day," Joe needled him. "It would go broke."

Chet downed the last mouthful of cherry pie. "That'll hold me for a while," he predicted.

The stewardess removed the trays and the boys dozed off until the plane ran into turbulence and began to wobble.

Chet opened his eyes, slumped in his seat, and placed a hand on his belt buckle. "I don't feel so good," he confessed.

As the turbulence increased, the plane bounced up and down. Chet turned plae. His freckles stood out and his eyes bulged. "What's happening?" he muttered fearfully.

"We're in the jetstream, that's all," Frank reassured him. "We'll soon be out of it."

Suddenly the plane flew into a down-draught and dropped a number of feet.

"We're gonna crash!" Chet cried. Desperately he clawed the life-jacket from under his seat, slipped it on, and pulled the strings, triggering the inflation mechanism. The life jacket ballooned out, pinning Chet between the seats.

A stewardess rushed up. "Sir, what are you doing?" she demanded.

Chet closed his eyes and gasped. "If we survive the crash, we'll all drown!"

·9·

The Porter's Clue

"NONSENSE!" the stewardess retorted sternly. "We are not going to crash!"

Chet opened one eye. "We aren't?"

"Certainly not. Turbulence in the air is routine! You are disturbing the other passengers."

Frank hastily assured her that he and Joe would take care of the situation. The stewardess thanked him and moved towards the cockpit. By now the jet was flying steadily on course. Frank let the air out of the life-jacket, helped Chet wriggle out of it, and stowed it under the seat.

Chet swallowed hard and looked remorseful. "I thought we'd crash for sure," he said.

"Forget it," Joe said. "No harm done."

"Get ready for Australia, Chet," Frank advised.

The freckle-faced youth regained his composure. His broad grin returned. "Kangaroos! Boomerangs! I can't wait!"

Finally they could see the coastline of Australia as the plane thundered down over Port Jackson, a large bay with long watery indentations into the land. Sydney Harbour came into view, spanned by a long suspension bridge.

"When we were reading up on Australia," Joe said, "I remember one of the books said the people in Sydney call that bridge 'the coathanger'."

The boys could see big ocean-going ships tied up at the docks, and clusters of tall buildings. The city and its suburbs lay spread out below them in a pattern of streets, squares, and parks, illuminated by the evening sun.

The plane landed at the airport. After getting through customs, the boys and Ponsley took a taxi to their hotel. They had booked rooms at the Australian Arms, where Dr Jenson had also made a reservation before he disappeared.

"May as well start our detective work right now," Frank decided.

As they got out of their taxi, he showed the hotel porter photos of Dr Jenson and Mike Moran.

"Recognize these people?" Frank queried.

The porter studied the faces and shook his head.

"I've never seen either of them," he declared.

They made the same inquiry at the hotel desk, but to no avail. During dinner, they discussed how they should proceed.

"We ought to check with police headquarters first thing in the morning," Frank decided. "By now they may have some news on Dr Jenson, and they may know something about Mike Moran, too."

"I'm going with you," Ponsley declared.

"Good. We'll meet for breakfast at eight," Frank said; then they retired for the night.

The following morning the Hardys got up bright and early. Chet did not feel well and decided to sleep a little longer.

"We'll see you when we come back," Joe told him, then he and Frank met Ponsley in the cafeteria. They had a quick breakfast and an hour later took a taxi to police headquarters. Here they explained their mission to a sergeant on duty.

"You'll have to talk to Inspector Morell," the sergeant replied. "He's in charge of the search for that missing Yank scientist. But he's not here right now. Should be back in half an hour."

"Okay, we'll talk to him later." Frank added that they were also trying to trace another missing American, named Michael Moran, whose face had been spotted in a Sydney newspaper photo.

"Hmm." The sergeant rubbed his jaw thoughtfully. "We don't keep tabs on all the tourists who come here—unless they get in trouble, of course. Let me just check with our Criminal Records Office."

He picked up the phone, dialled, and conversed for a few minutes. Then he hung up with a grin. "You're in luck. Our computer turned up his name straightaway. He's listed as a witness to an auto accident about a month ago. Gave his address as Flynn's Guesthouse on St James Road."

The boys and Ponsley thanked the sergeant and took another cab to the guesthouse on St James Road. They were disappointed, however, when the owner informed them that Mike Moran had departed about three weeks before, saying only that he was leaving town.

"So Moran's trail ends right here," Joe said glumly.

"And we haven't even picked up Jenson's yet," Frank added.

"What'll we do now, go round with the photographs?" Ponsley asked.

"Right. Let's start here," Joe said. He showed the owner Jenson's picture, but the man told them he had never seen the American before. Then the group walked out into the street. The boys returned to police headquarters while Ponsley took a taxi to their hotel.

After the Hardys had introduced themselves to Inspector Morell, he said, "I was just about to call Professor Young at the Aerospace Lab. We have traced Dr Jenson to a shabby place on sixteen Wallaby Drive. There was a fire there recently in the lobby that destroyed the hotel register and forced the owner to close for a while. That's why it took so long to track Jenson down."

The boys noted the address and thanked Inspector Morell. Then they took a taxi to Wallaby Drive. It was in a rundown section of town and number 16 looked like a decrepit apartment building. Only a small faded sign over the door indicated that it was a hotel. The blackened woodwork round the doors and windows showed signs of a recent blaze.

"I wonder if that fire the inspector mentioned was an arson job," Frank mused.

"That's an idea," Joe said. "Maybe someone was trying to keep the police from finding out Jenson stayed there."

The boys went inside. Two men stood behind the desk in the empty hallway that now served as a lobby. One was the manager, the other had "porter" stitched on the breast pocket of his threadbare jacket.

When Frank inquired about Jenson, the manager looked annoyed. "I've already told the police all I know," he said curtly. "Dr Jenson left with two Americans the day after he checked in and I never heard from him again. That's all I can tell you."

"Did he pay his bill?" Joe inquired.

"The men did."

"Why not Dr Jenson himself?"

"How do I know?" the manager asked gruffly.

There was a brief silence before Frank said, "Were you afraid of trouble if you told the police too much about Jenson?"

The man's face turned sullen. "Whatever gave you that idea?"

"You had a fire here, for one thing. And maybe you received some threats."

"I dunno what you're talking about."

Frank flashed a twenty-dollar bill. "Try to remember. Was there anything even the slightest bit unusual about Jenson's departure?"

The manager hesitated, obviously tempted. He glanced furtively round, then took the money and quickly put it in his wallet. "Well, Jenson seemed drunk," he told the boys. "He was sort of slumped between these two blokes. They paid and led him outside, then pushed him into a car and drove off."

"Do you think he was forced to go with them?"

"I dunno. I think he was drunk."

"Can we look in his room for a clue?" Joe asked. "We must find him!"

"Go ahead. I haven't rented it since." The manager gave him the key and the boys went into Jenson's room.

Joe looked into the closet while Frank went through a chest of drawers. They turned the waste-paper basket upside down, and lifted the mattress from the bed.

"Nothing here," said Joe, standing in the middle of the room and gazing around. His eyes fell on the door, which was covered with scratches and graffiti. Joe went over and bent down, staring at the bottom panel.

"Hey Frank, come here a minute!"

Frank looked at the initials and sentences scribbled on the lower part of the door. "Graffiti," he said. "Courtesy of the hotel's high-class clientele."

"Look close," Joe advised. "See this sign?"

"A bolt of lightning!" Frank exclaimed. "The same as we saw on Dr Jenson's desk!"

"Correct. And after it are the letters AL S. What do you think that means?"

"Maybe those are the initials of Dr Jenson's kidnapper!" Frank said, excited. "Could be his name is Albert Smith."

"Or Alfred Scott, or a million other combinations," Joe commented.

Their enthusiasm diminished as they realized the number of possibilities. "There are too many names with those initials," Frank concluded. "We'll have to find Jenson to find out whom he meant."

"Let's think about it as we go back to our hotel," Joe suggested. "What say we walk instead of taking a taxi?"

"Suits me," Frank agreed.

Before leaving, they wrote down their room number at the Australian Arms and asked the manager to call them if he remembered any other details. Then they walked towards the centre of the city, which was not far, and found that Sydney was built on a number of hills. Rows of houses painted in bright colours lined the streets, and cars whizzed back and forth through narrow thoroughfares.

"Why do you think Jenson checked into that

crummy hotel?" Joe asked his brother.

"Maybe he suspected he was being followed and wanted to hide," Frank replied.

"Or, if he's not on the level, perhaps he wanted to disappear and obscure his tracks," Joe concluded.

"I think he was kidnapped. I don't believe he was drunk when those guys took him out of the place," Frank said.

"You're probably right. Boy, these streets are all uphill or downhill," Joe said. "I'm getting tired!"

"Cheer up. We're coming close to level ground," Frank told him. He referred to Macquarie Street, where they saw the law courts before cutting over to George Street, the site of the magnificent Town Hall and St Andrew's Cathedral.

They stepped off the kerb and began to cross over to the cathedral, when a car swished round the corner and barrelled straight at them at top speed!

Joe barely had time to shove his brother out of the way. There was no chance to escape himself. He took a death-defying leap at the car, sprawling across the bonnet to avoid being run down!

The car zoomed past Frank, missing him by inches, and jolted over a patch of grass bordering the sidewalk. Joe was blocking the driver's view, but a sharp twist of the wheel sent the youth sliding off. He rolled over and over. Only the grass saved him from serious injury.

As Joe lay half-stunned, he caught a parting glimpse of the bearded driver, scowling at him through the open window as the car roared away. The man was wearing tinted glasses!

He continued up the street, rounded the corner, and vanished. Frank and Joe got to their feet, shaking their heads at their narrow escape. The few pedestrians ran to help, but nobody had caught the car's licence number.

"Thanks for saving me, Joe," Frank puffed. "Are you okay?"

"Yeah, except that fall rattled my eye-teeth." The younger Hardy waited till they were alone again before adding, "Did you get a look at the driver?"

"No. Who was he?"

"The guy who shadowed us in Princeton!"

Frank gave a long whistle. "He followed us to Australia! How did he know we'd be here?"

"He didn't follow us to Bayport," Joe said. "And I watched on the way to the airport. No one was behind us."

"Maybe he overheard our telephone conversation with Professor Young," Frank said. "Or he could have overheard Young and Smoky talking when the professor told Smoky to catch us before we left for Australia."

"Or Smoky could have told him!" Joe added.

"Right. Once he knew we were coming here, all he had to do was check with the airlines and take an earlier flight or even get on the same plane in disguise!"

"This is getting serious," Joe said. "The guy's out to kill. If we don't crack this case soon, he may succeed!"

Taking various detours, the boys returned to the Australian Arms Hotel. When they arrived in their room, Chet was still sleeping. Frank woke him up and told him what had happened. He was just about finished when the telephone rang. Joe picked it up.

He heard a muffled voice say, "If you want information on Dr Jenson, be at the Botany Bay Coffee-house in King's Cross in one hour!"

·10·

A Spy in the Crowd

"Who are you and how will we know you?" Joe asked.

"I'll know you, and that's all that matters." The phone went dead. Joe relayed the message to Frank and Chet.

"Sounds like a trap," he added. "Probably another one of our shadow's tricks."

"I think we should chance it," Frank said. "We don't have any other leads in the case."

There was a knock on the door. Frank walked over to it and asked, "Who is it?"

"Ponsley." It was their friend's familiar voice. Frank let him in and brought him up-to-date on the latest news.

"Suppose," Ponsley said, "I go along and trail behind you. If the crooks gang up on you, I'll call for help."

"Great idea!" Joe said. "How about you, Chet?"

Chet was awake by now, and felt better. "Of course, I'm coming, too," he said.

"Wait a minute," Frank objected. "I think it will be better if we split forces. You stay here, Chet, and if we're not back in an hour, alert the police. If you come along, they might get all of us and no one would know we're missing."

"Okay," Chet agreed readily. The thought of being caught did not appeal to him at all. Ponsley looked a bit doubtful, too, but did not retract his offer.

The three left, and just before the hour was up, the Hardys entered the Botany Bay Coffee-house, a popular gathering place for Australians of all types from Sydney businessmen to shop girls, office workers, and people in the arts. Like most Aussies, they seemed to have a sun-tanned breezy look about them that the boys liked. Over coffee and tea, a babble of cheerful voices could be heard.

Frank and Joe sat down at a table in a corner and ordered coffee. They surveyed the room without spotting a familiar face until Ponsley walked in. He took a table on the opposite side of the room, winked to indicate that he was keeping them under surveillance, and told a waitress to bring him a pot of tea.

"You're right on time," a voice said at Frank's elbow. "You must be interested."

It was the porter from the hotel Dr Jenson had stayed in!

The man sat down and accepted a cup of coffee. "Look, mates," he said in a low tone, "I know about Dr Jenson. I opened the door for him and the two blokes who were with him. I could tell from the look in his eyes that he was drugged. When they pushed him into the car, he began to struggle. I went out to see what was going on, and I heard him mutter something."

"What was it?" Frank asked eagerly.

"He said 'Alice Springs' just before they slammed the door and drove off!"

"Why didn't you mention this before?" Joe inquired.

"I told the manager. He said he didn't want any trouble, and that I might have made a mistake. That's why I couldn't tell you at the hotel that I recognized Jenson's photo. After thinking it over, I thought you should know that he wasn't drunk. He was drugged!"

The porter drained his coffee cup and, after accepting some money from Frank in payment for his information, he rose to his feet. He was due back at the hotel and strode off. The Hardys stared at each other in consternation.

Joe broke the silence. "Now we know what AL S stands for. Alice Springs! She must be the leader of the kidnap gang. Maybe she's holding Jenson a prisoner right now here in Sydney!"

"Joe, Alice Springs isn't a person. It's a place—a town way off in the Outback in the middle of the country. Jenson left a message saying that he was taken to Alice Springs!" Frank said.

Joe jumped up from his chair. "This is a hot clue, Frank! We'll have to go to Alice Springs!"

"That's the way I see it. We'd better get out there in a hurry."

Ponsley left his table and joined them. "Who was that fellow and what did he say?"

Frank told him and repeated the conversation.

"Where is Alice Springs?" Ponsley asked.

"Let's find out," Frank suggested and pulled a map of Sydney from his pocket that showed all of Australia on the reverse side. He spread it flat on the table, running a fingertip from Sydney west across New South Wales into South Australia, and then up into the Northern Territory. His finger stopped almost exactly in the centre of the continent, where the words "Alice Springs" were printed in black letters.

They could tell from the relief colouring that the town nestled in the foothills of the Macdonnell Ranges, at a point where a number of streams converged. The illustrations indicated that all round Alice Springs there were homesteads, mines, and cattle ranches.

Ponsley was aghast. "Impossible!" he cried, thumping the table with his fist until the ruby on his finger seemed to be a streak of red in the air. "That town is over a thousand miles from here!"

"A long trip," Joe agreed.

"Too long!" Ponsley snapped. "You have to stay in Sydney and continue the search for Mike Moran!"

Frank shook his head. "Mike will have to wait," he said firmly. "Jenson comes first. Besides, Mike said he was leaving town. Chances are he's not in Sydney anyway."

Ponsley groused and grumbled, but finally gave in. "I'll go with you," he decided. "I'm not the detective around here. I need you boys to solve my mystery. I'd better stay with you so I can be sure you start looking for Mike the minute you find Jenson."

"Fair enough," Frank said and paid the bill. He asked the waitress about the nearest travel agent's office, which happened to be around the corner.

The boys were unable to book a scheduled flight for the next day, but the clerk referred them to the pilot of a small private plane, who had just come in to pick up possible fares.

"I belong to the Royal Flying Doctor Service," the pilot told them. "The RFDS flies doctors, nurses, and medicine over the Outback wherever someone is ill or injured. Planes are the only way to get around quickly in that area."

"You must be like the bush pilots in Alaska," Joe surmised. "They cover a lot of territory."

"Quite similar," the pilot agreed. "Well, I operate out of Alice Springs and will be flying back there tomorrow morning. I'll be glad to take you."

"We'll need four seats," Frank said. "A friend of ours is coming, too."

"That's okay. I have enough room."

The boys thanked the man and left the travel agency. "What say we call Chet to tell him the latest news, and then see a few more of the sights on the way back to the hotel?" Frank suggested.

"Good idea," Joe and Ponsley agreed. They called from a public phone booth, then strolled along the Elizabeth Street shopping area, glancing at items in shop windows and enjoying the bustle of the city. They paused at a fishmonger's barrow.

"Anything on the menu from the Great Barrier Reef?" Frank inquired.

"Too far away, mate," the man laughed. "My fish come from Ulladulla, down south of here. How about some tasty snapper or John Dory? Blimey, you'll find 'em delicious!"

"Okay, you've convinced us." Joe chuckled.

They all bought fish sandwiches and munched them hungrily. Then they deposited their paper napkins in a litter bin and walked on.

Suddenly Frank spotted someone watching them from the opposite side of the street. The older Hardy boy recognized the man with the tinted glasses!

"Our shadow from Princeton!" he told his companions.

"The guy who tried to run us down!" Joe exploded. "Let's get him!"

The boys turned and hastened to the corner to cross Elizabeth Street. Ponsley brought up the rear as fast as he could. But the light turned red just as they arrived at the intersection and the flow of traffic compelled them to wait. By the time they got across, they could barely glimpse their quarry almost a block away.

"He's heading towards the waterfront!" Frank cried.

The Hardys and Ponsley ran after him. A sign, *Harbour Bridge*, pointed the way to the busy eight-lane steel span connecting Sydney to the North Shore.

Presently they came to the dock area, where ocean liners and tramp freighters were tied up at the piers to unload and take on passengers and cargo. Across the waters of Sydney Cove on their right could be seen the dazzling new opera house, looking like a cluster of pointed white concrete sails.

As the boys slowed to get their bearings, they almost bumped into a sailor who was hurrying in the opposite direction.

"Sorry, mates! I didn't see you coming," he apologized.

"Did you happen to pass a bearded man with dark glasses?" Frank asked him.

The sailor shoved back his cap and scratched his head. "Don't recall noticing anyone like that," he replied, "but if you want to come back to me ship for a minute, I'll find out if anyone saw him."

"That's mighty kind of you, but weren't you going the other way? We don't want to hold you up."

"That's all right, cobber. I was just going on shore leave. Nothing that urgent."

Ponsley sat down on a wooden bollard to catch his breath. "I need a breather after all that running," he said. "You two go on. I'll wait here."

The boys accompanied the sailor to his freighter, which was moored nearby. On its stern was the name *Sydney Cove.*

The sailor grinned. "Come on board. You can call me Salty, by the way. Everyone else does."

He led the way up the gangplank to the well-deck, where the captain was giving orders to his bosun and deck hands. One of the men was attaching a huge bale to a cargo boom near the open hold.

"What're you doing back aboard, Salty?" the officer bellowed.

"Just 'elpin' out these two Yanks, sir. They're lookin' for a bearded man with dark glasses. Anyone see 'im go by?"

The skipper and crewmen, who had stopped work, shook their heads. The boys thanked them and left the ship. They saw Ponsley coming towards them across the dock.

"I've seen enough of Sydney," he declared. "I'm going back to the hotel. Want to share a taxi with me?"

"May as well," Frank answered. "Looks like we've lost that creep we were chasing."

As they turned to go, the freighter's cargo boom swung out over the side with a heavy bale in its cargo net. The net opened just above the three and the bale hurtled down on them!

·11·

Chet's Clever Plan

FRANK caught a glimpse of the bale as it tumbled out of the cargo net. "Watch out!" he shouted.

Frank and Joe lunged into Ponsley, pushing him out of the way and knocking him over backwards. The three went down in a tangle of arms and legs as the heavy cargo slammed into the dock a few feet away from them!

The Hardys got up but Ponsley lay still. Joe leaned over and shook him by the shoulders. "Mr Ponsley, are you all right?" he asked, worried.

Ponsley groaned and stirred feebly.

"He's stunned," Frank judged. "He'll come round in a minute."

Salty hurried down the ship's gangplank to join them. "Blimey, I'm sorry!" he panted. "Someone swung the ruddy boom too far out. The net's not supposed to open till the operator presses the button. I don't know what 'appened. That bale might've 'urt you somethin' terrible!"

"It would have squashed us like beetles," Frank said. "But we're okay."

Ponsley sat up and opened his eyes. "Speak for yourself!" he cried. "I can hardly see! Good heavens, I think

I'm going blind! What am I going to do?"

Joe noticed that Ponsley's spectacles had been knocked off when he fell. The younger Hardy picked up the gold pince-nez, made sure the lenses had not been broken, and placed them back on Ponsley's nose.

"How's that?" he asked.

Ponsley adjusted the glasses with his thumb and forefinger. "Why, I can see again!" he said, relieved.

"We're not hurt, Salty," Frank told the sailor. "But I don't want to be in the way the next time your cargo net goes haywire."

Salty nodded and went back to the ship. Since Ponsley was more determined than ever to return to the hotel, they took a taxi to the Australian Arms.

When they stepped into the Hardys' room, they found it empty!

"Where's Chet?" Joe wondered.

"We'd better find out—fast," Frank replied tensely as he called the hotel desk. The clerk denied any knowledge of Chet's whereabouts. "Perhaps he went out for a newspaper," the man suggested.

The Hardys and Ponsley waited for an hour to see if Chet would come back, but there was no sign of him. Finally Frank jumped to his feet. "Joe, what if Chet has been kidnapped?"

"A dreadful thought!" Ponsley interjected.

As they considered what to do next, a key scraped in the lock. Somebody was trying to get in without being heard!

"It may be Chet's kidnapper!" Frank whispered.

The Hardys tiptoed across the room and stationed themselves on each side of the door, waiting for it to open.

The knob turned and the door swung inwards. The mysterious visitor stealthily entered the room.

"Chet!" Frank and Joe cried in unison.

Their rotund friend closed the door quietly. Placing a finger on his lips, he jerked his head in the direction of the window, and led them over to it. He motioned them to stand back so as not to be seen and pointed to a department store across the street.

Two men were standing in front of it, watching the hotel. Another joined them and pointed at the boys' window. He had a black beard and wore tinted glasses! When a policeman came along, the men pretended to look at the display of clothes in the store windows. When he had passed, they resumed their vigil.

Chet tugged Frank's sleeve and drew his friends away from the window. "I noticed them right after you left," he reported.

"Obviously they stayed here while Tinted Glasses shadowed us through Sydney," Joe said.

"Maybe we should call the police," Chet suggested.

Frank shook his head. "They can't arrest these guys just because they're standing down there watching us. Besides, Tinted-Glasses and his partners might not know where Jenson is. Their only job may be to keep us from finding him. If we get involved with these guys and the law, that may be just what they want. It'll keep us from looking for Jenson."

Turning to Chet, Frank explained the clue they had just received, which pointed to Alice Springs as the next focus of their search.

"Gosh, stop to think of it," Chet said, "those look-outs may even be trying to find Jenson themselves—by shadowing *us*!"

"That's possible." Frank agreed. "Either way, I think our best bet is to give 'em the slip."

"How?" asked Joe.

His brother turned back to their chubby pal. "Does the hotel have a rear door?"

"I checked that," Chet replied. "Two more guys are out there in the alley. They look like they're ready to jump us if we leave."

"The roof!" Joe said. "Maybe we can try that."

Chet shook his head. "I went up there. There's a lookout on the opposite building. He's watching the fire escape. And there's no other exit."

"Then we're trapped!" Ponsley exclaimed.

"We are," Chet agreed. "But I've worked out an escape route!"

"How?" Frank asked.

"Just grab an overnight bag with a change of clothes and come with me," Chet said mysteriously. "Hurry up!"

Ponsley went to his room and was back shortly. The boys had each packed a small bag and were ready. Chet motioned them out of the room and locked the door carefully. Then he led the way to the freight elevator. They took it down to the basement, and followed Chet to a storeroom.

A tradesman was lifting empty crates into a truck backed up to the exit.

"These are the friends I told you about," Chet addressed him. "Since we left our belongings in our room, you know we're not trying to defraud the hotel. We're coming back."

"Righto," the man replied. "You paid me. Now I'll carry out my part of the bargain. Get into the truck, all of you, and lie low. I'll tell you when we're clear."

Chet climbed into the vehicle and edged his way towards the cab. Ponsley came next, then Frank and Joe. They crouched down behind the load of empty crates and the driver slammed the tail-gate up. Then he went round to the cab, started the engine, and slowly moved the truck away from the hotel.

Through a crack in the tail-gate Frank could see the two men in the alley watching the back door of the hotel.

"We outsmarted them after all!" he said with a chuckle. "They'll be standing there forever!"

The driver took them to George Street, where he stopped and let them off. "This is as far as you go," he said. "Goodbye and good luck!"

The boys jumped out and thanked the man, then the truck sped away.

"I saw the truck coming up to the back door when I was in the basement," Chet revealed. "I figured the driver might make a deal with me, and he did."

"Good thinking, Chet," Joe complimented him.

Chet looked pleased. "What next?" he asked.

After a council of war, they decided to go to the airport and spend the night at a motel. From there, they phoned Inspector Morell and asked him to have the bearded man and his cohorts picked up for questioning. But an hour later Morell called back to report failure. Apparently the crooks had discovered that the Hardy boys and their friends had gotten away, and had abandoned their watch on the hotel.

Early next morning, the Hardys, Chet and Ponsley took off for Alice Springs. The green areas around Sydney disappeared, and they found themselves flying deep into the Outback, where sand and huge stones extended to the horizon on all sides. Clusters of rocks ballooned from the desert floor into fantastic shapes.

"If we were in the States," Frank said, "I'd guess we were over Death Valley."

"Or the Dakota Badlands," Joe added.

"Well, it's hot and dusty here, too," the pilot pointed out. "There aren't any rattlesnakes down below, but there are Australian brown snakes, which are nearly as deadly."

"You are not going to land, are you?" Ponsley asked, frightened.

The pilot laughed. "Don't worry. Landing in this part of the Outback is the last thing I want to do."

The plane crossed rivers where good farmland spread along the banks. Big cattle ranches occupied hundreds of square miles beyond the Macdonnell Ranges in Australia's Northern Territory. Finally they landed at Alice Springs, and the four Americans got out. They stretched their muscles, cramped after the long flight, paid the pilot, and took a bus into town.

They found Alice Springs crisscrossed by rows of hardy trees that managed to stay alive in the arid soil. The buildings were mostly small and roofed with tin. On Anzac Hill, a shining monument commemorated the Australians and New Zealanders who fell in two world wars.

The boys stopped at police headquarters and asked about Jenson and Mike Moran. The officer on duty could supply no information on either, but gave the boys a list of hotels and guest-houses where they could inquire.

"Good thing this town isn't big," Frank said. "We

won't have too much trouble checking these out."

"Are they all within walking distance?" Chet asked.

Frank had obtained a map of Alice Springs at the airport and looked at it. "I don't know. Let's start here and work towards the outskirts of the town."

Checking with various hotels on the way, the four walked through Gorey's Arcade, the shopping centre of Alice Springs. They went along the streets past bars and cafés and noticed that many men wore cowboy hats, shirts, trousers, and boots. Some of the men were dark-skinned aborigines.

"Those guys look like they came from Tombstone with Wyatt Earp after the gunfight at the O.K. Corral!" Chet commented.

"Except that none of them carry six-shooters," Frank added with a grin.

They came to a fenced-in enclosure where a competition was being held. Cowboys lined the rails, waiting for their turn to rope steer and ride bucking broncos. Three judges on a raised platform judged the performances and awarded prizes.

"A rodeo!" Joe exclaimed. "How about that!"

"Let's spread out and keep our eyes open," Frank suggested. "There's always an outside chance of spotting Mike or Dr Jenson in the crowd. While we're at it, we can chat with people, too, and find out if anybody has noticed an American answering either description. We'll meet here in half an hour."

"Good idea," Joe said, and the four separated and began asking cowboys and spectators for information on the two missing men. None of the Australians had heard of them.

They were on the way to their meeting place again

when the main event of the rodeo began. A rider came out of a chute, like a streak of lightning, on a coal-black horse that leaped and twisted in a savage effort to throw the man off its back.

Chet was fascinated by the violence of horse and rider contending to see who would win.

"I could get a better view from that fence post over there," he thought and climbed up. Carefully he positioned himself on the small post. But he got so involved in the show that at one point he lost his balance and dropped into the enclosure.

Frank, who saw the incident from a short distance away, muttered something about Chet and his ideas. Then the bronco threw its rider and charged full-tilt at Chet, who had just got to his feet.

"Watch out!" Frank yelled.

·12·

Kangaroo Confrontation

CHET froze as the black horse, glaring and snorting, galloped towards him, hooves pounding!

Frank moved like lightning. He snatched a lasso that had been used in the steer-roping competition and hurled the noose in a long flying arc.

As it settled over the horse's neck, he fastened the other end of the lariat to a fence post. The enraged animal was about to trample Chet when the rope tightened and brought it rearing to a halt in a cloud of dust!

Chet scrambled over the fence and fought for breath. "Frank," he puffed, "you're better than those TV cowboys any day!"

There were loud cheers and a round of applause for Frank's rescue. One of the contestants came up and spoke to him admiringly. "Good-oh, cobber! Your china would've ended up a proper mess if you hadn't come through with that rope trick!"

"China?" Frank looked puzzled. "Is that a word you cowboys use down under?"

The Aussie laughed. "It's good old cockney rhyming slang—'china plate' for 'mate'. And we're not cowboys down here, Yank. We're stockmen. My name's John Harris."

Shaking hands, Frank introduced himself and his companions. Together they watched the rest of the rodeo, and Harris captured first prize for bronco-busting. He invited them to join in the horseback ride round the ring. Ponsley quickly refused, saying he would rather wait on the viewing stand. He climbed up the few steps and sat down in a chair vacated by one of the rodeo judges.

Harris brought up three mounts. Frank, Joe, and Chet climbed into the saddles and trotted in the procession round the enclosure. The Hardys, who had ridden horseback many times, guided their mounts with practised skill.

Chet clutched the reins with one hand, waved the other, and shouted, "This is for me!" His horse, feeling the tug of the bridle, thought it was time to rear up on its hind-legs. The movement alarmed Chet, who slackened his grip and let the horse have its head.

Finally the ride ended, the rodeo broke up, and the boys joined Ponsley for a walk back towards the centre. They checked two more hotels without luck, then stopped at a luncheon-bar and ordered hamburgers.

Chet pitched into his enthusiastically. "Nothing like a horseback ride to set you up for chow."

Frank laughed. "Chet, who was in charge, you or the horse?"

"Maybe you'd like an encore," Joe needled him. "We can go back if you like."

"No, thanks," Chet said. "I showed the rodeo what I can do. That's enough for me."

Ponsley was becoming annoyed. "This trip has not been a success," he argued. "I'm sure Dr Jenson isn't here, and neither is Mike Moran."

Frank munched a pickle. "We only have a few more places to check, and we never give up prematurely."

Just then John Harris walked into the luncheon-bar, recognized the Americans, and came to their table.

"Mind if I join you?" he asked.

"Of course not," Frank said, inviting him to sit down. Harris ordered a hamburger. While he ate, Frank told him they were looking for two missing Americans. "Got any suggestions?"

Harris looked thoughtful. "I overheard a Yank talking to someone right here in the luncheon-bar not too long ago. He mentioned Cutler Ranch, a cattle station up north, owned by Americans."

Frank showed him the photographs. "Was it either of these two men?"

Harris shrugged. "He had his back turned to me. I just remember the accent, since it's rare in these parts."

Frank exchanged glances with his brother.

"Worth a try," Joe agreed.

"It's a long ride up north, beyond McGrath Creek and the Sandover River," Harris warned. "So pick a car that gets a lot of miles to the gallon. You won't pass any petrol pumps on the way."

Finishing his hamburger, he said goodbye and left. Joe seemed to be watching someone. Presently he got up and muttered, "Let's go!"

Frank and the others paid their bill and followed Joe outside. But they had gone scarcely a block when Joe suddenly whirled round. His three companions saw him grab a seedy stranger in a battered, greasy-looking felt hat, who had been walking close behind them.

"Why are you following us, mister?" the younger Hardy demanded angrily.

The stranger cringed when he saw the fighting look on Joe's face. "You've got me all wrong, mate," he mumbled. "I wasn't following nobody."

"Don't give me that! You were eavesdropping on everything we said back there in the restaurant."

"Well. . . ." The stranger hesitated nervously, then blurted, "I expect I did listen closer'n I should've done. But I was worried about what that stockman was telling you. Didn't know if I ought to warn you or not."

Joe frowned. "Warn us about what?"

"The Cutlers."

"What about them?" Frank demanded.

"They're strange blokes. From what I hear, they don't welcome visitors—especially visitors who ask questions."

"How come?" Joe pressed.

The seedy stranger shrugged. "All I know is what I've heard some of the aborigines hereabouts say."

"What do they say?"

"That they've seen nosy swagmen ride up to the Cutlers' cattle station, but they've never seen none of them ride away again!"

The four Americans stared at the seedy stranger uneasily. Before they could cross-examine him, he wriggled free of Joe's grasp and hurried off down the street.

"What did he mean by 'swagmen'?" Chet asked with a worried, wide-eyed look.

"Travelling cowhands, carrying their 'swag' or personal belongings in a blanket roll," Frank explained. "I remember that much from what I read about the Outback."

"They may be travelling cowhands," said Ponsley,

"but if what we just heard means anything, once they go nosing around the Cutlers' place, their travels come to a sudden end!"

Chet felt cold chills. "You really think the Cutlers polish off trespassers?"

"Suppose that guy was just trying to scare us off?" Joe suggested. "Suppose he doesn't want us to see something out there? Maybe Jenson is a prisoner at the Cutler Ranch and they don't want us to rescue him?"

Frank stood up. "It's still daylight. Let's go!"

Ponsley was against it. "I believe this will be another wild-goose chase," he protested.

"Mr Ponsley, we can't stop now," Frank urged. "We know Americans took Jenson to Alice Springs. The Cutlers are Americans, and someone's trying to keep us away from their place. We have to see what's going on at the Cutler Ranch!"

"You can stay here until we get back," Joe proposed.

"No, no!" Ponsley objected. "I don't want to stay alone. I'll go with you!"

The group went to the only car-rental agency in town and selected a small-engined car that gave them good mileage to the gallon.

"You're lucky," the agent told them. "We were all out of cars, but someone returned this one sooner than expected."

"Good," Frank said and paid for the rental. Then, with Joe at the wheel, they drove north from Alice Springs. The fertile region gave way to desert, after which signs of agriculture reappeared around McGrath Creek. They could see farmhouses with tall windmills pumping water from underground.

Soon the desert began again, and they were travelling along a dusty road through desolate country marked by the bleached skeletons of horses and cows that had succumbed in the waterless waste.

"I believe we should pause for a rest," Ponsley finally said. "Let's stop here."

Joe pulled over to the side of the road, where a strange formation of huge rocks rose above the desert. They noticed that one of the rocks was covered with painted figures. A serpent wound its way in long sinuous coils up from the base of the cliff. On the left, an owl perched in a flutter of feathers, as if terrified by the snake. On the right, a kangaroo hopped fearfully out of the way. Above these animals, a medicine man wielded a magic wand to ward off the serpent's poison.

Chet scratched his head. "How did this guy and his pets get here?"

"The aborigines painted them," Frank replied. "I read about their rock paintings when we were in Princeton. These could be hundreds of years old."

Ponsley nodded. "Terrific technique," he declared. "Compares favourably with modern art."

The four marvelled at the figures done in white, black, brown, and dark red. At last, the boys sat down with their backs against the cliff. Ponsley who complained about his stiff back, wandered away into the desert. A moment later he shouted frantically.

The boys scrambled to their feet and raced towards him, but stopped halfway, taken aback by what they saw.

Their portly friend was confronted by a large kangaroo!

The animal stood on its hind-legs with its heavy tail extended on the sand. Its fur was grey, shading to white underneath, and the top of the tail was black. It held its small front paws up in the air and stared at Ponsley, who raised his hand in a frantic effort to frighten it off. His ruby ring glittered in the sun.

Suddenly the kangaroo began to hop towards him. The more Ponsley waved, the faster it bounded forward, its eyes fixed on his hand.

Frank recalled that kangaroos are attracted by bright objects. Obviously this one was after Ponsley's ruby ring!

"Stop waving!" the boy yelled, but Ponsley did not seem to hear him. He backed away from the kangaroo, turned frantically, and ran as fast as he could. The kangaroo also increased its speed, caught up with, and sprang at him in a high bound!

Ponsley's feet became entangled with one another, and he fell headlong into the sand. The kangaroo leaped clear over him! The boys yelled at the top of their lungs to frighten the creature, and, after landing on its strong hind-legs, it hopped rapidly away into the distance.

The Hardys helped Ponsley up and brushed the sand off his suit. He was indignant about the kangaroo confrontation, and for the rest of the drive he kept insisting that they should never have ventured into the Outback.

They crossed the Sandover River and continued north until Frank spotted a large warning sign: *Cutler Ranch—Keep Out!*

"Maybe we shouldn't drive in there," Chet advised.

"Hey, we've come all the way from Alice Springs to check this place out," Joe reminded him. "Besides, it's almost dark already and no one will see us." He switched off the headlights and turned up a rutted drive leading to the property. He drove slowly till they reached a wire fence with a gate. Beyond it stood the ranch-house.

Joe stopped the car and the boys strained to look at the building. Suddenly a light snapped on in one window.

"I don't think it would be wise to barge up to the front door and knock," Frank commented.

"Right," Joe agreed. "We'll have to sneak in."

Ponsley shook his head. "You do as you please. I'll stay here."

"That's okay," Frank told him. "Joe, why don't you park behind that pile of rocks over there so the car will be out of sight."

The boys got out, leaving Ponsley huddled in the back seat. The three youths headed for a point well to the right of the gateway. The fence was made up of five, taut, wire strands.

When they reached the gate, Frank and Joe got down on their hands and knees and crawled under the lowest strand. Chet followed, but the wire caught him in the back. "I can't move!" he muttered to his friends.

"We'll get you loose," Frank whispered. "Just a minute!" Bracing himself with his feet, he lifted the taut wire as far as he could. Joe took hold of Chet's collar and tugged it. The wire released the boy, who shot forward on his face into the sandy soil on the opposite side of the fence.

"Okay, let's go!" Frank said.

"Wait. I lost a shoe!" Chet pleaded.

Joe slapped his forehead. "What a time to pick!" He felt around in the darkness, found the shoe, and pushed it into Chet's hand. "Tie it right," he warned. "You'll run like a lame duck with one shoe on and one off."

Chet tied his shoe-lace and the boys slipped from the fence across the yard to the lighted window, which was open halfway. Carefully stationing themselves in the darkness to one side of the light, they peered into the room.

A sofa stood against the wall, facing a big sideboard holding a number of decanters. In one corner a roll-top desk was open, revealing a series of pigeonholes filled with documents.

Six men sat round a table. Frank craned his head to get a better look at them. Then he whispered excitedly, "There's Tinted Glasses!"

"And Salty, the friendly sailor who almost killed us with his cargo!" Joe added. "And there's the guy who tried to scare us away from coming to Cutler Ranch!"

One of the men spoke, addressing Tinted Glasses. "I've got to hand it to you, Stiller. Everything's worked out just as you said it would."

Stiller nodded. "Sure, Bruno. But it would be better if Salty had picked the Hardys off on the dock!"

"I 'ad them set up," Salty declared. "They were lucky to get out of the way when I dropped that bale on them!"

"Well, make sure you carry out your assignments without any slip-ups in the future!"

"Sure I will," Salty said sullenly. "It's my neck as well as yours, you know."

"The next job is the most important of all," Stiller continued. "It's the last one. And everything's riding on it."

"I'll be glad when it's over," Bruno declared. "I want to get back to Wisconsin."

Stiller nodded. "I feel the same way. I'm tired of

trailing the Hardys halfway round the world.'

Salty chuckled. "Me, I'm luckier than you Yanks. Australia's 'ome to me."

Stiller frowned. "Your captain doesn't suspect you, does he?"

"No danger, mate. When you led the 'ardys down to the docks and tipped me the wink, I just slipped ashore long enough to get 'em off your back and set 'em up for the kill. All the skipper knows is, I'm an able seaman what knows 'ow to off-load cargo."

The door from the hall opened and a man and woman came in. The man was burly with long arms and large hands. The woman was short and dark with an intense expression. Both looked pleased as they shut the door.

Stiller addressed the man. "Well, Cutler, have you got the final marching orders for us?"

"I sure have," Cutler grinned. "I've just been on the phone to Sydney. We're to finish the job tonight!"

·13·

Daring Escape

"You finally got clearance to dump him in the Outback?" Bruno said. "Good. The desert will take care of him."

Stiller gave a wolfish grin. "That's right," he chortled. "It's as lethal as Death Valley back home in California."

"Dr Jenson will never see the Firebird fly," Mrs Cutler smirked.

"Right. The boss will come here to extract the missing information, then we'll dump him out among the snakes and lizards and leave the sun to finish the job."

The seedy man from Alice Springs shook his head doubtfully. "I'm not so sure that we'll be home free after the job," he spoke up. "I don't like the idea of the Hardys being in Alice Springs. I tried to scare them off when they started to get nosy, but we can't be sure it worked."

Cutler frowned. "Too bad that cowboy had to open his mouth about the ranch," he muttered.

"Well, they can't come out here tonight," the seedy man went on. "I called the car rental agency and they were all out of transportation. But the Hardys might show up here in a day or two and snoop around."

"By that time we'll be rid of Jenson," Stiller assured him. "And we'll destroy any incriminating evidence before tomorrow morning. I agree. We can't be careful enough. These guys are pretty smart. I still don't know how they got out of the Australian Arms Hotel without our seeing them!"

"And what gave them the idea to come to Alice Springs?" Bruno asked. "I know Jenson had no chance to leave word when Jim and I took him out of that flea-pit of a hotel on Wallaby Drive. He was so doped he couldn't have written his own name, even if he had had a piece of paper."

"Maybe they just guessed," Bruno suggested.

"I don't know," Cutler said. "I have a bad feeling about this. Stiller, you'd better burn the lists of clients. The stuff about our previous kidnappings and the smuggling job could send us all up for life. Also, for as long as we're still here, we'll post a guard down at the road."

The Hardys listened outside the window with bated breath. Chet felt a cramp in one of his legs. He turned to place his weight on the other leg, stepped on a twig, and made a slight rustling noise.

Those inside looked in the direction of the sound. "What's going on?" Cutler snarled.

"Maybe someone's outside the window!" Mrs Cutler cried. "Somebody might be spying on us!"

She rushed across the room to the window, while the boys ducked around the corner in the nick of time. Mrs Cutler lifted the lamp and thrust it through the opening. Leaning out, she surveyed the area for a minute or two. Finally she pulled her head in, put the lamp down, and said, "Nobody's there. It must have been the wind blowing through the bushes."

The boys tiptoed back to the window as Cutler turned towards the gang. "What about our new man—the one guarding Jenson?"

"He's okay," Bruno declared. "I recruited him myself."

The boys felt their hearts pounding with fear as they listened to the criminals. Frank plucked Joe's and Chet's sleeves and motioned to them to move back from the window. They stopped near the fence where they had sneaked in.

"We've got to help Dr Jenson!" Frank urged.

"How?" Chet queried. "We don't know where they're holding him. It could be anywhere in the farm-house from the basement to the attic."

"We'll have to climb into the house and search it," Joe suggested.

Frank agreed. "Let's case the place and see if there's a way in. I tell you what. I'll scout along the fence and see if there's an escape route. You two circle the ranch-house in opposite directions and check the windows and doors. We'll meet here in a few minutes and compare notes."

"Right," Joe said. "Come on, Chet."

The pair went off into the darkness while Frank walked up to the fence and began following the strands of wire to guide himself round the perimeter of the yard. About every twenty-five feet he came to a post, but there was no break in the fence until he reached the gate in front. It was fastened by a chain and a padlock, but no guard was at the gate as yet.

"They must think no one but the gang will ever get out here," he thought. He continued round the fence to the place where they had sneaked in.

Joe, meanwhile, had gone to the left of the house. His path took him to a cellar door, a sloping wooden oblong obviously covering a small flight of stairs to the basement. Taking hold of the metal handle, Joe strove to lift the door. It was locked!

Farther on he passed a pick-up truck and a station wagon. Noting that the keys were in both, he reflected, "These guys must really feel safe. Wouldn't it be something if the crooks' cars were stolen!"

Chet circled the house round the right side. He tried the dark lower windows only to find that they would not move. Then he stepped back for a view of the upper windows, which were inaccessible from the ground. "Not even a corner drainpipe to climb," he thought, disappointed.

Moving on, he met Joe sneaking towards him. Consulting in whispers, they decided to join Frank at the fence.

"If we can get Jenson out," Frank reported, "we'd better make a run for it down the road. Otherwise we could get lost in the desert."

"We may not be able to get him out," Chet said. "The ranch is escape-proof."

"I think the cellar door is our best bet," Joe stated. "Maybe we can spring the lock while they're all in the front room."

Frank nodded. "And then we'll have to jump the guy guarding Jenson before he can alert the gang. Let's hope it works!"

The three crept stealthily back to the house, edged round to the cellar door, and tried to wedge it open. Suddenly an uncanny scream made them jump!

"What's that?" Chet gasped.

A cat raced past, pursued by another. Noisily they vanished into the bushes and the boys breathed in relief.

"Wow!" Frank whispered. "They nearly gave me heart failure!"

The boys started to work on the cellar door once again. Joe took out a small set of pocket tools he carried for such emergencies, slipped the end of a tiny chisel between the edge of the door and the jamb, and levered skilfully until the spring of the lock snapped back. Elated, he began to lift the door.

A sound came from the rear of the ranch-house, and Joe immediately eased the cellar door down into place again. The boys sprang up, pressed themselves flat against the wall, and froze as the back door opened.

Cutler came out on to the patio. He held a torch in his hand and played it over the yard from the fence to the house. Foot by foot the light advanced across the ground to the cellar door. The boys stood stock-still, not daring to move a muscle! Now the beam shone inches from Chet's shoes, moving towards him!

At the last moment it wavered to one side because Mrs Cutler emerged from the house and joined her husband on the patio. "What was that screeching sound?" she demanded.

"That's what I'm trying to find out," Cutler replied. He flipped the beam from the ground to the bushes, barely missing Chet's belt buckle.

Suddenly two pairs of eyes gleamed through the bushes and one of the cats began to growl.

"Only a couple of cats," Cutler informed his wife. "Nothing to worry about." He snapped the torch off and they went back inside, closing the door.

Chet let out a sigh of relief. "Boy, that was a close call. I thought we were goners for sure!"

"If he'd aimed that torch a little higher," Joe whispered back, "he could have taken our pictures."

"There's no time to lose," Frank warned. "Let's make sure they're all in the front room. If one of them is prowling round, we're in trouble."

He led the way to the lighted window, where they could see that the Cutlers and gang members were assembled.

"Good," Frank declared. "We can go in——"

Wham! A window slammed over their heads and two men leaped down towards them from the darkness above. Instinctively the boys flattened themselves out against the wall. The men hurdled clear over them, hit the ground, jumped to their feet, and ran to the station wagon.

The Hardys got a good look at one man's face in the light from the window and recognized him from his photo. He was Dr Jenson!

They could not see the other man's face, but as he jumped his hand caught the light from the room and sparkling red rays were reflected from a large ring on his finger.

"That must be Mike Moran!" Frank gasped.

·14·

Frank Foils the Gang

A TUMULT of furious screaming and shouting broke out in the ranch-house.

"The room is empty!" Cutler yelled at the top of his voice. "They're gone—both of 'em!"

"Catch them!" Mrs Cutler screeched savagely. "Don't let them get away!"

"We'll head 'em off!" Stiller shouted. "Put on the searchlight so we can see 'em!"

A moment later a beam of yellow light from a look-out post on the roof cut through the darkness. It picked up Jenson and Moran as they jumped into the station wagon. Moran started the car. The engine turned over—and died!

Shots rang out and bullets flew towards the station wagon, clanging off bumpers and hub caps. One shattered the rear window as the men rushed out with Stiller in the lead. They pounded across the yard towards the fugitives.

Moran desperately turned the key in the ignition again. This time the engine came to life. He put the station wagon in gear, and the vehicle moved off just as Stiller grabbed the door handle on the driver's side. He glared angrily at the two men inside. He reached for the steering wheel and struggled with Moran for control, but Moran held on with an iron grip.

Stiller was dragged for about ten yards before losing his hold and falling off. He somersaulted in the dust and landed flat on his back. Cursing furiously, he got to his feet. The gang rushed up. Those who carried guns opened fire, but the station wagon was far ahead, moving quickly towards the gate.

"They'll have to stop!" Stiller snarled. "The gate's chained!"

The criminals ran as fast as they could, while the searchlight focused on the speeding station wagon. Moran stepped on the gas and smashed into the gate, causing it to splinter under the impact. The vehicle ploughed through, carrying broken boards with it, and disappeared down the road.

Frank, Joe and Chet observed the escape after sneaking to a corner of the ranch-house from which they had a view of the gate. They felt like cheering when they saw the station wagon vanish into the darkness.

"They got away!" Chet chortled.

Joe shook his head. "Those guys'll go after them in the pick-up truck unless we act fast!" He ran to the truck, followed by Frank and Chet, leaned in, and snatched the keys from the dashboard. "That'll stop 'em!" He grinned.

"They may have another set of keys," Frank said. "Better let the air out of this tyre." He tried to unscrew the valve cap, but it refused to budge.

Taking out his penknife, Frank gouged its point into the rubber and began carving a small slit in the sidewall of the tyre until air leaked out with a low hissing sound.

"Look out!" Joe warned. "They're coming!"

The boys melted into the darkness and hid behind tall shrubs.

"We'll take the pick-up truck and go after Jenson and Moran," Stiller ordered. "Don't stand there! Get in. I'll drive!"

As his henchmen obeyed, he squeezed behind the wheel and reached for the keys. His fingers hit an empty keyhole on the dashboard.

"My keys are gone!" he exploded. "Who took 'em? Which of you guys has been fooling around this heap? Fork the key over!"

Each one denied knowing anything about the key. Finally Bruno fished his own key from his pocket and gave it to Stiller.

"No use arguing about it, boss," he said. "They got a head start on us. We'll have to move if we want to catch up."

Muttering to himself, Stiller turned on the ignition and the pick-up took off with a roar. But by this time the leaking tyre had gone completely flat. The rapidly whirling wheel bumped and clattered loudly over the rough ground, throwing the flattened tyre casing half-way off the rim.

The truck lurched and bounced crazily from side to side while Stiller fought to bring it under control. One jolt broke the catch on the back gate, which dropped, and one of the men tumbled out. Finally Stiller brought the pick-up to a stop.

"We've got a flat!" he fumed. "Salty, I thought you were gonna put new tyres on so we could take Jenson for his ride!"

"I did, boss," Salty said defensively. "Look for yourself if you don't believe me," he added.

"Don't worry. I will," Stiller retorted. He got out along with the others. The man who had fallen joined them, rubbing his shoulder.

"I'm okay," he said, "but those guys won't be when we nab 'em." He waved his fist.

"If you ask me, the tyre was slashed!" fumed Bruno. "I'll bet Moran did it!"

"That's right," Stiller said. "He came out earlier to stretch his legs—or so he said. No doubt he punctured the tyre while we weren't looking. He's the only one who could have. But he won't get away with it. We'll track him down."

"What I want to know," Salty interjected, "is 'ow Moran became a member of our group."

Bruno shrugged. "My fault. I met him at a soccer game in Sydney and he told me he wanted a job in the Outback because the law was after him. I fell for his story."

"You stupid jughead!" Stiller grunted harshly. "We never should have listened to you."

"What do we do now?" Cutler asked.

"Change the tyre. What else?" Stiller hissed. "Get busy, you guys!"

"The jack's in the station wagon," Bruno said sheepishly.

"What! You've got to be kidding!" Stiller screamed furiously. A shouting match followed until Salty brought it to an end. "Mates, I've got it!" he yelled.

"Got what?" Stiller demanded.

"The station wagon's low on petrol. I forgot to top 'er up yesterday. They'll get stuck somewhere between 'ere and Alice Springs!"

Stiller was thoughtful for a moment. "That's right. And all they can do is hide in the Outback, close to the road. We can get in touch with Bartel in the morning, and——"

"We won't have any trouble finding them, boss," Bruno added. "Don't worry about that."

"All right. But I don't want any more slip-ups. Let's set up guards for the rest of the night. We can't be sure that these snoopy boys won't show up sooner or later! Go inside and get some more ammunition. Then position yourselves round the property. We'll do two shifts."

The men agreed and everyone went inside. Frank pulled Joe and Chet by their jackets. "Let's get out of here, quick!"

·15·

A Deadly Snake

THE boys raced through the darkness and wriggled through the fence. Then they ran round the rocks to the car. It appeared deserted as they approached.

"Where's Mr Ponsley?" Chet puffed. "Do you think he got scared and ran off?"

"We'll have to stay and look for him," Joe said. "We can't just drive away and leave him behind!"

A loud noise interrupted him.

"No need to look for Mr Ponsley," Frank observed. "He's here all right."

The boys peered through the window. Ponsley was sitting in the back seat with his hands crossed on his vest. His head was bent forward and his chin touched the enormous tie he wore. His mouth was open; and with every breath he snored.

Relieved to find he was still in the car, Frank, Joe and Chet piled into the small car, then Frank took the wheel as they moved off. He drove carefully, not daring to use his lights until they were round behind the rocks and well down the road.

"We're safe now," Frank said, snapping on the headlights and putting his foot down hard on the accelerator.

"As long as our car doesn't conk out," Chet stated. "I'll give three cheers when we get to Alice Springs."

"First we've got to find Jenson and Moran," Frank reminded him.

They came to a rough part of the road and bounced up and down over rocks and deep potholes. Frank shifted into low gear to manoeuvre past the worst spots. The jolting ride brought Ponsley awake with a start. He raised his head and looked around. "Where are we?" he demanded irritably.

"On the Cutler road," Frank replied.

Ponsley became peevish. "Well, you are driving this car as if you were riding a bronco at the rodeo."

"Can't help it," Frank said. "The Cutlers never built a paved highway for visitors to drive to their ranch."

Joe turned round and addressed their companion. "Mr Ponsley, did you notice anything after we left you in the car?"

Ponsley covered a yawn with his hand. "What do you mean?" he asked.

"The station wagon. Did it keep on going down the road past the rocks?"

"What station wagon?" Ponsley inquired. "I know nothing about a station wagon."

Frank was incredulous. "You mean a station wagon crushed through a board fence only a few yards from where you were and you didn't hear anything?"

"I don't recall a thing between the time you left and just now, when you woke me up."

Frank increased speed as they reached a better stretch of the road. "Unbelievable!" He chuckled.

"Why are you going so fast?" Ponsley complained.

Joe explained that they had to get safely away from

the gang of crooks at the Cutler Ranch.

Ponsley became cross. "I should think we are far enough away to slow down. I don't like being in an automobile at high speeds."

Frank turned on to the main road and increased his speed. "We have another reason for making time. Mr Ponsley," he declared.

"Oh, what's that?"

"We're trying to catch Dr Jenson and Mike Moran!"

Ponsley's mouth dropped open as the meaning of the statement sank in. The boys took turns describing events at the Cutler Ranch leading up to the climax, when Jenson and Moran leaped from the window of the house and fled in the station wagon.

"How did you know the man with Jenson was Michael?" he spluttered.

"He was wearing a ring with a red stone," Joe said. "It reflected in the light from the house."

Ponsley became excited. "Then it must be Michael! Frank, speed up! Catch the station wagon!"

Frank kept the accelerator pedal flat on the floor as the car raced forward. But trouble was in store. Several miles farther on, the car suddenly stalled. Lacking proper tools and light to work by, the boys looked over the engine for a long time before discovering that the distributor cap had sprung loose.

Later, after resuming their journey, they sighted distant figures silhouetted on the skyline. Ponsley insisted that they stop and investigate. The figures turned out to be wild aborigines hunting at night. Returning wearily to the car, they continued southwards to Alice Springs.

Dawn began to break. Shafts of sunlight glanced from the desert in shimmering rays. Near the Sandover

River, a group of kangaroos bounded away, and a rabbit shot across the road, seeking safety in scrub vegetation.

Then something caught Joe's eye up ahead. "The station wagon!" he exclaimed.

Frank hit the brakes and brought the car to a stop behind the vehicle they had been chasing. Rocks and gullies extended on both sides of the road.

"Salty was right," Frank said. "They must have run out of gas."

Ponsley got out of the car as fast as he could. "Michael! Michael!" he called out.

There was no reply. Ponsley groaned. "They're gone!"

"The keys are still here," Joe pointed out.

Chet squeezed into the front seat, turned on the ignition, and glanced at the dashboard dials. "The fuel needle's down to empty," he confirmed.

"Then they must be somewhere near here," Ponsley said hopefully. "But where?"

"Let's see if we can find their footprints and follow them," Frank suggested.

The four walked round the station wagon, but the terrain was too rocky for footprints.

"It's no use," Joe finally said. "We can't tell which way they went."

The boys shaded their eyes with their hands and scanned the horizon. Ponsley sat down on a boulder. Not a sound broke the silence of the desert, and not a movement could be seen among the rocks.

Joe was about to say something when he looked in Ponsley's direction and stopped short. Their friend was staring down towards his left hand, which was hidden by the boulder on which he sat. He looked deathly pale, his eyes bulged with fear, and a trickle of sweat rolled down his face. He seemed to have stopped breathing.

Joe stepped slowly round to see what was wrong. He noticed an Australian brown snake, about five feet long, coiled behind the boulder! The snake's neck arched in the air. Flashing wicked fangs only inches from Ponsley's hand, the serpent swayed menacingly back and forth, hissing ferociously.

Ponsley was mesmerized by the venomous creature. He sat as if turned to stone, too terrified to move.

Cautiously, to avoid startling the snake and causing it to strike at Ponsley's hand, Joe gave a danger signal to Frank and Chet. Responding, they moved up, and were horrified when they realized that Ponsley was in danger.

Chet picked up a dried branch, evidently blown from a far-off straggle of gum trees, made a wide circle, came up behind the snake, and brushed the sand with the stick. With blinding speed, the snake whirled and sank its fangs into the wood!

Frank and Joe instantly grabbed Ponsley and pulled him away from the boulder. He trembled and gasped for breath. Chet stepped back, dragging the snake, which maintained its grip on the stick.

"Look!" Joe cried suddenly.

Between the serpent's coils gleamed a piece of metal. When the snake released the stick and slithered off among the rocks, Joe retrieved the object, a key chain with the initial M on it.

"That's probably Michael's!" Ponsley exclaimed. "He must have dropped it here!"

"Most likely on the way up this gully," Frank observed. "So that's where we go."

The gully led to a point where the rocks were taller and more spread out, with defiles leading in several directions. They halted, not knowing which way to take.

Frank cupped his hands around his mouth. "Mike Moran!" he shouted. "Come on out! We're friends!"

His words echoed among the rocks and then silence fell again.

Joe called, "Dr Jenson! Dr Jenson!"

Again silence. A small stone tumbled from one of the tall rocks. Looking up, the boys saw a figure vanish over the top.

"There they are!" Chet cried out.

The four climbed over a pile of rocks and reached the top just in time to see the figure jump down on the other side and run into a defile.

"They think we're Stiller and company," Joe said. "They won't come out."

"You follow them," Frank replied. "I'll cut them off."

Noting that the defile curved round in a semi-circle, he scrambled down the pile of rocks, turned left, and met Moran and Jenson running through towards him!

Jenson was a slight, scholarly-looking man. Moran appeared to be the outdoor type, and he assumed a boxer's stance as soon as he saw Frank.

"Relax, Mike," Frank told him. "We're not in league with the Cutlers. Those crooks are a long way from here."

Just then the others came up. Ponsley hastened forward and cried, "Michael! Michael!"

Moran stared at him in utter astonishment. "Mr Ponsley, what are you doing here?"

"And who are these boys?" Jenson put in.

"Friends!" Ponsley said. Then he explained how they happened to be searching for Moran and Jenson.

When Ponsley mentioned that Michael had been accused of tipping off two bank robbers about the Mid-County Bank's alarm system, Moran shook his head in disbelief. "Dad needn't have worried about that. The alarm system they've got now is totally different from the one in use when I worked there. I know nothing about the present system."

"Can you prove that?" Joe asked.

"Sure. The old system had a number of flaws. I know because I checked it out. The manager called in a security engineering firm to install a new one. The job hadn't been finished when I left. The records will back me up on that."

"So the two men who were arrested must have been trying to frame you to cover up for someone else," Frank reasoned.

"You bet they were!" said Mike.

Ponsley heaved a sigh of relief now that he knew the senator's son could be cleared. The conversation reminded Frank of something. "You spoke about a bank employee named Thurbow, who helped to throw suspicion on Mike," he said to Ponsley. "What's his job there?"

"Security guard, I believe."

"Any idea what he looks like?"

"I have," Mike broke in. "He's a stocky, red-haired guy with a broken nose. I never did like him."

Frank turned to his brother. "Remember the man

who was in the chemistry shop talking to Mr Oakes when we ordered that methyl yellow?"

Joe's eyes widened and he snapped his fingers. "Holy smoke, you're right! He was a chunky redhead! I remember wondering if he might be a pro boxer with that broken nose. That must have been Thurbow."

"Check! Mr Oakes told us he was talking to a security guard when the mistake occurred. I'll bet Thurbow switched the methyl yellow with his own bottle of liquid gas."

"Probably because he heard at the bank that Senator Moran planned to call us in on the case."

The two boys told their listeners about their accident with the tear gas.

Later Ponsley inquired reproachfully, "Michael, why did you leave your home like that?"

"I wanted to see the world without my father's help. I decided to stop being Senator Moran's son for a while and try to make it on my own."

"How did you get involved with the Stiller gang?" Frank asked.

"I met Bruno at a soccer match in Sydney. He said he was from a ranch in the Outback and when I told him I was looking for a job, he hired me. I didn't know anything about the illegal operations till I got to Cutler Ranch."

Frank remembered that Bruno said Moran had claimed the police were after him, but decided not to mention it at this point.

"Mike was already there when they dragged me out of the hotel in Sydney," Jenson took up the story. "They drugged me to make it easier, but I heard them mention Alice Springs and wrote the letters AL S on the door. Did you read my message?"

"Sure did," Frank said. "But tell me, why did you pick that flea-pit of a hotel in the first place?"

"I had a feeling I was being followed. I had reservations at the Australian Arms, but I took a taxi at the airport and told the driver to take me to the opposite part of town. Unfortunately, it didn't help. They found me anyway."

"So after that you two met at the Cutler Ranch," Joe said to Mike.

"Right. That's where Bruno took me. He told me to guard Dr Jenson when they brought him in. Bruno handed me a rifle and ordered me to see that Dr Jenson stayed put in the upstairs room until his fate had been decided. When it seemed that they were going to drop him in the Outback, we escaped through the window. We didn't see you fellows. It was too dark. I had been in the yard, and I knew the keys were in the station wagon. That's why we used it for our break-out. We drove till the gas ran out."

"Then we hid in the rocks," Jenson continued. "When you came along and stopped behind the station wagon, we thought that you were Stiller and his henchmen."

"That's why we hid even deeper," Moran said. "By the way, how did you know which way we had gone?"

"We found this at the head of the gully," Joe replied. He handed the key chain to Mike Moran.

Moran took it and put it in his pocket. "I must have dropped it after we got out of the car. Good thing you found it!"

"Thank the deadly snake, Mike," Joe quipped.

"What's that again?"

Joe described the incident of the hissing serpent.

Moran became solemn. "I'm sorry you were in so much danger, Mr Ponsley."

The latter held up his hand. "Think nothing of it, Michael. I have found you, and nothing else concerns me at this point."

Frank turned to Jenson. "Do you have any idea why the gang kidnapped you?"

"None at all. It's a mystery to me."

"Could they be agents of a foreign government?"

"They might," Jenson confessed. "Professor Young and I received several messages warning us not to test the Firebird Rocket. It might be a plot to hold up our space programme."

A loud clatter broke out overhead and a helicopter zoomed through the sky. It was painted white, and bore no markings. The pilot made a wide circle round the two cars parked by the side of the road. Obviously interested in them, he returned for a second look.

"Chopper!" Chet cried. "If we can attract the pilot's attention, maybe he'll pick us up. Come on, we'll send him an SOS before he flies off!"

The rotund youth ran down the gully and out into the open. The others followed on his heels. Chet began to wave his arms frantically.

"Chet, be careful!" Frank warned. "It could be Stiller and his gang!"

Chet ignored the warning. Exultantly he realized that the pilot had spotted the group. "He saw us and is coming down for us!"

The chopper swung low towards them. Then machine guns chattered! Bullets kicked up puffs of sand on the desert floor!

·16·

Helicopter Hunt

"RUN BEHIND the rocks!" Joe shouted. "We're sitting ducks out here in the open!"

He raced back up the gully, followed by the others. The helicopter pursued them, its machine guns spraying bullets at their heels. They circled round the rocks until they found sanctuary under an overhanging ledge. Baffled by this obstruction, the chopper pilot hovered in the sky like a hawk waiting for its prey to emerge from a hole in the ground.

The six fugitives crept into a large cave at the end of the ledge. Ponsley sank down and mopped his brow with his handkerchief. Jenson sat down beside him. The Hardys, Chet and Moran peered through the mouth of the cave at their enemy overhead.

"We're safe for the moment," Frank said. "But the helicopter will keep hunting us."

Ponsley turned pale and gasped, "Then why are we staying in here? We'll be trapped!"

"We can't get back to the car while the chopper's in the air," Frank replied. "Let's wait until the pilot lands."

As if in response to his words, the whirlybird began to circle lower and lower, finally settling on the desert in a cloud of dust. The door opened and Stiller jumped out, followed by Bruno and another man. All carried machine guns.

"Run before they find us!" Frank called out to his companions. "Now!"

He was first out of the cave. Chet, Moran, Jenson, and Ponsley came after, with Joe at the end of the line to make sure no one was left behind. They took the reverse direction along the overhanging ledge, just making it round the rocks before a burst of shots rang out as the gang spotted them.

Quickly they ran down the gully to the car and piled into it. The gang pounded after them.

Frank took the wheel, and the car roared off amid a hail of bullets fired by Stiller and his henchmen.

"Anybody get hit?" Joe asked anxiously.

He felt relieved when everyone reassured him that they had not. Peering through the back window, he saw the gang turn and run up the gully.

"They're going back to the chopper!" he said grimly. "That means they'll be after us again."

"Oh, no!" Ponsley protested. He was squeezed into one corner of the car with his elbows pressed tightly against his sides. "It's bad enough riding like this! I can't breathe!"

"It'll get worse in a minute," Joe predicted.

He was right. The helicopter appeared in the sky and thundered after the car. One of the machine guns opened up again, kicking up sand behind the rear wheels of the speeding vehicle.

Frank swerved sharply from one side of the road to the other, presenting a moving target to the gunner. Reaching a row of hills, he dodged into them. He sped in and out among them, rocking the car violently as he took sharp corners on two wheels. The brakes squealed.

"We'll never get out of this alive!" Ponsley lamented. "We're done for!"

"Not yet!" Frank vowed. "We'll give them a run for their money!"

The hills ended, and the car was forced back out into the open. The chopper resumed the chase, throwing a shadow on the earth like that of a giant prehistoric bird flapping through the early morning sunlight.

Frank raced down the road. "How long can that guy keep missing us," he wondered.

"They're trying to draw a bead on us," Joe warned. "Here they come. Everybody duck!"

"Duck?" Ponsley quavered. "I can't even move!"

"What's that?" Chet cried, pointing down the road to a speck on the horizon that was growing larger by the second.

"It's a car!" Frank exclaimed.

The two vehicles raced towards one another. Frank blinked his headlights on and off as a signal to the other driver that he was in trouble.

"I hope he can help us!" Chet said.

"He sure will!" Frank replied. "That's a police car!"

The helicopter pilot, recognizing the police insignia, veered off and flew away, vanishing in the distance. Frank drew to a stop, and so did the patrol car. Two officers got out.

"Boy, are we glad to see you!" Frank exclaimed.

"What's the matter?" asked one of the officers.

Frank introduced himself and his companions, then explained that the helicopter had been chasing and firing at them.

"Why were the men in the chopper after you?"

Joe and Chet took turns describing what had occurred since they arrived at the Cutler Ranch. Moran and Jenson added their testimony, and told how they happened to be at the ranch.

The policemen listened in amazement. "We saw the 'copter and heard the gunfire quite a distance away, but we couldn't figure out what was going on," said one officer.

His partner added, "We'll call for reinforcements and drive to the Cutler homestead immediately."

"But the chopper will get there before you," Frank pointed out.

"True. But it's too small to fly out that many people. We should be able to nab at least some of the gang."

The two officers got into their patrol car and started up the road through the Outback, while Frank and the others continued to Alice Springs. They drove straight to the rental agency and returned the car.

Ponsley was so stiff that he had to be pulled out of the back seat by Chet and the Hardys. "Oh, my aching back!" he complained. "Mike, why did you ever have to come to a place like this?"

"I like this country," Mike said with a grin. "What do we do next?"

"Fly back to America at once!" Ponsley declared. "Michael, your father can't wait to see you."

Moran nodded. "And I can't wait to see him and Mom."

"I'd better fly to Sydney to check in with the Australian authorities and confirm my clearance at Woomera," Dr Jenson said.

Frank said, "And I think we should go with you in

case the gang tries to kidnap you again. Until they're behind bars, I know Dad would want us to act as your bodyguards, Dr Jenson."

The scientist smiled. "I'll be happy to have you. It makes me feel a lot safer."

On the plane to Sydney, Mike Moran told them about some of his experiences and how he had run out of money and immediately accepted the job Bruno offered him.

"Did you tell him the police were after you?" Frank asked bluntly.

Mike stared at him for a moment. "No. Why do you ask?"

"Bruno said you did."

"You spoke to him?"

"No. We overheard him saying it."

"Well, it's not true."

Frank had doubts but changed the subject. "Now you can help your father in his political campaign," he suggested.

"I'll be glad to," Mike said. "After my experiences down under, politics will be a tame game. But that's all right. I don't want to get involved with any more criminals."

At the Sydney airport, Ponsley and Moran said goodbye and went to catch a plane for the United States. The boys accompanied Dr Jenson to police headquarters and then returned with him to the airport to await a flight to Adelaide, where they would transfer to another plane for the Woomera rocket station.

While they were sitting in the terminal, a voice announced over the loudspeaker: "Call for Joe Hardy! Call for Joe Hardy!"

"Who can that be?" Joe wondered.

"You'll find out when you answer," Chet said.

After checking with the information desk, Joe went to the designated phone booth and picked up the receiver. "Joe Hardy speaking."

"Listen," growled a disguised voice, "you and your brother better get out of Australia! And take your fat friend with you—or all three of you will wind up in the hospital! Or in coffins!"

·17·

Woomera Welcome

JOE started to ask who the speaker was but the phone clicked off at the other end. Replacing the receiver, the boy returned to the others and quickly described the warning call.

"The helicopter gang knew we were with Dr Jenson," Chet said. "They could have called ahead to alert another member. He may follow us, so we'd better be on our guard."

Frank nodded thoughtfully. "But do you know what this means? Unless they called their accomplice while they were still in the air, they escaped the police!"

"I'm going to get in touch with the Alice Springs police right away," Joe said and hurried off to a phone booth. He managed to reach the officer in charge. "Did you capture the Stiller gang?" he asked.

"No such luck. We found the Cutler station abandoned. Obviously other gang members arrived with cars to help evacuate everyone. So far we haven't traced the helicopter or its crew."

Joe groaned in disappointment. "Any clues in the house?"

"Nothing. It was cleaned out except for some fingerprints. There were a lot of ashes in the fireplace and bits

274

of paper, but nothing conclusive. They obviously burned anything incriminating."

"And no hint to where they might have gone?"

"None. But we're working on the case and will find out sooner or later."

Joe thanked the officer and hung up. When he joined his brother and the others, they could tell from the expression on his face that something had gone wrong.

"The Cutler gang escaped?" Frank asked.

"Without a trace. They burned all the evidence and were gone when the police arrived."

"They must have been prepared even before the helicopter went off to chase us," Frank muttered.

"Do you think they'll make another attempt to kidnap Dr Jenson?" Chet asked.

"It's possible. We have to be very careful."

The scientist turned pale when he heard that his captors were still at large. "I'm glad you fellows are with me," he said. "And I'll feel even better once we get to Woomera. The security there is so tight, I doubt that any of the gang could get in."

His companions nodded, and they kept a sharp eye out for anyone who might be following them. They boarded the plane without noticing anything suspicious.

The plane flew over the desolate terrain of Southern Australia, then made a big circle to the coast over Gulf St Vincent and into Adelaide for a landing at the airport. There, a message was waiting for Dr Jenson.

"Professor David Hopkins is here to meet me," he declared after reading the note.

"Dr Jenson, who is this professor?" Frank asked. "Do you know him?"

"We can't take chances with strangers," Joe added.

Jenson laughed. "I've never met him, but I know he's a famous scientist. He's one of the experts I came to Australia to meet. Hopkins works out the astronomical tables for interplanetary probes and will help track the Firebird."

"The man who is meeting us here could be a phony," Frank objected.

"Don't worry," Dr Jenson assured him. "I know what Hopkins looks like. I've seen several pictures of him."

"Good," Frank said. "I'd hate to walk into a trap."

Jenson led the way to the waiting room, looked around, then waved to a man sitting on a bench. It was obviously Hopkins. Frank was relieved by the gesture.

The scientist was a short-sighted individual wearing steel-rimmed glasses. He came forward and introduced himself.

"Dr Jenson, the Sydney police informed us that you were coming," he said. "I couldn't wait to see you, so I flew down to Adelaide. We're all so glad to hear that you survived your ordeal unharmed!"

"So am I," Jenson said with a smile. He shook Hopkins's hand, introduced the Hardys and Chet, and gave Hopkins a brief rundown on his escape from the Cutler Ranch. "The boys came along as my body-guards," he concluded.

"That's a splendid idea in view of the danger," Hopkins declared emphatically. "Now then. We'll fly to Woomera in an official plane. The station's in the desert, where the rockets can be safely tested."

The plane was a medium-sized, propeller-driven craft, just large enough for them to squeeze in behind the pilot. After taking off, they headed north-west over Spencer Gulf and Port Augusta into a region of lakes that broke up the arid, sun-bitten terrain of western Australia.

As their long, cramped flight drew to an end, Hopkins pointed out of the window and said, "This is the Woomera prohibited area. It's a very large tract of land, absolutely barred to visitors who don't have official permission to enter."

"I know why," Chet boasted. "Your rockets are top secret! Space probes! Spy-in-the-sky! All that hardware!"

Hopkins smiled. "You seem to know about this."

Chet puffed his chest out. "I built a rocket myself and won the high school science competition!"

The Australian smiled again. "Perhaps some day you'll be working here as a scientist."

Chet looked pleased. "I would——"

"We're about to land," the pilot interjected. He manoeuvred the plane in line with the runway, set down the wheels, and taxied to the terminal. Hopkins looked after the details of his companions' clearance by the Woomera security staff, then took them in his car to their hotel.

"This town sprang up overnight," he said as they drove along. "Even the trees! Now we have homes, apartments, swimming pools—everything from a post office to a hospital. We'll go out to the rocket range in the morning," he added upon drawing up to the kerb to let his passengers out.

It was decided that Dr Jenson would share his room with Chet for security reasons, and the Hardys asked for adjoining quarters. However, the night passed without an incident, and Hopkins picked them up, as promised, early next day.

They drove to the central installation and saw rockets of all sizes at launch-sites. Some stood upright, ready to fly into orbit. Others were set at an angle that would keep them from reaching outer space.

Hopkins took the boys into a building and led them to its main room, which contained rows of sensitive instruments. Scientists and technicians were seated at consoles, checking the readings. "This is the control room," he said, "and these instruments monitor our rockets."

A man in a white coat was bending over a telemetry computer. When he heard Hopkins's voice, he straightened up and looked round. The Hardys stared in surprise. He was Professor Young!

"Adrian!" Young exclaimed, stepping over and shaking Jenson's hand. "I'm so glad the Hardys found you! Good job!"

Frank and Joe smiled and Chet looked a little disappointed because he had not been mentioned.

"Well, I want to welcome all of you to Woomera," Young went on. "I came here to follow the Firebird flight because I was afraid you wouldn't make it!"

"I almost didn't," Jenson said, and told Young about his experiences since he was last heard from.

Young looked grim. "NASA will do everything to see that your kidnappers are brought to justice. Please give me all the details of your capture."

He questioned Jenson and the boys very closely for an hour. At the end, he said, "Adrian, I take it you still have no idea why the Stiller gang kidnapped you?"

Jenson shook his head. "I wish I could tell you."

"When Cutler and his men are found, they may talk," Frank suggested.

"Let's hope so!" Young declared fervently. He invited Jenson to come into his office for a briefing about the Firebird. Then he turned to the boys. "While Dr Jenson and I are talking, I'll bet I know what you fellows would like to do."

"I'd like to see a rocket launching!" Chet said.

"I figured that," Young said with a smile. "You're in luck. There will be one in about five minutes. Come along with me."

He escorted the boys to a special observation window through which they could see a huge missile poised on its launch-pad. Then the two men disappeared while the Hardys and Chet waited expectantly, their eyes glued to the rocket.

The nose cone was painted green and the booster was white with the name *Wallaby* on it. A supporting gantry moved back, leaving the rocket standing by itself on the launch-pad.

An Australian scientist came up to watch. "You're Americans, aren't you?" he asked.

Frank said they were.

"I thought so from hearing you speak. That rocket is named for a small kangaroo, the wallaby. It will put a weather satellite into orbit." He stood near them while preparations for the launching continued. At last everything was ready.

"Here we go!" Chet cried. "The countdown!"

A voice intoned the numbers: "Ten, nine, eight, seven, six, five, four, three, two, one, zero! Lift off!"

Exhaust gases poured out on to the launch-pad in a dense white cloud. The rocket started straight up, slowly at first, then gathered momentum, and increased its speed. Soon it was hurtling through the sky high above the earth.

The scientists and technicians in the control room cheered loudly and the boys joined in.

"That's a beauty!" Joe said enthusiastically. "I hope she makes it into orbit!"

"So far, so good," reported Frank, who was following the flight through a pair of binoculars offered him by the Australian. "It looks like a perfect flight."

"I'll show you how perfect," the Australian said when the rocket had disappeared from view. He took them to a battery of instruments to check the moment the booster rocket fell away and the nose cone continued into orbit.

Young's voice sounded behind them. "Everything is going as planned. The flight is A-okay."

He and Jenson had come up without being noticed, and stood looking at the instruments over Frank's shoulder.

"It's an important flight for us," Jenson said. "The data it sends back will be used to plot the flight of the Firebird."

Everyone in the control room relaxed. They began to discuss the Firebird, its revolutionary nuclear engine, and the path it would take deep into space. Young showed the boys round, introducing them to Australians and Americans responsible for space programmes conducted jointly by the two nations.

Chet eagerly asked as many questions as he could think of and the scientists co-operated good-naturedly with the boy. Finally, in the late afternoon, the young detectives escorted Dr Jenson back to their hotel. They had a pleasant dinner, then retired to their rooms. Before going to bed, Frank telephoned Alice Springs again.

"Any clues yet?" he asked the officer in charge.

"We found the helicopter abandoned in the Outback," was the reply. "It was registered in the name of Bartel. At this point we haven't been able to establish yet whether that's a fictitious name or not. But there's no trace of the gang."

"I was afraid of that," Frank said. Slowly he hung up and told Joe what the officer had reported.

"I just hope that dodging the police will take up all the gang's time and attention," Joe commented. "This way they won't be able to follow us."

Joe's hopes, however, were dashed the following morning when a loud knock sounded on the door. Dr Jenson and Chet burst in. The scientist looked pale and shaken, and his hand trembled slightly as he held out a piece of paper to show the boys.

"This was slipped under the door of our room," he exclaimed. "They're going to kill me!"

·18·

The Trap

FRANK and Joe stared at the message. It was pieced together with letters cut out of a newspaper, a method the crooks had used before, and read: *The Firebird will die, and so will you!*

"They haven't given up," Joe stormed. "And they know where we are. It looks as if security isn't tight enough, even here at Woomera!"

"Maybe Arthur can help," Jenson said. Suddenly he sounded tired and depressed.

"Look," Frank told him, "don't worry about the gang. That's what we're here for."

Jenson smiled wanly. "Okay, I'll let you worry. Do you think it's safe to go downstairs and have some coffee?"

The group went into the cafeteria, and less than an hour later the official limousine picked them up. They were driven to the rocket range, where they met Young in the laboratory.

He was agitated when he saw the note. "This is unbelievable!" he exploded. "But they won't get away with this. I won't let them!"

"You didn't get a note like this?" Frank inquired.

"No," Young said, and he turned pale. "Not yet."

"What are you doing for your own safety?" Joe added.

"I travelled with the two men who guarded me in Princeton," Young replied, "and we're sharing a room. That, of course, may not discourage the gang from coming after me, too."

"What are we going to do?" Jenson asked.

"I'll talk to the security people here and arrange for a hide-out where the four of you can stay until the gang is captured," Young replied. "I'll figure out a way we can communicate with each other, and also request closer protection for myself. Just wait here while I make a few phone calls."

Young disappeared into his office and returned a short time later. "All set," he declared. "The private pilot who flew me here will take you to a safe place down in Port Augusta. No one will suspect you're there, and the local police will keep an eye on it. Please don't leave until I contact you."

Soon Jenson and the boys took off, and less than an hour later they landed at the Port Augusta airfield, where a car was waiting. The pilot himself drove them to a hotel on the outskirts of town. He pulled into the rear and backed up closely to the door.

The boys had noticed a large sign out front that read: *Captain Cook's Flagship*. The ancient three-storey building needed a coat of paint, the windows needed washing, and the lawn needed mowing.

"This is not exactly a first-class joint," Chet commented.

"Why did Professor Young send us to a place like this?" Joe wondered.

"Obviously he thinks no one would look here for an

eminent scientist," Frank suggested.

They went in and found a surly clerk at the desk. He glowered at them as they signed the register, and told them their room was on the third floor.

"The only phone in the hotel is this one on the desk," he snapped. "You can have sandwiches from the kitchen. Water and ice are in the basement. Take the stairs up, and don't ask me if there's a lift. There isn't."

"He's about as friendly as that brown snake Ponsley met in the Outback," Frank said sarcastically as they climbed the stairs. Finding their door number, they entered a dusty room with four cots, and a window that was stuck. Joe and Chet had to force it up by pushing together.

Jenson looked round and sighed. "I hope we don't have to stay here very long."

"Stiller and his friends might be rounded up at any time." Frank reassured him. "Then we can leave."

Joe punched one cot with his fist. "This'll be like camping out in the Bayport Woods," he grumbled.

Chet clicked his teeth. "I'm thirsty. I'll go get some ice water in the basement."

He went out, carrying a cracked jug that had been sitting on a small table. Joe locked the door and put the key on the dressing table. Frank and Jenson sat down on two cots and discussed the situation, wondering what would come next. Suddenly the floorboards in the hall creaked and footsteps approached.

"I didn't think Chet would be back that fast," Joe said.

The steps came closer and stopped outside their door. However, the caller did not knock.

"Whoever's out there must be eavesdropping on us!"

Jenson whispered nervously, his face strained.

"Shhh!" Joe warned, putting his finger to his lips. He and Frank tiptoed over to the door. Joe stationed himself flat against the wall next to it, while Frank turned the knob quickly and flung the door open.

Outside stood the desk clerk!

"What's the idea of eavesdropping on us?" Frank demanded.

"Who's eavesdropping? I came up to tell you there's a phone call for Frank and Joe Hardy. You can take it at the desk."

"Then why didn't you knock?"

"I wanted to make sure no one was around. I was told not to draw attention to this room."

"That sounds reasonable," Jenson spoke up. "Arthur doesn't want anyone to know we're here. He's being careful."

"It's possible," Joe commented.

The desk clerk glared at them. "I delivered the message," he grated. "Now I've got other things to do." He turned and disappeared down the hall. The Hardys followed him after warning Jenson to lock the door and not to open it for anyone except Chet until they returned.

"This call must be from Professor Young," Joe said as they descended the stairs. "Maybe the police caught the gang!"

They took the lower stairs two at a time and ran to the desk. The clerk was not in sight and the phone lay on its side off the hook.

Frank lifted the instrument to his ear and Joe stood close enough to listen in. "Hello?" Frank said.

A disguised voice replied, "Listen, Hardy! You and

that stupid brother of yours don't seem to have sense enough to save yourselves, much less protect Jenson!"

"Who is this?" Frank demanded.

"The same person who called Joe Hardy at Sydney airport."

"What are you calling about now?"

"You all disregarded my warning," the man retorted. "I gave you a chance to save your necks and you didn't take it. You decided to stay in Australia. All right, now you'll stay permanently. Six feet under!"

The man continued his threats. Frank put his hand over the mouthpiece and whispered, "Joe, do you recognize the voice?"

"It's disguised," Joe replied. "I don't know him from Adam."

Frank removed his hand from the telephone and said, "Who's going to make us stay permanently?"

The man hung up without answering and the Hardys stared at one another in puzzlement.

"This means we can't stay here either," Frank said. "We'd better phone Professor Young!"

Joe called and described the threat. Young was disturbed. "Good heavens!" he exclaimed. "I'll phone my pilot to go back for you right away. He's still in Port Augusta. All of you had better go to the airfield with him before the gang gets to the hotel!"

"Will do, professor," Joe said. "See you later." He and Frank hurried upstairs and knocked on the door of their room. There was no answer. Joe tried the knob and found the door was locked.

"Dr Jenson!" the Hardys called in unison.

Frank looked grim. "Something's happened. We'll have to break in!"

He kicked the door until a panel splintered under the impact. Reaching through, he turned the key in the lock and pushed the door open. The room was empty!

Footsteps in the hall made them whirl round. Chet came in, carrying his jug. "The ice water comes out in a trickle," he complained. "Say, what have you done to the door?"

"Dr Jenson is gone!" Frank said. "Did you see him downstairs?"

"Or anybody else?" Joe added.

Chet shook his head. "I was all on my lonesome."

"There's only one other way out," Frank said. "Through the window!"

The Hardys rushed over and saw that a sheet had been torn into strips and knotted together to form a rope. One end was tied to a radiator. The other dangled over the window-sill down to the ground.

"Dr Jenson got out through the window!" Frank exclaimed. "We've got to catch him!"

"But why would he do that?" Chet asked.

"I have no idea. All I know is that we must get him!" Frank said. He left a bill on the dressing-table for the damage to the door, then gripped the improvised rope, and dropped to the ground with the celerity of a squirrel. Joe followed at the same speed, then looked up.

Chet was hesitating.

"Hurry up or stay behind!" Joe urged.

Faced with the choice, Chet climbed down. He got hold of the torn sheet, and squeezed through the window, shutting his eyes tight. He dangled over empty space. "It's a three-storey drop," he quavered.

"Slide down! Let gravity take over," Joe advised. "You'll make it in no time."

Chet had almost reached the bottom when one end of the torn sheet snapped. With a loud yell he plummeted downwards. Frank grabbed his shoulders and Joe caught his legs, and the three ended in a tangle on the ground.

"Good show!" said a familiar voice behind them as they struggled to their feet. The boys froze. It was Stiller! He and his gang had them surrounded! In the background, Salty was guarding Jenson, whose hands were tied.

"We laid a trap," Stiller smirked, "and the smart Hardys walked right into it!"

Frank realized what had happened. "You guys must have sneaked in the back way before we ever got that call. And somehow you fooled Dr Jenson into opening the door while your confederate kept us talking down at the hotel desk."

"That's right." Stiller gloated. "We pounded on the door and pretended you two had had an accident. When Jenson opened, we grabbed him and left that knotted sheet dangling out the window before we ducked down the back-stairs again. One of my men actually climbed down the sheet so he could lock the door from the inside. You fools fell for the trick and plopped right into our arms!"

Jenson and the young detectives were taken to two parked cars. At the wheel of one was the hotel desk clerk!

"So you're in the gang, too," Frank accused him.

The clerk grinned. "I sure am now," he said as the captives were pushed into the cars. "It pays well."

"Where are you taking us?" Frank asked Bruno who sat next to him.

"Shut up!" his guard answered and jabbed him viciously in the side with his elbow.

Frank winced in pain and asked no more questions. The cars were driven to an abandoned warehouse several blocks away. It was a five-storey building. Most of the windows were broken or boarded up.

The gang marched the captives inside and up a flight of dark stairs to an attic at the top. One man was posted to guard them while his companions left. About an hour later, the other crooks returned with a new prisoner. The boys gasped as they recognized him.

"Professor Young!" they cried out in disbelief.

Dr Jenson stared at his partner. "Arthur! So they've got you too! How on earth did it happen?"

"A fake phone call right after I talked to Joe," Young replied. "The caller pretended to be with the Port Augusta police. He said they had a line on the gang and were ready to close in. He wanted me to fly here immediately to help identify them as soon as they were captured. But the person who met me at the airfield when I landed turned out to be my kidnapper."

"We tricked you as easily as we tricked your friends here," Stiller sneered at him.

"What are you going to do with us?" Chet asked.

"Finish you off, what else!"

·19·

The Rope Trick

FRANK and Joe looked at each other. Both realized that they would have to fight their way out. Frank counted the gang members that were in the room with them. Stiller, Salty, Bruno, the hotel clerk, and another man that Stiller had called Bartcl. "The owner of the helicopter, no doubt," Frank thought and wondered vaguely where the Cutlers were.

The Hardys knew they had a chance to subdue their adversaries if Young helped. Jenson was handcuffed. With a yell to Joe and Chet, Frank threw himself on the man nearest him. Joe did the same, and Chet, who caught on immediately, flattened Salty with a blow to the chin.

The next few minutes were bedlam. Stiller attacked Frank, while Joe took Salty with a flying tackle. Young seemed frozen and stood stock-still as Chet seized Bruno in a tight headlock. Even Dr Jenson got into the fray and tripped the other two men who were about to attack the Hardys.

Just then Mr and Mrs Cutler arrived. Cutler threw himself into the fight, turning the odds heavily against the young detectives. One by one the boys were overpowered. Jenson was lying on the floor, and Young stood frozen and helpless, as if in shock.

"Let's tie 'em up," Cutler panted, and his wife went to get a supply of rope. Soon the boys and the two scientists had their hands bound behind their backs and their ankles tied. Then the gang filed out of the room.

"They won't be here long," Stiller muttered to Salty on the way out. "And I'll be glad when we're rid of them for good!"

The door slammed shut, a key turned in the lock, and the men went downstairs. Slowly their footsteps died away.

"Work on the ties," Frank advised his companions. "If we slide up to one another, we can try to use our fingers to loosen each other's ropes. Here, watch me." He rolled up to Joe and wriggled until the two lay next to each other, facing in opposite directions. Then, with great patience, he worked on his brother's bonds. Jenson and Young followed suit, while Chet waited until Frank had untied Joe and was able to help him. Half an hour later everyone was free. Dr Jenson sat down in a corner with his head in his hands. He had gone through so much already that he had lost all hope.

Young, however, had overcome his panic and tried to encourage his partner. "Adrian, don't give up yet. Perhaps we'll all be saved, and the Firebird will be launched on schedule. Let's go over those final calculations again so we'll be prepared."

"You really think there's a chance?" Jenson asked, wanting to believe there was.

"There always is," Young assured him. "Here, I have some paper in my pocket. Let's write down the equations."

Frank, Joe and Chet, meanwhile, looked around the huge bare dusty room, seeking some means of escape. Aside from the door, which had been locked, the only other way out seemed to be through a single unboarded window. Its pane was cracked and the frame broken, but Chet managed to open the sash far enough to peer out.

"We can't climb down," he informed his friends. "Too high up."

Frank and Joe joined him and saw that the wall descended five storeys without offering a toehold anywhere along the way. Nor was there any possiblity of climbing to the roof, ten feet above.

"Are you sure?" Young called out, interrupting his discussion with Dr Jenson.

"Positive," Chet confirmed. He craned out as far as possible, surveying the wall to the left and right.

"Maybe if we tied all the ropes together," Young suggested, getting up to see for himself.

As he approached the window, he suddenly stumbled and fell heavily against Chet. The chubby youth lost his balance and, with a yell, started to plunge over the edge of the window!

Desperately Joe leaped forward and grabbed Chet's pants leg. He managed to hold on long enough for Frank to seize their friend's arm and clutch his shirt. Together the Hardys pulled him back into the loft.

Chet was as white as chalk and Joe's hands were shaking.

"I'm sorry!" Young said, staring at the boys. "I didn't mean to—it was an accident—I——"

Chet gulped. "That's okay, professor. It's just that I'm not built for flying." He tried a brave smile, and

Young turned around in embarrassment to sit with Dr Jenson.

The boys stood without talking for a while. Finally Frank said, "There's only one possibility and that is to clear the boarded-up windows. Maybe we can escape through one of them and climb down one of the other walls."

The young detectives wrenched the boards loose from each window, but were disappointed. The ground and the roof remained inaccessible.

"There goes our last chance," Joe said, discouraged. "We can't climb up or down, and the only stairs are guarded!"

Suddenly Frank had an idea. "Do you have a pencil?" he asked his brother and Chet.

"Yes, here," Joe said. "Why?"

Frank pulled a piece of paper out of his pocket and scribbled a hurried message. *"Help. We are being held prisoners in the warehouse!"* Then he leaned through the window and tossed the paper out. It drifted down on to the deserted street.

"Do you have any more paper?" Joe asked, excited.

"No. Do you?"

"No."

Chet did not have any either, and Frank said, "Let's ask the others."

The two scientists were involved in a serious conversation. Dr Young had scribbled a number of equations on a piece of scrap. He looked up in surprise when the boys approached him. "This is all I had," he declared. "What do you need it for?"

They explained, and he said, "Forget it. This place is so deserted that no one would find it anyway."

"It was a good try," Chet said. "And we have nothing to lose, right?"

"I suppose so," Young muttered, but he did not seem convinced.

They sat in silence for a while, overwhelmed by the hopelessness of their situation. Joe stared out of the small window, his mind desperately trying to find a solution. Suddenly he sat up straight.

"Hey, did you see that?"

"See what?" Frank asked.

"The rope! In front of the window!"

"What?" Everyone looked in the direction of the opening, at the same time noticing a scuffling of feet on the roof.

"Someone's up there!" Frank exploded, as the rope came into view again, swinging wildly back and forth in the empty space.

"He's climbing down!" Joe shouted.

Young and Jenson stood up. They were about to rush to the window when a man shinned down the rope, braced his foot against the wall, pushed back, and swung forward in a wide arc through the opening into the attic.

Everyone stared in amazement as the newcomer landed and bounced in an upright position. He looked at them with a big smile.

Jenson and Young hastened over, and Frank cried out, "Dad!"

"Mr Hardy?" Chet mumbled, his mouth agape. "Is it really you?"

"Mr Hardy!" Young stammered. "Are—are you here alone?"

"Yes," the detective replied, looking at the scientist.

"Dad, how did you get here?" Joe asked. "We thought you were still in Florida at the Space Flight Centre!"

"I discovered a clue that led me to Australia. Then I got a line on the gang ringleader. I followed him till I came to this place."

"Why did you post yourself on the roof?" Joe wanted to know.

"I knew the gang was using the warehouse as a hide-out, and I had reason to expect them to bring you here. When they left this morning, I followed them but lost them. So I came back and decided to wait. I climbed up to the roof, tied a rope round the big weather-vane, and eventually saw the gang taking you up to the attic."

"You think we'll get out of here safely?" Jenson asked anxiously.

Fenton Hardy nodded. "We will, except for the one rocket scientist who's at the bottom of this mystery."

Jenson turned pale. "I don't understand. Are you accusing me?"

"Not you, Dr Jenson."

"Then what do you mean?"

Fenton Hardy looked straight at Young. "Professor, you're facing criminal charges in Australia and the United States!"

·20·

Surprise in Port Augusta

As THE boys and Jenson stared in utter astonishment, Fenton Hardy pointed a finger at the professor. "You were behind the whole thing!"

"Prove it!" Young sneered.

"I will, and you'll spend time in prison! You're under arrest!"

"That's what you think, Hardy!" Young snapped viciously. "This is your last case. We've got you outnumbered. You're finished!" Pulling a whistle from his pocket, he blew a shrill blast that echoed through the whole building.

Bruno's voice responded from the landing at the top of the stairs. "Okay, chief," he said and turned the massive key in the lock. He pushed the door open and entered, covering the group with a revolver while Young moved over to join him.

Footsteps pounded up the stairs. Led by Stiller, the rest of the gang came in. The Cutlers brought up the rear with puzzled looks on their faces. "What's going on?" Cutler asked.

"We caught a real big fish this time," Young chuckled. He pointed to the Bayport detective and asked Stiller, "Do you know who this is?"

Stiller grinned. "Sure. That's the detective Fenton Hardy, who sent me to jail ten years ago. I've been itching ever since to get even!"

"You were guilty," Mr Hardy reminded him. "You got what you deserved."

Stiller scowled. "I'd have got away with it except for you. Now I'll take care of you and your sons, too."

"This is your chance for revenge," Young said. "Get them out of here. I don't want to see any of them again, ever!"

"It'll be a pleasure!" Stiller snarled.

He and his gang moved forward. Frank doubled his fists. "We may as well go down swinging!"

Joe assumed a karate stance with upraised palms and challenged the gang, "You won't take us without a fight!"

Stiller looked at Cutler. "Shall we finish them off here?" he asked roughly.

Cutler shook his head. "I had to rent this dump. Any evidence of a crime committed here might be traced to me. We'll take them to the woods out in the back. There'll be plenty of cover out there."

Cutler glanced at Young. "Sure you've got all the dope you need from Jenson?"

Young nodded impatiently. "Don't worry about that. He's given me the final equations. Come on—let's finish this job so I can get back to Woomera."

The gang began to circle the boys and Mr Hardy held up a hand. "Don't resist," he told the boys.

The advice surprised the three so much that the gang members were able to break through and overpower them after a brief struggle.

"Tie 'em up again and do a better job this time," Mrs

Cutler commanded as Bruno picked up the ropes and handcuffed the prisoners.

"Dad!" Frank cried out. "Why did you tell us not to fight?"

"There's no need to resist," Mr Hardy said. "Didn't you hear tyres screech down below?"

The gang froze in dismay, then Cutler dashed to the open window and looked down. "It's the cops!" he cried. "Let's get out of here!"

He and Mrs Cutler ran from the attic and down the stairs, followed by other members of the gang. But the police already had the building surrounded. A detective sergeant and several uniformed constables arrested and disarmed the crooks as they tried to escape. The prisoners were herded back upstairs, and the captives were untied.

"You're right on time, sergeant." Fenton Hardy grinned.

"No trouble, sir. Mr Moran alerted us a couple of hours ago."

"Mr Moran?" Frank asked incredulously.

"That's correct," Mr Hardy replied. "Here he comes." He pointed to Michael, who had followed the police to the attic.

Chet's mouth dropped open. "Mike! Wh-what are you doing here?"

"It's a long story," Mike said with a smile as the criminals were handcuffed and taken downstairs by the officers.

Professor Young stared at the newcomer. "You double-crossing rat!" he fumed. "You were supposed to be working for *us*!"

"Sorry, professor." Mike grinned coldly. "I happen

to be working for the US government. And it was my assignment to investigate the Cutler-Stiller gang for a series of international kidnappings and other offences. I didn't know then they were behind the Jenson disappearance."

"Fantastic!" Frank exclaimed. "So you got a job with them—saying the law was after you?"

Mike grinned. "I'm sorry I couldn't tell you the truth, Frank. Now I can because my assignment is over and I'm a free agent again."

"What about Mr Ponsley?" Chet asked.

"I had to let him know because I wasn't going with him."

"But how did you meet with Dad?" Joe inquired.

"After I left Ponsley at the airport, I phoned my superior at the US Consulate," Mike went on. "He instructed me to assist Mr Hardy in the Jenson case and the rounding up of the gang. So I met your father in Sydney and told him all I'd learned. We combined forces and flew into Port Augusta yesterday evening. By pooling all we knew, we were able to trace Stiller's mob to this warehouse—but we still didn't have the evidence to convict Young."

"You've got it now," said Chet. "Boy, what a case! So that's why you couldn't let your dad know what you were doing or where you were."

Mike nodded. "But it's all over now." He glanced at the two Hardy boys. "By the way, your deductions about that bank security guard were correct. Thurbow has confessed that he was the one who tipped off the robbers about the alarm system, and that he switched those chemicals in the hope of putting the Hardys out of action."

By now all the crooks had been taken downstairs except for Young. When a constable approached him with a pair of handcuffs, the scientist made a sudden break for the window. He squirmed through, grabbed the rope still dangling outside, and in seconds had shinned down to the ground.

The constable leaned out the window and took aim with his gun.

"Don't shoot!" Mr Hardy warned. "We want him alive!"

Frank edged past them and went down the rope after the fugitive. Young headed for the woods behind the warehouse, and Frank followed at top speed. Joe, meanwhile, flew down the stairs, hoping to head Young off. The others followed.

The prisoners were being loaded into police cars in front of the warehouse. The constable paused to explain the latest turn of events to the sergeant, while Mr Hardy and Chet followed Joe round to the rear of the building, just in time to see Frank disappear into the woods.

"Young must be ahead of him!" Joe said as they hurried after the young detective.

Frank lost sight of Young among the trees, but a path led him through the underbrush and he went forward until he came to a fork, where he had to guess which way Young had gone. He decided to take the left branch. A hundred yards in he caught sight of the fugitive.

Young, glancing over his shoulder, noticed Frank. Puffing from exertion, he darted from the path into the underbrush. He stumbled and tripped in the thick shrubbery, but he refused to slow down because he could hear his pursuer forcing his way through after him.

Young reached the right-hand path, looked round, and then ran back towards the fork, hoping to confuse Frank.

Joe, meanwhile, had taken the right-hand path, his father and Chet the left. The boy ran until he reached a towering tree, where he paused to get his bearings. He heard a rustling sound and looked up.

Young leaped down on him!

The rocket scientist hit the younger Hardy between the shoulders, and the pair went down amid leaves, vines and plants. Stunned by the collision, Joe felt Young's hand closing around his throat and choking off his breath. Grimly he struggled to break the hold. The man had a strategic advantage over him, and Joe gasped convulsively. The branches of the tree above him seemed to swing wildly as if whipped about by a heavy storm; then everything darkened and Joe went limp.

Suddenly he felt a hand pull him by the shoulder. He seized a wrist with his last bit of strength.

"Hold it," Frank said. "It's me!"

"Where's Young?" Joe croaked.

"He ran off when he saw me coming—back towards the warehouse. We've got to get him. Think you'll make it?"

"Sure, now that I can breathe again!" Joe rubbed his throat and the boys raced up the path. They reached the open space behind the warehouse and spotted Young jumping into the gang's pick-up truck. Two policemen hurried round the corner, but Young got the truck going and roared straight at them, forcing them to spring out of the way to avoid being run down.

The man powered towards a side road near where the Hardys emerged from the woods.

"Don't get in front of him!" Frank warned his brother. "He'll run you down!"

"I won't," Joe replied, "but this will! Give me a hand, Frank!"

Together, they levered up a fallen log from the ground and hurled it under the front wheels of the speeding truck. The vehicle struck the log with a thump, careered wildly to one side, and jolted to a halt in the underbrush.

The Hardys pounced on Young and dragged him out of the driver's seat. Realizing he could not escape again, he surrendered without a struggle. He, too, was loaded into one of the police cars in front of the warehouse, where Frank and Joe rejoined their father and Chet.

The Australian police detective complimented the Hardy boys on their quick thinking and fast action. "Now we have the whole gang," he added with satisfaction.

Young gave Fenton Hardy a venomous stare. "What made you suspect me?" he rasped.

"Frank and Joe asked me to check out Smoky Rinaldo. He'd found all the clues at the Aerospace Lab that seemed to incriminate Dr Jenson, and he could easily have planted them himself. But he turned out to be clean, as far as I could tell. Then I realized you could have planted the clues just as easily. What's more, you were the only person who could have kept the gang tipped off about Frank and Joe's moves. For that matter, you were probably the one who stole that pass Stiller used to get into the Aerospace Lab."

"So Stiller followed us around the lab," Frank commented. "And, on orders from Young, he shadowed us at the Nassau Club."

Joe looked at Young. "You put on an act at the Princeton Library! You told me Stiller got out of the elevator and ran upstairs. Instead, you probably warned him to leave through the front door while you sent us on a wild-goose chase!"

Young glared at him but said nothing.

Frank spoke up. "And you told Stiller that we would be flying to Sydney so he could resume his job in Australia. By the way, was it you who phoned us at Sydney Airport and threatened us after we'd returned there with Mike Moran and Dr Jenson?"

"What do *you* think?" Young snapped.

"I think he's right," Chet broke in. "I also think it was you who made that phone call to the hotel here in Port Augusta to keep Frank and Joe busy while your gang kidnapped Dr Jenson from our room."

"Right," said Joe. "By that time, his private pilot was probably already flying back to Woomera to pick him up and bring him here."

"And later," Chet said to Young, "you tried to push me out of the warehouse window. If you weren't handcuffed, I'd punch you right in the nose!"

Dr Jenson spoke up with indignation. "Arthur, why did you go through that miserable play-acting up in the warehouse attic just now?"

"Because I needed the last Firebird equations you'd been working on. That's why. So I pumped you for the information in order to handle the project on my own."

"But I don't understand. Why was that so important to you?"

"I can answer that," Mr Hardy said. "In case you didn't realize it, Young's been working for a foreign power. When their intelligence agents picked up news of the Firebird's development, they approached Young and paid him to eliminate you, Dr Jenson, so *he* would be the one controlling the project. He was then to devise a scheme to foul up the launching in such a way that it would take NASA a long time to find out what went wrong. Young was supposed to turn over all our plans to this power so they could build a Firebird rocket of their own before we could recover from the foul-up and thus be ahead of us in this area of our space programme."

Frank shook his head in disgust. "It's a good thing we prevented him from going through with his scheme," he said. Frank was proud that he had had a part in solving the case, but also felt the familiar emptiness he always experienced when a case was finished. Would there ever be another mystery for the Hardy boys in the future?

"Well, Dr Jenson," Joe said, "now the tables are turned. You'll be in charge of the rocket launching."

"And it'll be right on schedule!" Chet added enthusiastically. "I'm sure it'll be a great success!"

Frank nudged his friend and grinned. "Not like yours at Bayport Meadow, Chet!"